THE
MISSION

FIONA PALMER

ACKNOWLEDGEMENTS

Once again, I have Jim to thank for his amazing input. Also to my friends and family who read my work. To my writing buddies Rachael Johns and Cathryn Hein, such wonderful ladies, thanks for being just an email away. Cathryn, this book wouldn't be in print if it wasn't for your help, thank you! As always, my family are so supportive, especially mum. Big thank you to Jordan Weaver-Keeney for your help and Claire de Medici for the edits. And as always, the readers. Thank you.

For Jim Jim

CHAPTER 1

'I'm going to kill him,' said Ryan through gritted teeth.

If Jaz hadn't felt Ryan's muscles stiffen under her hand and looked up to see him say those words, she probably wouldn't have heard him. The noise in the Burswood Casino was loud, but Jaz's lip-reading skills had been improving under Ryan's guidance. Now she wished she hadn't picked it up so well.

Jaz held his arm firmly, making sure he wouldn't take off to kill whoever had upset him. Upset was maybe a too soft a word – pissed off and ready to kill fitted so much better. She could see the pain and anger churning through his hate-filled gaze, distorting his sharp, handsome features. She flicked her long silky black hair over her shoulder as she turned to see the man Ryan Fletcher wanted dead. He was across the room, past the blackjack tables and a row of pokie machines. He was standing by a doorway that led to the high-stakes games, laughing with the bouncer guarding the door, his hair dark and his skin a smooth light-coffee colour. Apart from his expensive taste in suits, Jaz couldn't see what all the fuss was about. He seemed just like any other cashed-up gambler in this room.

'Him? The one in the nice suit and big gold watch?' she asked, turning back to Ryan.

His sharp jerks indicated she had found the source of his fury. Ryan was breathing hard, and Jaz knew it was taking all his effort not to cross the room and knock the guy out.

'Ryan, do we need to go back outside for a moment? Maybe get you a drink until you've cooled down?' Jaz put her hand on his chest and felt the heat pulsing through his white dress shirt. She rubbed her fingers across his racing heart to get his attention. 'Ryan?' Man, she didn't need him going ballistic and blowing their cover. Jaz needed him to be calm and in control because she was out of her league right now and needed him. She could not complete covert missions on her own. She'd only just joined the MTG Agency, and she needed Ryan to take the lead as she learned how to bring down bad people – killers, drug dealers and traffickers, and the like – to keep Australia safer.

Ryan's dark brown eyes finally shifted to her. 'A drink. Yes. Now. Over here,' he said, firing out each word like an automatic rifle. He nodded to the nearby bar, which had a raised floor. No doubt he wanted to use the vantage point to watch over the room, and especially the guy who had freaked him out so much.

Jaz got them both a club soda and they sat at a small table, Ryan's gaze never straying far from its target. Jaz gulped down her cool drink and watched him watch his prey. How was it possible that just eight hours earlier she was at school trying to get through a mock exam? Now she was in the Perth Burswood Casino dressed up in black pumps, a skin-tight red dress she'd stolen from her mum's wardrobe and enough make-up to look twenty-five, not seventeen. At least that's what Ryan had told her when he first saw her. Jaz could tell by the glint in his eyes that he'd approved, even if he hadn't told her so.

It was the first time they had been together since her school ball; they had shared a kiss that night, actually quite a few, just before he left for an undercover operation, and she had spent the intervening weeks wondering just where they stood with each other. Of course she was attracted to him, had been from the moment he walked into her gym a few months earlier. Well, it was actually her friend Pax's gym, but to Jaz it was her place. She'd grown up in that gym and could fight as well as any of the guys who trained there. It was one of the reasons Ryan had taken such a quick interest in her. They had sparred together, laughed together – and then he'd dropped the bombshell that he belonged to a secret agency that worked on bringing down bad guys. And he'd recruited her. Just like that. The weirdest part was that Pax – her best friend's grandfather, and in fact just like her own grandfather, who owned The Ring – was also a part of this MTG

Agency as their computer guru. Pax, whom she'd known her whole life, had kept this secret. The same secret she was now keeping from her family and her two best friends. If Jaz wasn't sitting across from Ryan now, she'd almost believe she'd dreamt up the whole thing. Seriously. But Ryan had shown up after school earlier today, proving just how real he was.

A month had gone by since she'd last seen him, since their kiss and since she'd agreed to join the Agency. In that month, she'd thought of nothing else.

The first thing he'd said when she finally saw him again was, 'Do you still want to be a part of this?'

'Of course I do,' she'd replied, when really she'd just wanted to jump into his arms and kiss him. But he'd been cold, wearing an emotionless mask, and kept his distance from her. She'd never felt so rejected. It was a rude awakening from the dream reunion she'd imagined.

Jaz slid her palm across the table and held his hand. His body jerked with her touch and he pulled his hand away.

'Jaz…'

'Can we talk while you work? He's gone now,' she said, as the man stepped through the door. 'Who was he to you anyway?'

Ryan cleared his throat. His eyes still shone, but his lean body had calmed, his muscles relaxing as tension rolled away. 'That was Sal. You remember the guy I was telling you about.' Ryan pointed to his arm, where his tattoo was hidden under his long-sleeved shirt.

Jaz nodded. She had seen the word *Forever* etched there, and she also knew there was more to that tattoo that met the eye. Under a black light, angel wings appeared down the length of his arm, along with initials and a year: *CC 2013*. Jaz shuddered at the memory of the night she'd first seen it. She'd been alone with Ryan in his bathroom, she was wet, he was shirtless, she was bleeding and he was sewing up her knife wound. She would never forget it.

Jaz pushed the memory aside. 'Your friend, Chris?' she managed to squeak out. 'That man was the one who— ' She glanced around. 'Hurt Chris?' Hurt was a euphemism for shot point-blank in the head.

'Yep. He's the one. And Chris isn't his only victim. No one has ever seen him carry out his dirty work, mind you; it's always one of his henchmen.

But I don't care. He's the one I'm going to take down. He's the top man behind it all.'

'Did you know he would be here tonight? Aren't we supposed to focus on watching Nicko Serveyous?' Ryan's brief had told her only what she needed to know: Serveyous had been running a drug operation in Pakistan and importing his product to Australia, and they were to watch him and paint a clearer picture of his contacts and operation. 'Now I'm starting to think these two could be more closely linked than we thought,' Ryan now mused. 'Sal's a big-time fish, and his connections stretch far beyond Australia.'

'So, is that where you've been for the last four weeks – in Pakistan?' she whispered.

Ryan's nod was minimal but she knew his body language by heart. After all, she'd dreamed about their kiss nearly every night he'd been gone, dreamed of holding him and being together. But seeing him now, she knew she had fooled herself well. He didn't want the same thing.

'I'm so glad you're back safe,' she blurted out. She felt a blush burn under her skin, no doubt turning her face the colour of her dress.

Ryan sat up awkwardly. 'Jaz, about how we left things. I— ' His hand ran down his face. 'I shouldn't have done… *that*. You understand we have to work together now. I can't compromise our missions.'

Jaz prickled over his choice of words. How could he call their amazing kiss *that*, as if he'd accidently kicked down a door in a fit of rage? Was she the only one who thought their connection ran deep? She looked out towards the pokie machines to hide the sudden humiliation that pulsed through her, her dreams crumbling away as reality stamped its foot.

But then she shook herself off. She had been hand-picked to join this secret team of do-gooders. And she had joined to help save the world — not to find a date.

'Yep, I get it.' She turned back to him with determination. 'So, tonight you needed me as cover?'

'Yes. I'd draw attention sitting alone watching a door, but with you it's different. We can chat and drink. We blend in.' He glanced at her dress. 'Well, sort of,' he mumbled before turning away.

After a long stretch of silence, Jaz asked, 'Can you tell me more about your trip?'

'Not here. And it's probably better the less you know.'

'But how am I supposed to learn?'

'By being on the job and by watching me. We'll give you exercises to hone your skills, like following people, gathering information. Jaz, the Agency doesn't want to risk your life doing the things I'm doing. It takes time to get to my stage.'

'I understand. But I know how to fight. I know how to use a gun.' She could thank her best friend Taylor for that skill. He was probably a better shot than Ryan too, but that came from having a cop for a dad and practically living at the firing range. 'I can take care of myself,' she said leaning forward, causing the table to groan.

Ryan met her eyes, holding them with a scary, scary gaze. 'Are you really ready to pull the trigger and kill someone, Jaz?' His voice was almost a growl.

She remained silent but shivered at the thought of actually taking another life. She swallowed.

Ryan freed her from his stare and checked the room again. 'I didn't think so.' It wasn't said arrogantly, more truthfully. 'And until then, we won't risk you in those situations.'

Jaz sat back and watched Ryan. His strong jaw was clenched and his eyes carried so much weight, yet he was still gorgeous and attracted glances from women.

'I'd like to think if it came to that I could do it,' she ventured.

When his eyes came back to her they weren't as frightening; if anything, they seemed sad and heavy.

'That's just it, Jaz: it changes you. I don't want that for you, at least not yet. You're too young. Too innocent.'

Blah, Jaz felt like groaning out loud. She didn't like being treated like a princess, protected as if she couldn't take care of herself. He must have known she was ready to disagree, because he spoke quickly.

'But there are other things you can do.' He glanced back to the door before continuing. 'We need you to go into the Agency to go over that mission we talked about before I left. Can you meet with James tomorrow morning at ten?'

Jaz nodded. 'Yep. Now that Pax knows I'm with the Agency, I can use him as an alibi. Mum doesn't worry when I say I'm staying with him. Lordy, would she have a pink fit if she knew what either of us was up to.'

'I know.' Ryan finished his drink and stood up. 'Time to move. Shall we go play?'

She knew they weren't thinking of the same games. 'Really? While we're on watch?'

'Yeah, we'll just take turns at watching for Nicko.'

'All right, cool. I've never been inside the casino before. What do I do?' She was still using her fake ID that Anna had made them after sneaking into Pax's 'secret work' office.

'Well,' said Ryan with a smile, 'I'll go get some change if you watch the door, and then we'll play those pokies. It should give us a good vantage point.'

'So, do I watch for Nicko or Sal?'

For a moment, Ryan looked torn. He rubbed his jaw before replying. 'Nicko's the one we want tonight, so if he comes out, follow him like I've shown you and call me straightaway so I can catch up. Okay?'

'Yep. Got it.' Jaz walked towards the pokies Ryan had pointed out, and tried to visualise Nicko's features from the photo Ryan had shown her before they got into the taxi. Bald, mid fifties, liked expensive suits and had a burn mark under his left ear. Shouldn't be so hard.

As she was about to take a seat, she caught the back of a man walking near the door. Bald. Expensive suit. She quickly stepped to the end row of pokies and spotted the guy. She breathed a sigh of relief. This bloke was late thirties at most. Not Nicko. Back to watching the door. She spun around to make sure she hadn't missed the real Nicko waltzing out of the door, when she collided with a man.

'Oh, I'm so sorry,' she said, looking up and trying not to gape as she recognised the dark hair and and coffee-coloured skin. He was holding her arm, his gold watch sparkling.

'No, *I'm* sorry. It's my fault, I wasn't watching where I was going,' he said apologetically, his voice as smooth as silk.

Sal, the man Ryan wanted dead. Jaz was lost for words as she gazed at his piercing black eyes. How many kills had they seen? He was watching her intently and she realised she would have to say something.

'Well, that makes two of us, then. Sorry, again.' Jaz gently pulled her arm, so he let it go. There was something weird about him, something she couldn't quite put her finger on; did she just feel funny because she knew he was this big scary bad man, or was it the fact that he seemed so normal. He was polite. He had a nice smile. She was suddenly conflicted.

'Can I buy you a drink? To apologise properly?' He smiled again and she automatically smiled back.

'No thanks, my partner is waiting for me. I better go.' Jaz stepped past him and walked down the row of pokies. Her skin prickled and she knew he was watching her leave. When she got to the end of the row, she sat down and then very slowly checked to see if he was still watching. Gone. Relief flooded her just as a hand came down on her shoulder and she just about screamed. Swinging around, she saw Ryan. 'Oh, it's you, thank God.' She breathed deeply. Too many shocks at once.

'What the bloody hell were you just doing?' Ryan glanced at the door she was supposed to be checking. His face was flushed. 'Shit, that's Nicko. Come on.' He pulled Jaz up off her seat and led her away. He passed the plastic container full of coins he was holding to an old lady with a short perm. 'Here, next game's on us,' he said. They were gone before they could see the delight on the woman's face.

As they made it to the end of the aisle, past the pokie players, Ryan wrapped his arm around Jaz, pulling her in close as they walked. Just like a happy, loved-up couple. She wished.

'He's up ahead, past the guy with the green shirt,' said Ryan. It was a busy night and they had to squeeze together to pass groups of people.

'I've got him.' Jaz was too afraid to blink in case Nicko vanished.

'Good,' he said before his voice dropped to a grumble. 'Now, tell me what you were doing talking with Sal. Did I not explain how dangerous he is? Christ, Jaz. What the hell were you thinking?' His breath rushed against her ear with each word.

Without taking her eyes off Nicko, who was making his way out of the casino, she talked through her teeth to Ryan. 'I thought I saw Nicko, but it wasn't him and as I turned around I ran into you-know-who. I didn't plan it.'

'He was touching you.' His voice seethed.

'I know. He was apologising.' Jaz felt ridiculous, as if she were defending this awful killer. 'I got away as fast as I could without causing suspicion.'

Ryan let out a breath as they headed outside into the cool night air. Nicko had stopped and was waiting for someone. Ryan pulled Jaz into him, circling his arms around her. He dropped his head on her shoulder as if they were about to kiss.

Jaz's heartbeat raced with anticipation, but she knew this was all for show.

'What happens now?' she said against his cheek.

'We wait.' Ryan pulled back and laughed aloud. Jaz went along and giggled. 'Come here, beautiful,' he said before pulling her back into his arms. 'He's getting into a black car. One Foxtrot Echo Golf six five nine. Try and remember that. Pax can run it for us later.'

'Hmm,' Jaz mumbled noncommittally. Now was not the time to let Ryan know that her memory wasn't the greatest. Cramming for her exams never worked, so she highly doubted she'd remember the number plate. But just for good measure she repeated it over in her mind a few times. Two minds were better than one.

'Let's go,' he said, holding her hand and pulling her to the taxi stand.

Ryan held the door open for her, still playing along, and she climbed, smiling to keep up appearances. Who knew who would be watching? Maybe Sal? She shivered with the thought.

'You cold?' asked Ryan as he closed the door and pulled her against him. He rubbed her arms and then paused, as if realising how close they were. He dropped his hands and sat forward, trying to spot the car. 'Can you follow that black car, the one that's turning right up ahead, please? Our friends are in it,' he said to the cab driver, who smelled like old cigars and sweat.

Jaz tried to relax back in the comfort of the taxi and left the watching to Ryan. His aftershave smelled divine and she missed the warmth from his arms. At least pretending to be his partner she could be close to him. It was better then when he was away on missions doing God knows what with God knows whom.

After twenty minutes, Ryan gave the taxi driver Pax's address.

'Nicko's gone straight home,' he replied when he saw Jaz's raised eyebrows. 'Nothing exciting tonight. We were hoping he'd stop by a warehouse or go to a meet.'

'Could he have been meeting Sal?' Jaz asked. 'And what if he leaves later, in another car?'

'I'll let them know about Sal being here tonight. And don't worry; someone's already watching Nicko's house.'

'Oh, okay.' Jaz felt like a very small piece of the puzzle. But it was also reassuring to know she had joined something real and that there were others working hard out in the field to bring these bad people down. They took the rest of the car trip in silence, and when they arrived back at Pax's place, outside The Ring, Jaz felt better. She was home and safe. Ryan paid the huge taxi bill and followed her inside the big, flat white building past the fading 'The Ring' sign that she should repaint one day. Inside, the smell of leather, sweat and plastic mats welcomed her. She'd been coming to this gym since she was a baby. It started with her mum teaching her karate, and then moved on until she was training with all the regulars in everything from boxing to street fighting. She loved it all.

Inside the office light was on. Pax was sitting by his computer still at work or, more likely, waiting for them.

'Great, you're back,' he said, pushing his steel-rimmed glasses onto his head. He held out his arms to Jaz and she stepped in for a hug. His teddy-bear body wrapped her up warmly, softly, just how an adopted grandparent should be. 'You don't look like my little Jasmine anymore,' he said letting her go. 'All grown up. It's so hard to believe.'

'Pax, come on,' she said, embarrassed that Ryan was a witness to this display.

'So, it all went okay?' Pax asked, looking to Ryan for an answer.

He nodded. 'A relatively quite night, really.' Ryan picked up a pen and wrote down the number plate. 'Look, I've gotta go and report and then see what our next move is, in the meantime can you run this plate and send the details through. I'll see you all later.' He turned to leave but Jaz called out to him.

'Ryan, will you still be around? Wanna come spar sometime soon?'

His smile was tight. 'I'd love to, Jaz but I'm tied up for a while. I might not be around for a few weeks, or even months. But I'll be in touch when I get back. I hope all goes well tomorrow with your briefing. Good luck.' Ryan lifted his hand as if he were going to touch her shoulder, but then it morphed into a wave, leaving Jaz feeling ripped off. 'Bye.'

He shared a nod with Pax before he turned and left. Jaz was still gazing into the dark when Pax spoke.

'Come on, I'll make you a cuppa while you go and have a shower. You'll feel better.' Pax's warm arm came around her shoulders and together they headed to his house, which was attached to the end of the gym. Pax locked up The Ring and then set the alarms. Jaz had always thought it was because The Ring was in a bad neighbourhood, but now she realised it was to protect all the computer hardware he used for the Agency.

As Jaz walked into Pax's dark house, feeling for the light switch, she couldn't help but feel abandoned. She just hoped Ryan would be back sooner than expected. Until then, she would go into this briefing and be the best agent she could. She was going to have her very own mission and she wanted to make them thankful for selecting her. And maybe she wanted to make Ryan proud too.

CHAPTER 2

Jaz woke to the sound of Pax whistling an old Elvis song while he made breakfast. She could smell coffee and cinnamon. What better reason to get out of bed? She threw back the covers and put her ugg boots on. There were two single beds in this room; one was hers, the other belonged to her lifelong best friend Anna Johnson. Pax was Anna's great-uncle and the reason they'd become friends.

Back home, both girls had rooms three times the size of this one, with queen-size beds and expensive plush carpets. But that was never something they missed here with Pax. They loved the small room with its old patterned carpet and all the little personal bits they'd accumulated here over the years. From the stuffed animals Pax had given them to the things they'd created with him, like the computer cable curtain that hung over the doorway, and the light cover made from parts from a motherboard that glittered in the light. Pax's place was certainly a world away from the glitzy life they had at home. But it was his love that made it so homely.

As Jaz walked down the narrow passage towards the kitchen in her blue pyjamas, she wondered if Pax was the reason they weren't stuck-up snobs like the rest of the girls at their fancy private school, St Christian's. He came from wealth yet had turned his back on it.

'Morning Jaz. How'd you sleep?' said Pax, handing her a cup of coffee. He gestured for her to sit at the table, where fresh pastries were laid out. Pax's favourite, which meant he'd already been out to the Vietnamese bakery down the street. He wore his old Kmart runners with his threadbare jeans and a big brown polo shirt that stretched across his podgy middle. Jaz found his non-designer-brand clothes refreshing and real. To the untrained eye he might have seemed like a poor old man, but Jaz knew the computer equipment and printers he had were state-of-the-art. She'd also seen one of his bank statements and knew he was as rich as his brother's family. After all, the Johnson computer empire was a well-known business in Perth, but Pax had taken a different path. One that finally made sense to her now. Anna's father now ran the family business and it would probably be Anna's in time if she wanted it.

'Like a log, Pax. Thanks,' she replied, before sipping her coffee. 'Ah, that's better.'

Pax sat across from her at the seventies-inspired table, his focus set on her. 'Now, tell me all about last night. Did you see Nicko?'

'Yes. He didn't do anything out of the usual. But this guy Sal was there, which sent Ryan a little loopy.'

'Sal?' Pax said loudly. 'The bad boss Sal? Did you see him?' His eyes grew wide.

'Yep. I actually ran into him by accident—'

'WHAT!'

Jaz ignored Pax's outburst, which was just as overprotective as Ryan's, and continued. 'And when Ryan saw us exchanging words... well, he blew his stack just like you're doing now.' She smiled at Pax, who was a little pale. In fact, he looked like he was about to be sick.

'What did he say? Did he look at you? Do you think he'll remember you? Please tell me you didn't give him your name!'

'Geez, settle down, Pax. It was nothing. I said sorry, he said sorry and that was it. I must admit, it was rather strange meeting him.'

'W-why?' Pax stuttered.

'I don't know. It was like he was a normal person. It's so hard to picture him as a drug-trafficking cold-blooded killer.'

Pax breathed deeply and pushed his plate away from him, his pastries untouched. She really must have shocked him – usually nothing stopped Pax from his favourite treat.

'Jaz, one thing you'll soon find out is that everyone has a secret. People aren't who you think they are, and most are really good liars.'

Jaz pushed her own plate away, suddenly losing her appetite. 'I guess I'm one of them now too. Lying to my friends and family. Hiding secrets.'

'Some choose to lie and others do it to protect those they care about. Don't feel bad, Jaz. You and I, we want to traverse this world with our eyes wide open. And sometimes that means we see the world for what it really is. The human race can be disappointing; some people have no conscience, and they allow greed and power to rule them. I believe in what I'm doing, and I know you do too, otherwise you wouldn't have said yes to joining.'

Jaz smiled. 'You're right, Pax.'

'Right about what?' asked Anna as she walked through the door. 'Oh yum, pastries.' Her strawberry-blonde hair was pulled back into a neat ponytail but it still slipped over her shoulder as she reached for the plate Jaz pushed towards her.

'Here, have mine. It's apricot.'

'You don't mind?'

Jaz shook her head. 'Go for it. I'm happy with just coffee. So, what are you up to? Miss me?'

'Yep. Thought I'd swing by and say hi,' said Anna, giving Pax a hug and kissing his balding head. 'Wish I could have stayed over too, but I wasn't sure how long I'd be stuck at Dad's big work dinner. Who wants to celebrate a new merger with another company? Not me.'

'It can't have been that bad,' laughed Pax.

'Oh, it was. You know Dad, he was loving it.' Anna rolled her eyes. 'So, what did you guys get up to?'

'Um, well, we just did some stuff in the gym and then watched a movie,' said Jaz.

'You wanna hang out today for a bit?'

'Oh, I'm busy this morning, but we can do something after lunch?'

'Yeah, okay. I think Ricky was going to call today, so I'll let you know.'

'How is the Rickster?' Jaz asked. Anna had gone with him to the ball and now they were dating. Jaz tried to be happy for her but she couldn't help but get a little annoyed by how much time Anna was suddenly spending with him. But, then again, it gave her freedom to pursue her other pastime, with the Agency.

'Great. He's so nice.'

And boring, thought Jaz.

'I'm glad you're happy, sweet pea,' said Pax, whose colour had returned, but he still didn't reach for a pastry.

'I am, thanks, Pax. So Jazzy, what's got you busy this morning? Hot date? Is Ryan back?'

Jaz shot Anna a glance. She absolutely did not need Pax hearing about her desires for Ryan. He'd hit the roof. 'Oh no, haven't heard from him,' she lied smoothly. 'But I am off to a job interview.'

'What?' Anna glanced between Pax and Jaz. 'Is she for real?'

Pax smiled and reached for his coffee, his hand shaking slightly. 'Yes, Jaz is going for a job.'

'Why?' Anna screwed her face up. 'Isn't your job here at The Ring?'

Jaz laughed. 'Anna, this is a love job. I want a job that is going to pay me money. Mum refuses to buy me a car, or even lend me the money, so I'm going to get a job and buy my own bloody car. She can't stop me then.'

Anna's eyes lit up. 'Cool. You should get something awesome like Taylor's Mustang.' She brushed some pastry crumbs from her lips. 'Maybe *I* should get a job. Mum and Dad have been talking about getting me a little beep-beep Barina. I would just *die* in one of those. Taylor wouldn't get in it,' she said with a chuckle.

'Anna, do you know how much that Mustang cost? I'll be lucky if I can get a second-hand clapped-out Barina!'

'You'll just have to work longer. So, what's this job?'

Pax reached for the sheet of paper he'd printed out this morning. 'She'll be an office girl. One of my mates mentioned they had a position going.' Pax handed Anna the fake job application at MTG Agency.

'Aw cool. What hours do you have to do?' said Anna.

'After school for a few hours and some weekends.'

Anna's face dropped. 'Life's about to get very sucky.'

'Yep. That's the problem with growing up.' Jaz checked her watch and then sighed. 'Speaking of which, I better go and get ready. Until I get my car, I'll have to take the bus into the city.'

As Jaz headed back to her room to get dressed, a great big ball of guilt twisted in her gut. She hated lying to Anna; the worst part was how easily she did it. But it felt awful. Would she ever be able to be truly honest with her best friend again?

Jaz only had to walk a block from the bus stop to the MTG office in the city. She remembered the building from the last time, when Ryan had taken her in to meet with James, the boss. This time around, though, she didn't have Ryan for comfort. This time she was going in alone. And this time she wouldn't be afraid.

She tilted her head back as she stood outside the tall building. The noise of the city drowned away to a hum. It looked just like the other high-rises around, windows and steel. MTG owned the whole building, just the bottom two floors were used for agency while the other floors were a front with other businesses, as far as she knew. Someone walked past her through the front automated doors. He wore a suit and looked like a regular busi-nessman, but Jaz couldn't help but wonder if he was an agent, or maybe he really was just a guy who worked on the fourth floor.

With a deep breath, she walked into the foyer. Two elevators were front and centre, with steps on the left, but Jaz knew to walk around to the right and head down a passageway to the front office of MTG. This time it was a different woman at the reception desk.

'Can I help you?' she asked. Her face was covered with make-up, but it only accentuated her wrinkles. Jaz preferred this fifty-something woman to the last younger, prettier one who'd made goo-goo eyes at Ryan.

'Yes, my name is Jasmine Thomas and I have an appointment.' Jaz wasn't sure how much information to give her. Did this receptionist know what the MTG Agency did, about all the covert operations and overseas missions? Jaz's first guess would be no, but then she thought of Pax and reminded herself how deceiving looks could be. Maybe this woman was one of the originals; maybe she even knew Pax.

'Sure, take a seat.' She gestured to the four red chairs on the oppo-site wall.

Jaz sat and tried to smooth her black pants straight. She'd dressed up as if she were going to a real interview, nice pants and a blue silk cap-sleeved top. But it just made her feel more uncomfortable with her lie. In her bag she carried a folder with her résumé. Just in case.

'Mr Montenegro, Jasmine is here.' The receptionist's voice was clear and professional. She hung up the phone and gestured to Jaz. 'You can go in now. Second door on the right,' she said with a smile.

Jaz heard the lock click as she got close, and pushed her way through the heavy door. When she came to James's door she pulled her shoulders back and breathed in before knocking.

'Come in.'

Inside the familiar office, she found him sitting behind his large desk.

'Hello, again,' she said.

James waved her to a seat by his desk. 'Hi, Jaz? Jasmine?' he asked.

'Jaz is fine.'

'Great. It's good to see you again. We have lots to discuss today, and a few forms to sign as well.' James smiled, his blue eyes instantly making her feel at ease. He was much like her step father Paul, similar age and a warmness to him.

'I'm ready.'

'I'm sure you are.' He paused, appraising her. 'We've never had anyone like you before, Jaz. Yes, we get kids as young as you, like Ryan was, but they never come ready to go into the field, if you know what I mean. Ryan is convinced you can handle yourself, and he tells me you've quickly picked up the techniques he's taught you already.'

Jaz thought back to the time Ryan had taught her how to observe and to follow a target while remaining unobserved. 'Yes, he's a good teacher.' *Among other things*, she thought. It warmed her to know that Ryan had faith, that he believed in her ability and knew she wanted to make a difference. He knew her well.

'Normally we wouldn't have assigned you to a mission so soon, but you open up a perfect opportunity for us to connect with a target's family. Ryan backs you all the way. Marcus is around your age, and we're confident you can gather information from him and his family without putting yourself in too much danger.'

'So, that's all you will need me to do – befriend him, find out personal info, get access into his house and have a look around?'

James leaned back into his chair and smiled. His dark blue suit brought out his eyes and contrasted his blond hair. 'Well, it seems you have a good handle on what's expected. I'm impressed.'

Jaz tried not to grin like fool at his praise. 'I'm getting the idea. Ryan is helping with that, and last night's job helped.'

'Ah yes, the casino.' He sighed. 'You may feel like a piece of jewellery, like you're just there for show, but do know, Jaz, you are playing an important part.' He opened the folder on his desk. 'Janice has given me all this paperwork for you to fill out.' James began to pass over sheets and a pen. 'Also we've set up a bank account that you will have access to, and where your payments will go. And yes, you can claim all your expenses relating to your work.'

That was the last thing on Jaz's mind as she started filling in the sheets. 'Is Janice the one at the front desk?' she asked.

James nodded. 'We have a few who work the desk, and they're all aware of who the agents or operatives are. But the less discussed the better, if you know what I mean. Except with Pax, of course. Now, we've worked out a safe drop for you while you're on this mission. We can't have you being followed back to MTG, so your sister's grave will be your drop.'

Jaz jerked up. 'You know about my sister?' she asked. It was one of those things not talked about, even at home. Almost a secret.

'Yes, we know about Rebecca,' he replied, his voice softer as he looked up from his file. 'Your brother's twin, yes? She died from SIDS when she was just eighteen months? I hope you feel okay about this, Jaz, but can we make our connection point her grave at Karrakatta Cemetery?'

Jaz squeezed her hands together, feeling like a line was being crossed and yet she knew this would be a big part of this job. It was her sister and even thought she didn't remember Rebecca, it just made her feel a bit uncomfortable. And yet she could understand why.

'You will put any information you find inside flowers, and we'll do the same if we need to talk to you. Use the code Ryan showed you, but we'll use this to communicate.' James picked up two books from the floor; both were Richelle Mead's *Vampire Academy*. 'I'm told this is popular with kids your age.'

'Yep, I've read the whole series twice.'

'Good. It won't look out of place in your bag or room. This folder is what we have on Marcus Sinclair. His parents, Carl and Diane, run the most successful art dealership in town, and we think they may be using it as a way to smuggle drugs in and out of the state.' James continued. 'Everything you'll need is in here. The home and business addresses, details on Marcus's favourite spots, hobbies, daily habits, recent photos of the whole family.'

'You've had someone watching him already?'

'Yes, we've had eyes on the family. Once we knew you were a possibility for this mission, one of our guys, Jaxon, collected some info for you.' James slid across another sheet. 'Read this, memorise it, because you can't take it. Marcus likes to surf, so you could try to run into him at the beach.' James waved his hands around. 'I'll leave it up to you, a test of sorts,' he said with a wink.

Jaz felt her pulse jump at the thought of a test but at the same time there was a thrill about this one, a deep need to prove her worth.

'But if you need some guidance, go to Ryan. Pax doesn't do field work, he's more behind the scenes, so Ryan can help you when he's back. But if something's up, then send us a message as soon as you can, and I can have Jaxon meet with you if Ryan isn't around.' He paused, waiting for her nod before continuing. 'There's no time limit on this, Jaz. Just take it slow. Don't pump him for information, let it flow naturally. Be cautious and treat it like a normal friendship, treat him like a normal kid.'

'Got it,' said Jaz, but she wondered if she really was capable of this mission. There were a lot of lies and secrets and opportunities to be caught out.

By the time she'd filled in the forms and taken in everything she could on Marcus and his family, her head felt like an overwatered melon about to burst. 'Thanks, James,' she said as she tucked the *Vampire Academy* book into her bag.

'No, it's I who should be thanking you, Jaz.' His eyes burned with a new, sudden passion. 'My grandad started this Agency years ago to rid the world of criminals who slipped through the system, the ones who can hide behind money and power while they spread drugs and kill people.'

She could see that James believed in the cause, and that was enough for her. 'I'll let you know when I make contact,' she said before heading to the door. Jaz glanced around James's neat, warm office and wondered when she'd be back.

'Be careful,' said James, as he followed her to the door.

They shared a glance. He looked like a businessman upfront, but his eyes gave him away. She could see how big his heart was, and she liked him for it.

'I will. Bye.'

As she walked away from his office, she felt a weird sensation, as if she'd just become a different person. In reality, she'd just found herself.

CHAPTER 3

Jaz glanced at her watch, counting down the seconds as she waited for the school bell. One minute left with her short, bald maths teacher and his constantly squinting eye. One minute left of having Minka behind her throwing bits of paper at her back. One minute left of the bad body odour coming from the guy on her right who clearly hadn't heard of deodorant.

Finally, the siren for lunch went and the sound of scraping chairs filled the room. Jaz threw her books in her bag and headed to the cafeteria.

'Hey, Jazzy, how was maths?' said Anna, who jogged to catch up, her hair in a neat braid.

Just seeing her best friend improved her day. Together they grabbed lunch and sat at their usual table by the big window. It wasn't where the popular people sat, but that just made Jaz like it ten times better. And at least they could see the sky.

'Hey, Taylor,' said Jaz as she watched her other best friend sit next to her, his plate loaded up with sandwiches and fruit.

'Hey, ladies, how's it goin'?'

Taylor gave his gorgeous celebrity smile, the same one Jaz had thought she'd loved. Turns out, she didn't realise what real love was until she met Ryan. It made what she felt for Taylor obsolete. She still loved Taylor – he was her best friend and he was still handsome and kind and popular – but she didn't want to date him. And when he'd kissed her at the ball, it had totally proved they were meant to be just friends.

'Not too bad. Wanna hang out after school?' Jaz asked, as she glanced at Anna who was scoffing her food down like a starving bear.

'So-rry,' Anna mumbled as she tried to swallow her big bite. 'Ricky's asked me to hang out with him. As a matter of fact, I've gotta go meet him in the library now.'

Anna shoved the last bit of her sandwich into her mouth, put her apple in her pocket and picked up her tray. Taylor had stopped unwrapping his lunch to watch Anna, who shrugged and waved goodbye to them as she left.

'And that was Anna Johnson,' said Jaz, a little disappointed. She turned to Taylor. 'You know I'm happy she's happy, but geez it would be nice if Ricky could share.'

Taylor grunted a reply and pushed his tray away from him, leaving his lunch half-unwrapped, and picked up his can of Coke.

'So? You and me after school? You doing anything?' she asked.

'No.' Taylor was staring into his Coke as if it held the answers to the meaning of life. His hair flopped forward and his shoulders were slightly hunched. Suddenly he looked across to her, his face serious. 'Hey, Jaz. If I ever get a girlfriend and end up like that, you *will* tell me that I'm being an arse, neglecting my friends. Won't you? Seriously, how hard would it be to take ten minutes out to eat with us?'

'Yeah, I know. But Anna's never had a real boyfriend before. She's still figuring things out. The novelty will wear off at some stage and she'll come back to us.' Taylor chewed at his lip. 'Come on. How about we hit the firing range after school and see if I can beat your arse,' she said, hoping to cheer him up. It worked. A spark flitted across Taylor's blue eyes.

'You're on, Thomas. It's a date.'

'What! I must be going crazy,' said Minka, who'd paused by their table.

Jaz groaned. Minka, a rich spoiled platinum blonde, hated Jaz, and even more so after Jaz saved her from some drunken louts in an alleyway a few months back. It was like Minka was punishing Jaz for helping her. But Jaz figured Minka just didn't like owing anyone any favours. It didn't help that Minka had always wanted Taylor hanging from her arm, like one of her Gucci bags.

'You two on a date? Hilarious,' Minka added.

Jaz leaned across the table to hold Taylor's hand. 'Of course, Minka. Surely you're not the last to find out?' she said with a smile.

Minka swished her hair over her shoulder as she turned and continued on her way. Jaz let out a chuckle and she glanced at Taylor.

'You were just kidding, right?' he said, his eyebrows raised.

Jaz squeezed his hand before letting it go. 'Of course, Tay. I just love watching her squirm. Besides, you know my heart is elsewhere.'

Taylor sipped his drink before speaking. 'So, how is Ryan? Seen him lately? Does he want to come shooting with us?'

Now it was her turn to slump in her chair. 'I wish, Tay. I haven't seen him for ages. His work keeps him busy, but one day he'll stop by The Ring and surprise me.' She hoped for that every day.

'Don't you text him? Or call?' he asked.

'No. He told me not to,' she said, while scrambling to think up a lie. Her friends didn't know that Ryan was a secret spy and she had to keep it that way. 'He doesn't think it's a good idea while I'm still at school.'

'You're nearly eighteen. The age difference is nothing. Does it worry him?'

'Look at you, Dr Phil. Since when did you become a relationship guru?' she teased, hoping to shift the topic of conversation.

'Ha, I wish. I know nothing, Jaz. Absolutely nothing.' He got that far-away look in his eyes again. Jaz was glad he'd stopped talking about Ryan, but she felt bad he was upset again.

'Shall we go shoot some hoops? I've had enough to eat,' she said.

'Yeah, let's go.'

The tyres of Taylor's Mustang screeched out of the school's car park as Jaz wound down the window to let the air slide through her hair. As they rounded the corner she saw a guy with black sunnies and car watching them. Again. At first he'd seemed creepy and she'd been curious, but now she'd seen him so often that he was like a permanent fixture outside their school. She'd since come to the conclusion that he was someone's dad who had taken a fancy to Taylor's Mustang. He moved to his car as they drove away, and Jaz turned her attention to her driver.

'Now, now, Mr Stewart. You don't want to attract the attention of the police. What would Daddy say?' she said with a laugh.

'Nothing,' he said, before bursting with laughter. 'It would probably be the first time my name got a mention down at the station. Doubt Dad talks about me to his officers and detectives.'

'Aw, come on, Tay. He probably goes on and on about how his son could outshoot all of them.' That put a smile on Taylor's face. 'Oh, I love this old song.' He cranked up the radio and they sang along to Linkin Park's 'The Catalyst'.

Right now, life was perfect. It was a beautiful afternoon, the sun was warm, the breeze was fresh, she was with Taylor and they were singing like they had no cares in the world. Only, she had lots to worry about. Starting her first solo mission was one of them. But for the moment, it was nice just to be a kid.

When they arrived at the range on the outskirts of the city, they parked near the building that looked like an old clubhouse, aged red brick overgrown with shrubs and tall gum trees. Taylor walked in as if it were his home.

'Hey Jaz, great to see you back,' said Stewie from behind the counter as they signed in.

'Great to be back, Stew. I'm looking forward to giving Tay a run for his money,' she said to the officer on duty.

Stew threw back his shaved head and laughed. 'Oh Jaz, I wouldn't go betting money on that just yet. You know he practically lives here.'

'Yeah, yeah. Don't worry, you'll be seeing more of me too. I have a lot to catch up on,' she said with a nod.

'Come on. We better get started, then. This could take a while,' said Taylor with an exaggerated sigh.

Jaz elbowed him in the ribs. 'Thanks for the wonderful encouragement, Tay.'

They entered into the close-range shooting area where stalls were set up. Jaz couldn't see Derik, who wasn't hard to miss with his short orange hair. She looked through the small serving window into the office and found Derik engrossed in a game on his phone. 'Can we get some service here?' she said with a grin.

Derik looked up and smiled. 'Hey, you're back. Good to see, Jaz. Hey, Tay. So what will it be for you both today?'

'I'll go the Browning 9-millimetre, thanks, Derik.'

'Make it two,' said Taylor.

'Do you have a Starfire 9-millimetre in there?' she asked, remembering that Ryan said it would be the gun she'd get to use eventually. For now the Browning was the one to practise with, because it was heavier and would make the Starfire seem easy.

'Yes, we do. That's probably a better, lighter fit for you. Do you want it?' said Derik.

'Ah, no. I'll stick with the Browning.'

'Geez, Jaz. Watch out, you're starting to sound like a gun know-it-all,' said Taylor.

'Just like you, hey?' Jaz laughed. 'You thought I never listened when you talk guns, did you?'

Taylor scratched his chin. 'Nup. You're a girl.'

Jaz rolled her eyes and took the gun and ammunition. 'Thanks, Derik.' She took a set of earmuffs and helped herself to a stall. Then she focused on her target at the end of the room while she loaded the gun. Keeping her breathing steady, she took aim and fired.

When the eight shots were spent, she checked her aim on the target sheet as it whizzed towards her.

'Not bad, Jaz. You're just holding yourself too rigid and tight. Try to relax your shoulders more,' said Taylor.

She took her stance. 'Like this? What else?'

Taylor adjusted a few other things, like her stance width, before she reloaded and went again. Jaz kept going through the rounds while taking on board the advice. Even Derik put his two bob in, but Jaz was happy to listen. She had more riding on this than either of them knew.

'Should I have another go with a different gun, Tay?' she asked as they emptied another clip.

'No, you're better off getting good with that one before you try to adjust to others.' Taylor and Jaz handed the guns back to Derik while they put away the earmuffs. 'What's up with you today anyway?' he asked.

'What do you mean?'

Taylor squinted as if he were trying to see through to her thoughts. 'I've never seen you so focused on shooting before. When you're kicking my arse at fencing or fighting at The Ring, I sometimes see that same focus. But today – today you were somewhere else. Has someone pissed you off?'

The last part made Jaz smile. 'Yeah, you,' she teased. 'I just thrive on the competition Tay. See ya, Derik. We'll be back soon.'

'I'll hold you to that,' he said as he waved them goodbye.

Taylor put his arm around her shoulders as they walked out. 'Come on, Jaz. I know you're competitive, but there was more than that today.'

Jaz didn't reply as they signed out and headed to his car. Only when she'd put her seatbelt on did she speak. 'I guess I really want to learn. I want to be great at it like you. And maybe I'll go into the armed forces after school and do something with it. Have you thought any more about what you'll do?'

Taylor pulled at a thread on his black school pants. 'Not really. I could join the police force and follow in Dad's footsteps, but I want something more than writing fines and going to domestic disturbances. If only I could go straight in as a detective, or maybe join the Federal Police. I want a bit more action.'

'I hear ya,' she said. 'Well, until we figure it out, will you help me with my shooting?'

'Jesus, Jaz. You just have to be a crack shot at everything. You've already beaten me at fencing, now you want to take over the range too?' he teased.

'Come on, Tay. All the practice in the world couldn't get me to your level.' She smirked. 'Please?'

He grinned. 'How could I say no? Besides, I've been trying to get you girls to come here with me all the time.'

'Oh poor, Tay. It can't be that bad? Being St Christian's golden boy isn't enough?'

Taylor laughed as he drove them back into the city. 'It was all right in the beginning but now it just seems tedious. Like I have to put on a performance.'

'More like you've finally seen through Minka's fake personality. Half of them are like that. I'm glad you've opened your eyes. *So*, can we do this again next week?'

Taylor's face lit up like she'd promised him the world. 'Hell yes. Do you think Anna might come next time too?' he asked.

'Yeah, she probably will.' Jaz was doubtful, but who was she to upset Taylor?

'Hey, you. Was that Taylor's rumbling Mustang I heard?'

'Yep, we were just at the range.' Jaz glanced at her mum, who was elbow deep in the takeaway menus, their Tuesday-night ritual. Tasha was looking back at her with a whimsical smile. 'What?' Jaz asked.

'Nothing. You just look really happy.' Tasha's blonde hair was out of her normal tight bun and cascaded around her shoulders.

'I am.' Jaz went up to her mum and gave her a hug. She had her mum's lean body and her blue eyes, but that was where the resemblance ended. Jaz's dark hair and tinted skin made her stand out in her family. Her father was dead and Tasha refused to tell her about him. But her stepfather, Paul, had been her dad since she was two and she had her half-brother, Simon. So, she wasn't lacking in the family department, but still she wished she knew something more about her father. More than just the medallion of his she wore around her neck.

'Aw, thanks honey. I love you,' said Tasha, as she caressed Jaz's face in her hands. 'Now, it's do-or-die decision-making. Italian or Chinese?'

Jaz sat on the stool behind the large marble kitchen bench, her hand automatically feeling for her father's medallion. As usual, Tasha saw her but didn't comment. Tasha knew how to avoid the whole 'father' situation with perfection. 'Italian, I'm thinking. Where's Simon and Dad?' Jaz asked as she ran her finger over the circle. She loved the carving of St Michael, the archangel, his wings out, sword raised as he stood on what looked like a demon he was about to slay. Around the edge of the pendant were the words *St Michael Pray for Us*. Jaz wasn't religious, but had her father been?

'Simon's still with your dad at the office. They should be back in half an hour. So, it's just us,' said Tasha as she handed over the Italian take-out menu.

'Hey Mum, was my real father religious?' Jaz asked.

Tasha went rigid. 'Um, maybe a little, I think. Why?'

'This was his, right? Or was it given to him by someone who was religious?' said Jaz.

Tasha sighed. 'I think his mother may have got it for him when he was little and he wore it every day as a good-luck charm. I think it was special to him.'

'Is that why he gave it to you?'

Jaz studied the faraway look on her Mum's face. She almost seemed in pain. Did she miss him? Or had he hurt her? 'Did he love you, Mum?'

Tasha nodded, a small smile of memories on her lips. 'Yes, I believe he did, Jasmine. But sometimes that's not enough. You'll find out in life that you have to make some hard decisions, and I hope you choose what's right for you. No matter how much you love someone, sometimes they're just wrong for you.'

Ryan flashed through Jaz's mind and she shook it away. Would her mum think he was a wrong choice? She certainly wouldn't consider the idea boyfriend to be a guy who carried a gun, sought out drug lords and possibly killed people. Damn. Still, Jaz didn't feel in her heart that it was wrong. Maybe she was optimistic or naive, and maybe she wasn't thinking about her future in the same way her mum was. Tasha probably had dreams for Jaz of marriage, a career and kids. Jaz wanted that, just not now. Right now she wanted to make a difference.

CHAPTER 4

'Is she okay?' asked Anna as she joined Taylor and Jaz at the front of the old brick school.

Jaz had been staring off into space; actually, she had been staring at the school gates at the spot where she'd last seen Ryan. If she concentrated really hard she was sure she could make him appear in his favourite worn jeans that hung from his lean hips. He would be wearing a snug T-shirt that showed his muscled physique, and his clipped hair would give him that tough, edgy look that she loved so much. She squeezed her eyes shut and opened them again. Still no Ryan. Damn. With a sigh she turned to Anna. 'I'm fine,' said Jaz, but even she wasn't convinced. 'What took you so long?'

Taylor brushed his fringe back absentmindedly, but Jaz could tell by the way his eyes were locked onto Anna that he wanted to know the answer to her question too.

'Oh, um.' Anna's pale skin turned rosy red, making her freckles fade. 'I was just saying goodbye to Ricky.' She adjusted her bag on her shoulder. Taylor looked at his feet and Jaz just felt lonelier. She missed Ryan.

'So, what shall we do this afternoon now that we're all free?' said Anna.

Taylor looked like he was going to say something but swallowed it. Just as well, because Jaz wasn't up to snarky comments.

'Shall we go to the range?' Anna tried again.

'Jaz and I have been twice this week already, including yesterday,' said Taylor, his voice verging on grouchy.

'Oh, okay.' Anna looked slightly put out. 'Shall we go to The Ring?'

Jaz found herself searching for Ryan by the gates again. But no one was there, not even the students, who had all left, leaving the three of them about to get a hurry-up from the teachers. 'I don't feel like going to The Ring today, can we do something else?' To tell the truth, Jaz was dying to get to The Ring and see if maybe Ryan was there, or had been. But all week she'd been disappointed. She needed to change that. She couldn't live her life on tenterhooks, waiting.

'Oh, Jaz. You look so lost. Have you still not heard from Ryan?' Anna put her arm around her shoulders. Trust Anna to notice, even when she was in her Ricky lover-boy bubble.

'No, but I didn't expect to.' This was making Jaz feel worse. Then an idea struck. 'Hey, you guys wanna go to Cottesloe and chill out at the beach? Grab a coffee?'

Taylor and Anna shot each other confused looks and then shrugged.

'I guess so,' said Taylor.

'Something different,' said Anna, whose skin was sensitive and so she never ventured to the beach. Jaz could just see her screwing up her nose at the sticky white sand.

'We don't have to sit on the beach, Anna, but it would be nice to get a coffee and watch the waves.' *It might be calming*, she thought. It also might give her a chance to run into her target, Marcus Sinclair. And quite possibly scare herself to death. But how scary could an eighteen year old be? It's not like he was the one carrying guns and trafficking drugs.

'All right, to the beach it is,' said Taylor, who finally smiled. 'To the 'Stang.'

With a squeal, Anna ran to his car yelling, 'Shotgun!'

Jaz ran behind them and couldn't help laughing.

'Tay, can you go slowly down Marine Parade, I wanna take in the view,' said Jaz later, starting to feel better.

'Yes, ma'am.'

Jaz was on the right side of the car, so she could look out at the houses along Marine Parade. Anna had her eyes left, where the ocean rolled back and forth beside the road. The sun was sitting low in the sky; three more hours and they'd be able to watch a glorious sunset over the water.

For now, Jaz was watching the houses on the right, trying to catch the numbers. Suddenly she found Marcus's house, with its two-storey greatness surrounded by a fancy slat fence. She couldn't see through it but it looked in keeping with the million-dollar waterfront property. Having the Indian Ocean at their doorstep must be perfect for a surfer.

'Where to, Jaz?' asked Taylor as the golf course appeared on the right.

'See if you can find a park near Indiana's.' It wasn't overly warm, so the only beachgoers were the diehard ones, while the rest walked, rode bikes or mingled around in groups chatting.

'I'm the first to say I'm not a beach fan, but it really is gorgeous here. All the green grass and pine trees,' said Anna wistfully. 'We should come more often.'

Taylor found a car park, and together they walked along the path to Indiana's for coffee. The large off-white building with its pale green roof and masses of windows, some of them arched, was situated on the beach side of the road. If you stepped out the front of the large building, you were on sand and metres from the water.

Inside they got their coffees, while Jaz searched every male face.

'Jaz?' Anna repeated. 'Hello?'

'What?' Jaz took the cup Anna was waving in her face.

'You okay, you seem distracted?'

'Sorry. Just been a while since I've been here. Trying to take it all in.' Man, were her lies getting worse? 'Lets go sit outside under the trees.'

She led them to a nice spot where they sat on the grass and shared the large chocolate biscuits Anna had bought.

Taylor leaned back on his elbows, his tie hanging loosely around his neck and his shades firmly in place to block out the sun. 'This was a great idea, Jaz.' Two girls walked past in their bikini tops and sarong skirts. 'Brilliant, actually,' he added as his head turned to follow the girls.

'Oh my God,' mumbled Anna. While Anna and Taylor began a debate about suitable beach attire, Jaz strained to see the faces on the guys at the beach. There were so many, how would she find Marcus? Especially when he might not even be here? She pictured him from the Agency file: he was tall, with dark green eyes and dark straight hair that sat just above his shoulders. She wondered which operative had staked him out and how did they find out his eye colour? On his driver's licence, looking through binoculars, or did they stop him to ask a random question and study him?

When her eyes started to smart with tears, she gave up straining them. She couldn't expect to just find him with a click of her fingers.

'I'm going for a walk.' Taylor held out his hand and took their empty coffee cups with him.

'Thanks, Tay.' As he walked away Jaz couldn't help but admire her friend. 'How did we end up with a friend as hot as Tay?' she said to Anna.

'I don't know. He's always been handsome, Jaz, and nice. It's not often you get those two things together. Aren't we the lucky ones.' Anna was watching Taylor too.

'So, does Ricky do it for you?'

Anna startled. 'What? What do you mean?'

'Just wondering. You guys have been going out for over a month now. That's the longest relationship any of us has had,' said Jaz with a snort.

'Yeah, not for lack of trying, hey?' Anna agreed. 'But yes, I'm happy with Ricky. Sure, he's no Taylor in the looks department, nor does he have a body like Ryan's, but Ricky is smart and so that keeps us interesting.'

Jaz nodded.

'Why, what do *you* think about Ricky?'

'It's not for me to say; he's your pick, Anna. Besides, I don't really know him. We haven't really seen you lately, let alone had time to get to know Ricky. Why don't you bring him to eat lunch with us?'

Anna sat forward and picked at the grass. 'Ricky doesn't really feel comfortable eating in the caf. That's why we stick to the library.'

'Yeah, but we aren't going to bite him. Tay and I miss you, Anna, and if you hadn't noticed, Taylor sits at our table every day now.'

'I'd noticed that. And I'm glad I'm not leaving you to sit on your own.' She thought for a moment. 'I'll ask Ricky if he'll join us. I'd really like for you to get to know him. He's quite serious at times, but he does like me and is so thoughtful.'

'I'm happy for you,' said Jaz.

'So am I. Wait, what am I happy about?' said Taylor as he rejoined them.

'That Anna's happy.'

Taylor nodded.

'Hey, I meant to ask about the job. When do you start?' said Anna.

'She starts this weekend,' said Taylor. 'On Saturday.'

Jaz wondered if Taylor was rubbing it in. They had become closer now that it was just the two of them most of the time, and she'd needed his company more than she realised. 'Yep. It will be great. My own money.'

'What will you be doing?' asked Anna.

'Bits of everything, really. Sometimes at the front desk and other times out the back, filing.'

'Can we come and visit?' Anna looked hopeful and it made Jaz feel hot and sweaty.

'Um, I don't know. I'd hate to get fired. Maybe just warn me when you're coming in?' James had told her not to worry about this, that they could just say she'd gone to run an errand and then she'd have time to get the MTG office. He said there was usually only an initial visit at the beginning, but once everyone saw where she was working they'd let her be. Jaz just hoped he was right.

'How long until you can afford a car?' asked Taylor.

'Why? Are you sick of driving me around in the 'Stang? Would you rather me drive you around in some old clumpa?' said Jaz with a smirk.

'Really? You would buy some old bit of crap?'

'She's going to get a bright yellow Ford Fiesta,' said Anna with a laugh.

Taylor pulled a face. 'No. No. Let me help you, please.'

'Well, I could get a loan now that I have a permanent job. So, after a few pays, maybe you could help me find something? I know I could never get something as cool as your Mustang, but I won't be seen in a Ford Fiesta of any colour.'

Anna and Taylor went on trying to find the right car and colour for Jaz while she took the opportunity to do some more people-watching. She looked behind her, along Marine Parade where the rows of buildings sat on the other side of the road. She could just make out the blue shade on the Bluewaters Cafe. That was supposed to be one of Marcus's favourite places for early breakfast and late-afternoon meals. Had he visited already today? Maybe she could get her friends to drop in? And then there was the Cottesloe Beach Hotel, which was behind them. Marcus was now eighteen, so apparently he liked to get a beer and watch the sunset from the

Verandah Bar. Must be nice to live down the street, not having to drive home and miss the view. It seemed such a world away from The Ring, when in fact they were roughly a suburb apart.

Jaz wasn't worried that she hadn't spotted Marcus. After all, she started work on Saturday, so until then she wasn't going to sweat the small stuff. Right now the sun was dipping lower in the sky and her friends were laughing together. Anna had hit Taylor on the arm for suggesting she get a pink VW beetle. Their smiles cleared the heavy thoughts from her mind. This is how it was meant to be, the three of them, together having fun.

CHAPTER 5

THE MORNING AIR still had a chill to it at six o'clock. But nearly an hour later, Jaz was covered with a film of sweat.

'Harder, Jaz,' said Bags as he urged her on.

Grunting, Jaz put force behind her jab. Still, it wasn't enough to move Bags. He was strong, solid and tall. And he was also a trained boxer.

'That's it. Now uppercuts,' he added.

Jaz felt the sweat run down her forehead, pausing on her eyebrows before dropping and landing on her gloves or the mat below. The same mat she would have to clean at some stage. But that was a love job – well, a love of Pax, not the cleaning. She hated seeing him down on his knees, scrubbing away.

'All right, Jaz. Another ten. Make them count.'

Trying to keep her breathing even, she pounded out the last ten uppercuts with as much force and strength she could muster. And maybe she let out some of her frustrations and fears along with it.

After the tenth, Jaz stood trying to catch her breath. Bags had dropped his pads and began to take her gloves off for her. 'Thanks, Bags. Great workout. I enjoyed that, even if I can't feel my arms.'

Bags reached over and squeezed her bicep. 'Well, I can and they feel and look great. You have such strength, Jaz, hidden in those lean arms and legs. I wish I could go back to being so young and fit. It was much easier then.'

'Aw, come on Bags. You've only just made forty. That's still young, really.'

Bags chuckled, a sound that was deep and infectious. 'Oh, sweet thing. I love you, thanks. And thanks for the early morning workout. Great way to start a Saturday.'

'Yeah, great way for me to get rid of some nerves before work,' said Jaz as she wiped her face with her small towel.

'Ah, well, that makes sense. I could feel some tension coming out. Those last jabs were hard.'

Jaz smiled. Bags was straight down the line. If you were throwing half-baked punches, he'd tell you. But he'd also tell you if you were impressing him. That didn't happen a lot, so when it did happen you knew you were doing well.

'Thanks, Bags. Means a lot.'

'You better go and get cleaned up for work, and I have another willing student in fifteen minutes,' he said.

'Let me guess, another middle-aged man trying to reclaim his youth?'

Bags laughed with a nod. 'I think we've both been in this gym for too long, Jaz.'

Jaz's laugh matched his. 'Thanks again, Bags. We'll have a proper bout sometime soon, yeah?'

'Anytime, angel.' He gave Jaz a hug and then she stepped off the mat and headed to the change rooms, where she had a special area sectioned off; they didn't get many women at The Ring, but if they did come, they also used Jaz's shower and change area. It was a little on the rustic side, but Jaz loved its uniqueness. And it gave her the privacy she needed.

Jaz picked up her bag, which she'd left just inside the change-room doorway, and went to her cubicle. As she flung her towel over the door, she spotted it: a large sticky note with a numbered code all over it. Jaz felt her legs threaten to buckle beneath her as she realised what this was, and who had written that code. Ryan. He'd left her a note in here before. Jaz could hardly contain a squeal of excitement. She put the note in her bag so the steam wouldn't ruin it, and then quickly went about her shower.

It was probably the fastest shower in the history of humankind, but Jaz wanted time to decipher the note before she had to head to Cottesloe and find Marcus.

She changed into a pair of denim shorts, a black sports crop top that she covered with a blue holey T-shirt and her black Converse trainers. Jaz left her hair out to dry and, grabbing her bag, headed to Pax's office. The door to his house was still closed, so he was probably enjoying a sleep-in or a walk to the bakery. *Good*, Jaz thought; she wanted some alone time to work out her message.

In the bottom of her bag she searched for the *Reps* magazine Ryan gave her ages ago. She'd actually enjoyed some of the articles, which inspired her to stay healthy as well as toned.

'Okay,' she said as she pulled out the crumpled publication, 'let's see if I can remember this.' Jaz stared at the first few codes.

45-13-6/68-3-7

Page, line, word. She worked her way through the numbers.

All the best for today.

Jaz figured he'd had trouble trying to find 'good luck' in the fitness magazine. But still, it was nice that he'd thought of her and remembered her first official day as an Agency employee. She sighed and looked up towards the main floor of the gym: Ryan had been here at some stage, to deliver the note. Did he stay for a workout, as cover in case anyone was watching him? Was it while she'd been at Cottesloe, or maybe when she was at the firing range? She felt an ache in her chest at the thought of missing him, but maybe he'd done that on purpose. Did he know how hard it was for her to let him go? Was she that transparent?

Jaz glanced at her chunky watch on the leather band. She'd better get a move on if she was going to get to Cottesloe by eight when Marcus's favourite coffee shop opened.

Quickly she jammed the magazine back into her bag and returned it to the change room. She held the sticky note in her hands, running her finger over the numbers Ryan had written. Part of her wanted to put it in her pocket and keep as a memento, but the other part of her knew she shouldn't keep any trace. Not because she thought someone was following her and would find it but later on, but down the track when she was undertaking operations like Ryan did, she would have to be very careful. So, she may as well start now and get into the habit of not leaving a trail.

Back in the office, she put the note into Pax's fancy shredder that practically minced the paper. There was no way someone could piece anything back together, and now that she knew what Pax did for the Agency, she realised just how important that shredder was. Not to mention the metal drum he had out the back, which he used to burn most of his rubbish. Funny how you don't question things about the people you love. It made her realise how easy it was to keep secrets.

Jaz opened her phone cover and made sure she still had her fifty-dollar note and bus card in the slit, and then pushed it into her shorts' pocket. She waved goodbye to Bags and stepped out into the bright sunshine, the air no longer fresh but warm and filled with city smells. Jaz put on her sunglasses: they were silver-rimmed, large and reflective, much like what the pilots wore in *Top Gun*. Jaz loved them, and she liked being able to see everyone without them knowing she was watching. Perfect for today's mission. She could even use them as a mirror if need be. Next, she fished out her music player from her back pocket and put in the earplugs while she headed to the bus stop.

She was listening to Avicii's 'I Could Be the One' when she got off the bus and walked along Marine Parade. It was a lot quieter than the last time she was here. Most were probably tucked up in bed after a big Friday night. But still there were those who were out, walking dogs, exercising or just enjoying the morning beauty of the beach. It was tranquil.

Jaz headed to Bluewaters Cafe and ordered a coffee, the whole time her eyes searching for Marcus. She was well aware that she might not even see him. He was eighteen, after all, so he was probably sleeping off a hangover.

She found a table by the window to enjoy her drink. She knew she couldn't stay here all day; once she'd finished her coffee, she'd have to move on. Damn, she should have brought a book and could have pretended to read. She'd just have to lean up against a tree and pretend she was dozing. God, if only her friends knew that this was her new job: lying in the dappled sunlight trying to spot a certain Marcus Sinclair.

Realistically, she knew it would get harder. She hadn't even tried to think about what could happen down the track. How far had Ryan gone on his undercover missions? Did he sleep with people? Maybe killed others to be a part of the gang? Jaz shuddered as her mind spun cogs.

'This is going to be a long day,' she mumbled under her breath.

But the intel that had been gathered was right. Marcus did like his

Saturday stop by the Bluewaters for breakfast. He walked in alone. Dark, almost-skinny-leg jeans hung low on his waist and he wore a rustic red T-shirt. It was weird seeing the target in the flesh. But he was just like the photos they'd shown her. His hair was longish but clean. Jaz resisted the urge to run and hide as he walked past, but Marcus only had eyes for the counter.

'The usual, Marcus?' the guy behind the counter asked.

'Yeah, cheers, Russ.' Marcus handed over money before sliding his wallet into the back of his pants. Jaz had nearly finished her coffee and had to figure out a plan.

The cafe was almost half-full, mainly couples eating together. Marcus went straight to a corner table. Presumably his regular one.

Jaz took out her earphones, leaving them on the table by her coffee cup. Then she pulled out her phone and pretended to type a text message. Out of the corner of her eye she saw him get his order of bacon and eggs. When her stomach groaned she realised she should have got herself breakfast, but with her nerves she didn't think she'd be able to eat.

Okay, she had an idea, she just had to see if it would work. Standing up, she put her phone in her pocket, walked to the counter and asked for a takeaway coffee. Marcus still hadn't finished his breakfast by the time the barista had made her coffee, so she continued out the door. She stopped just outside and leaned against the wall of the cafe, far enough so Marcus couldn't see her through the window.

Her heart was pounding and her hand was shaking so much that she was worried she'd spill her coffee before it was time. *Deep breaths*, she told herself as she fought the war with her nerves. Jaz was lucky enough to have a reflection of the open glass door that let her see into the cafe. She pulled out her phone so she had a reason to be standing where she was without drawing attention to herself.

The blood in her head pulsed through her ears, almost like a clock counting down. Her muscles began to tense and then she saw movement. Without second-guessing what she saw, or if her plan would work, she headed back into the cafe with her head down.

She was relieved to see his black Converse shoes just as she walked into him. To make sure it was dramatic enough, Jaz squeezed her coffee cup, causing the lid to fall off as the cup contents splashed back against her. She did too good a job, as hot coffee scalded her skin through her shirt.

'Ah. Ohmygod! Sorry,' she blurted out.

'Sorry,' he said at the same time.

Jaz practically shoved her phone and the coffee cup, with whatever was left in it, into Marcus's hands.

'Sorry, thanks. I've gotta… ouch,' she mumbled out as she pulled her T-shirt off over her head. 'Boy, that was hot.' Jaz used her T-shirt to wipe the coffee off her skin. She could see the hot drink had left her chest slightly pink. At least she was making all this seem real and accidental.

Jaz finished mopping up then held her T-shirt in front of her, scrunched up like a stained coffee ball. 'I'm so sorry, it's really not my day,' she said. Finally, she had the chance to look at him. When they said he had deep green eyes they weren't wrong. He was much cuter in person.

He was smiling at her, a little dimple forming in his cheek. He was fresh-faced, no stubble.

'Nice abs,' he said. His eyes lifting to hers. 'Are you okay? Weren't you just in the cafe?' he asked. His eyebrow raised slightly.

'Um, yeah. I forgot my earphones. See, I told you. Bad day. I should have stayed in bed.' Talking to him came easily. She just had to think of him as a normal guy, not a target. Jaz pointed to the table she'd been sitting at, her earphones still there. She left Marcus there, holding her stuff while she stepped into the cafe to collect them. 'I'm sorry again. I really need them for the bus.'

'They would have been all right here. The guys would have kept them behind the counter for you.'

Jaz nodded and shivered slightly as the breeze gusted past.

'Here, let me help.' Marcus handed her back her phone and coffee. Then, before she knew it, he'd pulled off his own shirt.

'Nice abs.' It was the first thing that came out of her mouth and she chuckled. Marcus smiled as he handed over his T-shirt. His chest was smooth and tanned, as if he got around without a shirt on, and his abs were defined. She wondered what he did to get them. He was probably thinking the same thing about her.

'Thanks. Here, take my shirt.'

'Oh, are you sure?'

'Yep, I live just down the road. Not a problem.'

'Really. That would be great. I don't fancy riding home on the bus like this, or smelling like coffee.' Jaz pulled a face. 'Hang on.' She quickly chucked her coffee cup into a nearby bin, along with her shirt, and stuffed her phone into her shorts, then took the shirt offered. 'I can't believe you're giving me the shirt off your own back. Thanks…?'

'Marcus,' he supplied.

'Thanks, Marcus. I'm Jaz.' She pulled on his red T-shirt. It smelled nice and manly. It made her think of Ryan, not the cute guy opposite her. 'Comfy,' she said, as he admired his shirt on her. Jaz turned toward the street, wondering what to do next.

'Hey, don't you want my number?' he asked.

Jaz turned back, her brow crossed.

'So you can return my shirt?' he said.

'Oh, you want your shirt back? I figured that since you live here in Cott, and with those designer labels—' She indicated his jeans and shoes. 'That you wouldn't miss one little shirt?' She was being cheeky but she hoped he liked cheeky.

'Is that so?' he said, putting his hands on his hips. It just made his shirtless body look more appealing. 'It just so happens you're right, I can afford to lose a shirt, but that shirt also happens to be my favourite. That shirt and I have seen some awesome things together. And it's lucky.'

'Lucky, you say? I could definitely use some of that today.' Jaz fished out her phone and held it out to Marcus for him to enter his details. 'But I can't steal your luck, so I'd best return it.' She smiled as he took her phone.

She read the contact entry when he handed it back. 'Marcus Sinclair. Hi,' she said.

As she put her phone away, Marcus pulled out his and held it out to her. She raised an eyebrow curiously.

'I need yours too. What if my shirt brings you too much good luck and you forget to return it? I need to be able to bombard you with calls and texts until you give it back.'

Jaz nodded and reached for his phone. As she entered her details, she wondered if his phone held any secrets. Phone numbers of his dad's business partners. Maybe they had Marcus pick up things. Who knew how involved he could be. She liked to think no parent would include their kid in anything like this, but she wasn't naive enough to not know that bad people didn't make money from having ethics.

Marcus's fingers brushed against hers as he took his phone back. 'Jaz Thomas – shirt girl.' He glanced at her. 'Nice to meet you,' he said with a grin. 'But you didn't need to add that. I won't forget you.'

'Because I have your favourite shirt?'

'No, because one, you took your shirt off in the main street of Cott and two, I've never seen a chick with abs before.'

He didn't run his eyes over her body or come across as creepy. It was like he was just stating a fact. 'Thanks. I work hard to keep them.'

Marcus glanced at his watch and then sighed. 'I'm sorry, I've got to catch up with friends, but I hope to hear from you soon.' He bent down and picked up a skateboard, which had been by the doorway. 'See ya, Jaz. Take good care of my shirt.' Then he smiled, turned and launched onto his skateboard. He didn't look back, but when he picked up speed he flipped his skateboard in the air and kept going down the path. Yeah, he knew how to use a skateboard. Probably how he kept his own abs tight.

Lifting her head, she followed Marcus, who was rolling down the street half-naked. She looked down at his rusty T-shirt and tucked the front section into her shorts. Well, she'd certainly come away from this meeting with more than she expected. A shirt and a phone number. Now she just had to report her morning's work and wait until it was time to meet Marcus again. Next time though, she wouldn't be as scared. After all, he was just a boy.

CHAPTER 6

Jaz went back to The Ring to collect her bag. She was also hoping for another note from Ryan, even though she knew it was unlikely.

The Ring was still open when she got there late in the morning, though Bags was long gone. 'Pax, you here?' she called out, as the smell of leather and sweat got stronger the further into the gym she went.

'In here,' he called out. Pax's head stuck out of the storage room. 'I'm just getting ready to scrub some mats.' A wicked grin spread over his face. 'And you're just in time to help me, aren't you?'

'Yeah, I guess.' Jaz returned his smile then left her phone, sunnies and music player by her bag and went to help Pax carry out the buckets and sponges.

'So, you're back early?' he queried. 'I'm not sure if that's a good or bad thing.'

'It's good. I met Marcus and got his number.' Pax's eyes shot open. 'Oh, and his shirt,' she laughed.

Pax's jaw dropped as he took in her shirt. 'Really? How did you manage that?'

Jaz begun to scrub down the mats beside Pax and told him how it had gone down.

Pax sat back on his heels when she finished. 'Wow. You really get how this stuff works, don't you?' Jaz paused and he rushed on to explain. 'I mean, just for you to plan that out and for it to work. Obviously Ryan has rubbed off on you.'

Jaz wanted to say that Ryan hadn't rubbed off on her enough; she'd gladly take more. Instead, she simply shrugged. 'Or maybe I just watch too many spy movies,' she said with a smirk. 'It wasn't that hard. He seems nice.'

Pax's eyes narrowed. 'You just be careful,' he warned. 'If his family is up to no good, then you don't want to be caught up in it. And don't let yourself like him too much. Many an agent has been warned about that. It does happen but it never ends well.' He looked so serious and worried.

Jaz almost wanted to tell him there was no chance of that because she was hung up on Ryan. But that admission would be ten times worse.

'It's okay, Pax. I'll be careful. Shall we finish these mats? I have to get home and pass on my notes, so to speak.'

'I understand. Just know that if anything feels funny you can come to me. I'll be here for you, Jaz. I know I don't do rescues or play with guns. I'm just the computer guy. Need a new ID or to get into a country, that's me. But I can help you in other ways. I just hope you don't get into a position where you need any of that.'

Jaz grabbed Pax's hand. 'I know you don't like that I've joined and I know that you'll worry about me. All you can do is trust that I'm capable of looking out for myself. It'll be okay, Pax.' It was so sweet that he cared. He could have told her mum and made it hard for her to join, but he didn't. He'd supported her, and that meant the world. 'I'll be okay.'

When she got back to her house, her mum was leaving.

'Hey, Jasmine, I'm taking Simon to the shops. Do you want to come? Or do you want me to get anything?' Tasha was in jeans, ballet flats and a designer top. Her hair was whisked up in a sexy bun.

'No thanks, Mum, I'm fine. And I've got some homework to catch up on.'

Tasha paused as she reached for the car keys. 'Are you sick?' she joked.

'Ha ha.' Jaz smirked.

Tasha cast her eyes over Jaz's shirt and then shrugged, as if giving up over her daughter's choice of attire. Jaz preferred Adidas, Lonsdale and the Bad Boy MMA clothes to her mum's choice of Lisa Ho and Alex Perry.

'Dad's at work but we'll be back this afternoon.' Then Tasha put on the biggest pair of Gucci sunglasses Jaz had ever seen – they hid half her face – and walked out the door, calling for Simon.

Simon came running down the stairs. 'Hi, sis, bye, sis,' he said as he ran past.

'Hey, what are you going to get?' she asked him as he paused by the door. That was the most running she'd seen Simon do in the past month. He may have tended toward the computer geek, like his dad Paul, but Simon also had Jaz's coordination. He could play sports, was quite good at it, just chose not to. It was a waste. But Simon did adhere to their mum's fashion tastes, which was evident with his designer jeans, polo shirt and expensive leather shoes.

'The new Final Fantasy game is out, and the latest iPhone.' He shot her a grin like he'd just won the lottery. 'You want anything?'

'Actually, can you get me a skateboard?'

Simon screwed his face up. 'Say what? Punching people isn't enough, now you want to hurt yourself on a skateboard,' he teased.

'Ha ha. Just go and ask for one that would suit me, please? I don't care what it looks like, just as long as it's a good one. Okay?' Jaz hoped Simon didn't bring back some pink or fluoro one. But it didn't really matter. It was just an idea that had occurred to her, a way to get closer to Marcus. She didn't want to look like a complete fool on a skateboard, so practise she must.

'Righto, sis. I'm sure I can manage that.'

'Thanks, Si.' As he left the house, Jaz felt the warmth of love for her half-brother. He was a good kid. It made her think of his twin sister Becky and how much different life would be if she had survived. Would she have been more like Jaz or like Simon? Knowing she would be visiting her grave soon made Jaz feel sad and wistful. They didn't go to her grave anymore, well maybe her mum and Paul did but they didn't tell them. Jaz's only memory of Becky was visits to her grave site and her baby photos. Jaz hadn't been since she was maybe ten, which made her feel like a bad sister.

'Let's get back to work,' she said to herself. She grabbed a Coke from the fridge and a chocolate bar from her mum's secret stash behind the flour tin in the pantry, before heading up to her room.

Automatically, she began to put away the folded clean clothes her mum had left on her bed. Her room was no longer a cave of darkness and mess. Now she loved leaving her heavy dark purple curtains open, letting the light fill her large room. The carpets and walls were grey and the room was accentuated with deep purples and black. She'd realised, after seeing Ryan's spotless organised home, that if she wanted to be treated like an adult, she had to behave like one. Her messy room had been the first thing to fix.

Jaz put her Coke and snack on her study desk and caught her reflection in the full-length mirror. Marcus's shirt looked good on her. She lifted the material up so she could smell the earthy male scent. Spending time with Marcus would be good. It would keep her mind off missing Ryan. Closing her eyes, she inhaled one last time before taking the shirt off and finding Ryan's jumper, which she still had. It no longer smelled like him and had been washed many times, but it was as close to him as she could get.

'Okay, where did I leave that book?' Pulling open the drawer of her desk, she found the copy of *The Vampire Academy* that James had given her. Then, with a piece of paper and a pen, she began the long task of recording today's events for her boss. She knew the basics of what she wanted to say. 'Have made contact with target. Have phone number and will meet again soon.' Only it wasn't that easy to find those words in the book. At times, Jaz forgot she was looking for a certain word and found herself actually reading the book, getting swept up in Rose and Lissa's story. Who knew searching for words such as 'contact' and 'target' would take so long.

Next time she caught up with James she'd have to ask if they could switch to an ebook. Then she could just search for the word she needed and – boom – there would be the page number. It would save them both loads of time.

Jaz heard voices from downstairs and was surprised to see it was well after lunch. Her stomach groaned as if to remind her food was needed to function. She'd just been so engrossed in her task.

Putting her note into her book, she slipped downstairs. 'Hey, did anyone bring back any food?' she asked. Jaz started looking through the bags full of shopping, hoping to find something edible.

Tasha pulled out a bacon-and-cheese twist roll from a bag. 'How did I know you'd be hungry,' she said. 'Please use a knife and not pick at it like a barbarian.'

Jaz was just about to pull apart a handful of the roll but quickly put it on the chopping board.

'Here, sis, will this do? S'posed to be top notch.' Simon lifted up a skateboard. It was red and black underneath, with the word Habitat in the design.

'Cool, cheers, bro. I like that.' Jaz took it off him and spun one of the wheels. 'Now I just have to figure out how to ride it.'

'Why on earth would you want a skateboard?' her mum asked.

Jaz shrugged. 'Just saw some kids with one and it looked like fun. I could get to The Ring faster on it too, especially seeing as someone won't help me buy a car,' said Jaz, with a big dramatic eye roll.

Jaz was about to tell her mum that she had a job and could buy her own car soon but she stopped, remembering that Pax said not to mention her job just yet and to say he was paying her now. 'Besides, Pax is paying me at The Ring. I'm in a more permanent role, so I'll have a car before too long.'

Tasha's frown lines appeared.

'Come on, Mum. You can't keep me off the road forever. I'll be an adult soon and you won't have any say.'

'I know, Jaz. I know.' Tasha put her hand to her forehead as if she was getting a headache. 'I'll talk to your dad tonight and see what we can do to help. I like that you're saving for your own car, but I would still prefer to help you get something that's reliable and safe.'

Jaz groaned. 'Please not a Volvo.' Simon burst out laughing.

Jaz grabbed her bit of bread, shoving in a mouthful as she went outside with her new skateboard. She'd have a bit of a practice before she headed to the cemetery. Maybe Taylor would come and drive her, save her taking the bus.

Just as she was about to stand on the skateboard, she felt eyes on her back. 'What do you want?' she asked Simon.

'Seeing if you stack it. Maybe I should have got you a helmet and knee pads too,' he said with a smirk.

'Bugger off, Si,' she said, teasingly. Finishing the last of her bread, she pushed off the ground and rolled along on the board. Simon got bored of watching after five minutes, especially when she hadn't stacked it, and went back inside.

With him gone, she attempted the thing she'd seen Marcus do and quickly realised it took a lot of skill to get the board off the ground, let alone as high as he had. Maybe she should watch a few YouTube 'how to' clips. That could be her job tomorrow.

After putting the skateboard in her room by the door, she texted Taylor and asked him if he was busy. His reply was instant.

Nup.

Cool. Can you give me a ride to the cemetery pls?

Sure. C U in 5 J

Jaz pulled out one of the fake plastic hydrangeas in a vase on her desk. She'd bought them a few days ago because they had a stem perfect for hiding a note in.

Jaz pulled out the coded message hidden in her book and rolled it up tightly enough to slide it into the fake flower stem, then plugged the end. When Taylor turned up and honked his horn, Jaz was still sitting there looking at the flower, so many things running through her mind. The message, her job and, most of all, going to the cemetery to see her sister. Simon didn't like to visit anymore, he said she was gone and visiting wouldn't bring her back. But on the anniversary of her death Jaz had noticed that her parents would disappear together and had realised they still came to talk to her. Maybe Jaz would have gone too, but it was hard to mourn someone you couldn't really remember.

Shaking herself from her daze, she headed downstairs. Simon was in the kitchen raiding their mum's chocolate stash – he looked like a kid caught stealing, guilt all over his face. Simon never was good at lying or being bad. Jaz chose to ignore an opportune time to tease him. 'Can you let Mum know I'm off with Taylor for a drive? Be back later.'

Without waiting for him to answer, she pushed through the large French doors to the side driveway where Taylor was waiting.

'Hey you.'

'Hey yourself,' she replied.

Jaz put on her sunnies and slid onto the front leather seat.

'Nice flower,' he said as he reversed out of the driveway. 'For Becky?' he asked.

Jaz nodded as she touched the soft blue petals. 'Yeah, it's been a while.'

He didn't say anything but Jaz could sense that Taylor was wondering why she had chosen now to visit the cemetery.

They drove in silence, radio playing in the background and the breeze blowing in through their open windows on the warm Saturday afternoon.

'I just got a skateboard,' she said out of the blue. 'Have you ever tried it?'

Taylor turned to her at the red light and gave her a look as if to say *Who are you?* 'No. Guns are my thing, remember?' he said with a smile.

Jaz laughed. 'You're a guy, I just thought you might have done it at some stage.'

'Gee, thanks, Jaz. You just made that sound like you were asking about my sex life.' They both cracked up and were still joking about it when he pulled into the cemetery.

Taylor turned off the car. 'You want me to stay here?'

She shook her head. 'No, I'd like you to come. Please,' she added.

Later, when she would be picking up a message, she would go alone, but for now, she was grateful for Taylor's presence.

Jaz took the path, letting her memory guide her. She passed the gardener who was trimming some of the lawn and tending to a flowerbed. 'Do you think he finds this job lonely, or do you think all these people keep him company?' she whispered to Taylor.

'Who knows. To me it feels eerily quiet and a little creepy, but I can't say I go to cemeteries a lot. The last time I was here was for Mum.'

Jaz nodded as they came to stop by Becky's grave. Taylor's mum had passed away four years ago. 'I'm sorry, I didn't think to ask if this would be hard for you.' She reached for his hand as they stared at the large headstone. It was big for such a tiny grave.

Taylor squeezed her hand. 'Maybe we could go to Mum's next?'

'Of course, Tay.' She gave him a smile before letting his hand go and stepping towards Becky's grave. There was a little vase at the base, which was incorporated into the headstone. Jaz put in the flower and said a silent hello. How much different would their life be if Becky had lived? There were enough people dying from disease and medical conditions, let alone from man-made deaths like drugs and gang wars. Jaz hoped that her message inside the flower would somehow be the start of something amazing. Something to be proud of and something that would help many others.

She couldn't save Becky from her fate, nor Taylor's mum, but she could certainly try her best to save others.

'See you next time, Becky. I'll be back,' she said after a few minutes before turning to Taylor. 'Come on, let's go visit your mum.'

CHAPTER 7

IT WAS TUESDAY afternoon and school was nearly over for another day. Jaz leaned her arm on her desk and flinched as her grazed elbow connected with it. Damned skateboard. She much preferred fighting; bruises didn't bleed and scab.

Jaz had been toying with the idea of texting Marcus, not wanting to leave it too long in case he forgot her, when she felt her phone vibrate in class. They were supposed to be using the last ten minutes to finish their essay but Jaz couldn't concentrate. Luckily her teacher was working back through her notes, so while her head was down Jaz slipped her phone out of her pocket and read her message.

I'm hoping you haven't lost my lucky shirt?

Jaz felt a grin spread across her face. Marcus may be her target but she found herself keen to catch up with him again.

With a glance at her teacher, she typed out a reply.

What lucky shirt? Do I know you?

She waited half a second before sending another message.

Just kidding. Can you afford the ransom price???

Depends what it is? Where are u now?

At school for the next few minutes.

Me too. What class?

English. ZZZZ

LOL It's better than calculus. Wanna meet & talk terms of ransom price?

The siren went, and Jaz hurried to stash her things away in her bag and rush out the door with her classmates like fish escaping a torn net.

Jaz leaned against a wall, as students filtered out the hallway to the exit, to continue texting.

Sure, why not.

Cottesloe Arch Monument, it's by the car park. Meet you in 20? I'll bring coffee.

Sweet.

'Why are you smiling like that?'

Jaz glanced up to see Anna and Ricky standing in front of her. They were holding hands, but Ricky was standing back, trying to be invisible.

'Hi Ricky,' she said, in her nicest voice. He nodded and half-waved back. Was he scared of her? Her reputation wasn't that bad. Was it?

'Was that Ryan?' Anna asked.

'Um, no. I wish.' Jaz's smile fell from her lips.

'Oh sorry. I didn't mean to remind you. I'm going home to Ricky's place. What are you doing now?' said Anna.

'I'm going to go to The Ring, as usual.' Jaz wasn't ready to mention Marcus yet. Maybe she wouldn't have to. For now, Jaz wanted to keep it quiet for as long as possible. Things would only get harder when her two worlds collided.

'Okay. Hey, is Tay all right? He hasn't been replying to my texts.'

'Yeah, as far as I know. He's playing basketball with the guys this arvo, so he's probably just preoccupied.' But Jaz realised he hadn't replied to any of hers today either.

'That must be it,' said Anna as she turned back to Ricky. 'See ya, Jaz.'

'Catch ya tomorrow.' Anna and Ricky headed to the bus stop, hand in hand.

Jaz checked her watch, a big silver dial on a leather band. Twenty minutes was not long enough to dump her schoolbag at home, change and get to Cottesloe. She'd just have to go as is. Jaz went around the corner to wait for a different bus on the other side of the road and hoped it wasn't late.

Twenty-five mintues later she found Marcus standing by the large pine tree beside the arch monument with two coffees in his hand. She nearly didn't recognise him in his school uniform.

'Hey, sorry I'm late. Bus,' she said rolling her eyes.

They stood looking at each other for a moment. 'Glad you made it,' he said eventually. 'You look different in uniform.'

'You too. Scotch College, I see.' Jaz tugged on his maroon tie with the gold and blue stripe. He also wore a white shirt and school pants. It was weird seeing him like this, and he probably thought the same about her white shirt, black tie and checked skirt.

'Yep. Saint Christian's?' he asked as he handed her a coffee.

She nodded. 'Thanks.'

'Come, let's sit down on the stairs near the beach.' They walked down a path that sloped towards the ocean. It was quiet here, not like further up the street where the Life Saving Club and the shops of Cottesloe begun. The only thing opposite them here was the small car park and the golf course. It was also overcast, so not many were out enjoying the beach.

Marcus stopped about halfway down the steps and sat on some rocks just off to the side. Jaz put her bag down beside her and joined him, drawing her legs up together. The sand clung to her black tights.

'I don't suppose you have my shirt with you?' he asked with a raised eyebrow.

'No, sorry. You're out of luck.' She laughed.

'At this point, I don't think so.'

Jaz quickly took a sip of her coffee as she felt her cheeks grow warm. She glanced at his hair, which was pulled back into a ponytail at the base of his neck. A few long strands had fallen free and moved across his face in the afternoon breeze coming offshore. It was a beautiful spot and the rhythmic sound of the waves over the rocks nearby had a soothing effect on her.

Jaz had pulled her ponytail out on the bus, letting her hair fall down around her shoulders like a sea of black silk. Hopefully he liked long hair.

'I'm glad you came today, Jaz,' said Marcus.

'Me too. I'd do anything for a free coffee.' She laughed as she tucked her hair behind her ear. 'So, what's it like going to Scotch with only boys?'

'Boring,' he said. 'Mixed would be heaps better. You would have to fend the guys off at your school, right?'

Jaz almost choked on her coffee. Marcus patted her on the back as she coughed. 'Oh, you are way off,' she said. 'I scare them all.'

'Get out of here.'

'No, it's true.'

'Don't believe it for a second.' He smiled and Jaz felt the honesty in his gaze.

'What about you?' Jaz wanted to change the subject. 'Which one of these houses is yours?' she said with a wave to the opposite site of the road.

'Why? You plan on visiting me?'

'I have to drop your shirt off somewhere. Or maybe I could just post it?' Marcus was shaking his head before she could finish.

'No,' he said seriously. A little pink flush appeared on his cheeks. 'I was thinking you could hand it over on Saturday, over lunch?'

'Were you now?' Marcus was a flirt but he wasn't over the top, more cheeky and fun. It felt nice to have someone's attention.

'So, are you free on Saturday?'

'Maybe,' she said coyly.

'You don't give much away, do you?' He tilted his head as he studied her.

They chatted for nearly an hour, everything from school subjects, sports, movies. Jaz couldn't help but think that Marcus would be great boyfriend material, if his parents weren't possible drug runners. Sadly, she couldn't have Ryan either because they were both on the same spy team. Life was never easy.

'You fence, really? Like, with swords? That's… different,' he said.

'I like different things. And our school has a fencing team. I do martial arts as well.'

'Ah, that explains your abs.'

'And yours are from surfing?' she said, gesturing to the expanse of ocean in front of them. 'Or skateboarding? I tried doing that flip thing you did on mine and it's not as easy as it seems.'

Marcus raised his eyebrows and his dimple reappeared. 'You have a board? Sweet. You'll have to bring it on Saturday and I'll show you a few things. I also surf as well. Hard not to when you wake up to this every morning.'

'Yeah, rub it in, why don't you.' Jaz rolled up the sleeve on her right arm and showed Marcus her graze. 'Maybe you could show me how *not* to stack it on a skateboard.'

His hand reached out and caressed her arm gently. 'Ouch. That's a good one.'

Jaz didn't pull away from him. Instead, she enjoyed his warm touch. She didn't have to pretend. Marcus was good company. Jaz shivered, the breeze off the ocean had turned cold without her realising. The salty air carried the freshness of the approaching night.

'You're cold.' He pulled his hand away reluctantly. 'Can I drive you home? I take it you don't have a car, seeing as you took the bus here.'

Jaz pulled her sleeve down and nodded. 'I'm saving for one. Hopefully I can get one soon. Mum's decided to actually help me get something decent. She's worried I'll be stranded on the freeway or in some seedy suburb with engine trouble. My friend has a classic Mustang and I'd love to get something like that, but Mum will want something more reliable and modern.'

'Mustang. Nice. A guy friend?' he asked curiously.

'Yeah. My best mate, Taylor. He, Anna and I have been best friends since we were kids.' Marcus seemed pleased with her answer.

'Come on, my car's just up here. It's no Mustang, though.' He stood up and held out his hand. Jaz took it and he hauled her up to her feet, and then he reached for her bag and slung it over his shoulder.

'Thanks.' Jaz brushed off the sand, took one last look at the beautiful beach and walked back up the steps to the car park by the road.

She heard the beep of a car unlocking and then saw the lights on the sleek black BMW in front of her. 'That's your car?' It had dark tint and big shiny rims. Jaz loved it.

'Kind of.'

Marcus put her bag in the back and they got in. The leather seats hugged her body.

'It's my dad's car, well, one of them. He's always in his Jag, so I get to use this one.'

'It's cool. My folks don't appreciate a good car. I guess Taylor has rubbed off on us girls,' she said with a laugh.

As he started the car, Imagine Dragons' 'Radioactive' blared through the speakers. 'Shit, sorry.' He turned the volume down and then pulled out of the car park and headed away from Cottesloe. 'That's my house there,' he said pointing to the two-storey with the big fence.

'Fancy,' she said, trying to look as if it was the first time she'd checked out his house.

'So, where to?'

Jaz's mind began to spin. Should she let him know where she lived? If she was supposed to get close to him, become his girlfriend, then he'd expect her to share basic things like her address. He'd want to meet Taylor and Anna, her parents. This thought scared her, and suddenly she wondered if she should have gone with a fake name.

She watched Marcus driving. It was hard to believe he could hurt her, especially when he seemed so normal and nice. Better than nice, even.

Jaz gave him directions to her house and actually felt a little sad when he pulled up out the front.

Marcus whistled. 'Not bad digs, Jaz. Which room's yours?' he said teasingly.

'Ha, as if I would share that with you. I'll run up and get your shirt while you're here?' she said, and went to leave but he grabbed her hand.

'No, leave it. Bring it on Saturday. That way I know you have to turn up.'

'Marcus, you don't have to worry. I turned up today, didn't I?' She gave him a big smile as he let her go. 'Besides, I really need some skateboard lessons.'

'Maybe we could swap and you could show me some of your moves?' He lifted his hands into a karate chop pose. 'I only know *The Karate Kid* moves,' he said with a smirk. He started to move his hands in circles. 'Wax on, wax off.'

Jaz covered her face with her hand. 'My God, you're as loony as I am. You'll fit right in with my friends,' she said. Jaz got out of the car and leaned in the open window. 'I'll see you Sat. Thanks for this afternoon. I had a good time.'

'Me too, Jaz.'

As he drove away, Jaz couldn't help hoping Saturday came quickly. Talking with someone new was refreshing and exciting. It helped fill the void of missing Anna. For the first time in weeks, Jaz could overcome her desire to go to The Ring to check for a message from Ryan. Instead, she went to get the skateboard for some practice. And it was kind of fun.

CHAPTER 8

JAZ SPOTTED TAYLOR out the front of the school. His shoulders were slightly hunched, not his normal square strong stance. Minka was beside him talking – maybe she was causing the deflated posture? She always made Jaz feel like ripping her own ears off so she didn't have to listen to Minka's fake nasally voice.

But as Jaz arrived at his side she realised, from Taylor's glassy-eyed expression, that he wasn't hearing a word Minka was saying. Personally, Jaz thought Minka brought that on with everyone.

'Hey Tay,' Jaz said touching his arm. 'Minka.' It was as close to a 'hello' that Jaz could muster.

Minka was the Barbie doll image but with an evil Morticia inside. Her nails resembled talons and her perfect blonde hair would turn into slithering snakes, given half a chance.

'Hi Jaz,' said Taylor softly. Minka turned her head away from them as if someone had called her, but Jaz was past taking offence at Minka's bitchy ways.

'You wanna do something this arvo? Anna's with Ricky.' Taylor flinched and Jaz wished she'd kept that last bit of info to herself.

'We can go out on our boat, or the jetskis, Tay,' said Minka, who apparently was now involved in their conversation. Minka gave his arm a squeeze. 'Come on. It will cheer you up. Some of the crew are coming too.'

By crew, Jaz knew Minka meant her loyal minions and the guys they thought deserved their attention. But she didn't know Taylor very well, because when he wasn't happy the last thing he wanted was a crowd.

'Na, I'll think I'll pass, Minks. I said I'd drive Jaz home anyway,' said Taylor as he glanced at Jaz.

'Oh, okay. Well, you just text me if you change your mind.'

Minka would ooze into a pool of maple syrup if she were any sweeter. Maple syrup laced with an acid-eating component, more like it.

Taylor nodded and looped his hand in Jaz's as they walked to his car, through the crowd of leaving students.

Jaz nudged his shoulder. 'You okay, Tay? You've been a bit quiet lately. Even Anna's worried.' That got his attention.

'Really? I didn't think she knew what happened outside the Ricky atmosphere.' Taylor saw her expression and lowered his eyes. 'Sorry, it's been a weird few days, that's all.' Taylor unlocked his car and they threw their bags in the back before getting into the front. 'You wanna come back to my place for a bit? I don't feel like doing much but I don't want to do it alone.'

'Sure, why not. I have no plans. So, tell me, what's been going on with you?' Jaz wondered if it was just Anna that was getting to him. Did she dare ask?

Taylor started the car and let out a sigh that would fill a hot-air balloon. 'It's Dad. He's been a bit stressed lately and I'm worried.'

'Oh, in what way?'

'His fuse is short, he seems scatty and preoccupied.' He shrugged, pulling onto the main road. 'I've never seen him like this, but he assures me it's just work getting a bit thick at the moment. I guess it's hard work when you're the Deputy Commissioner of Operations. I guess I forget to stop and think about just what he deals with every day, you know. We go to school and he's doing all the hard cop stuff.'

'Yeah, and your dad being at the top would make him accountable for so much. Maybe he just needs a bit of space and time?'

'That's what I'm hoping. Anyway, enough about me and my woes. What about you? Who have you been flat out texting in class, and don't try to deny it. It wasn't me and wasn't Anna, cos we were all in that class.'

Her heart lurched and her palms felt clammy. Jaz glanced out the window as she decided what to say. Keep it normal. That's what James had said. Okay, then. Turning back to Taylor she smiled. 'Well, aren't you just

Mr Clever Pants. Anyone tell you you'd make a good cop?' she said with a laugh.

'My dad. Constantly,' he said with a smile. 'So, fess up. Who was he – and don't try to tell me it wasn't a he. You were smiling, and no one smiles in English. Was it Ryan?'

Well, Jaz had been smiling. Now she felt awful. Taylor knew she liked Ryan. What would he think about her and Marcus? 'No, it wasn't Ryan. We… well, let's just say that we will never be a "we".' Taylor's concern splashed across his face as he glanced at her. 'But don't worry, I'm okay. I've actually met this guy, Marcus. He goes to Scotch and he seems nice.'

'Oh, I see. How did you meet him?'

'Let's just say I bumped into him, spilt my coffee, I had to borrow his shirt and we've been talking ever since. But it's just new. It isn't anything worth mentioning yet. I'm not sure if we've even defined it yet, you know what I mean?'

'So, no hanky-panky then?'

Jaz flung her arm across the car and slapped his shoulder. 'Taylor Stewart, is that all you think about?' she teased.

He laughed, and Jaz was glad to see him a little more relaxed and happy. It was like that for the rest of the drive to Taylor's house. He parked the Mustang in the empty double garage; his dad wouldn't be home until late. Taylor practically raised himself. Some days she envied him, not having a parent around to boss you, but then she realised how lonely he must feel. No wonder he went to the range.

'Come on, I'll put the cappuccino maker on. I'm sure we have choc biscuits somewhere too.'

Jaz got out of the car and followed Taylor to the back door. He unlocked it and held the door for her. She stepped inside the familiar house, which felt a little cold and empty. Just as she was about to turn back to Taylor, she saw something dark move, and then everything went black.

The first thing she noticed was the thump in her head, second was the angry voice. Slowly Jaz realised she was sprawled on the floor. Her hair was draped across her face as she lay stomach down, the hard tiles cold and uncomfortable. She kept her body still except for her eyes. Through her hair, she could see Taylor held at gunpoint. Her heart skipped a beat. What the hell was going on! Literally, the nozzle of the gun was at his temple. It was held by someone wearing black clothing and a balaclava. His voice was deep and intimidating.

'Want to die, boy?'

She was swamped with fear. What did this guy want? Would he kill them? Was she about to watch Taylor be executed? Her fear began to twist into anger. How dare someone threaten her best friend's life? *What would Ryan do in this situation?* she wondered. It took everything Jaz had not to jump up to try to save him, but she didn't know if she could stand yet without dizziness and she didn't want to startle the guy into shooting Taylor. What the hell could she do? *Think!* Whatever she did, she had to do it slowly so not to cause any kneejerk reactions.

'Do you value your life, boy?' The gunman kept asking as he held Taylor in a headlock.

Taylor was petrified, his face pale. What the hell did this man want? Was this a home invasion? Was he after Taylor's dad's gun collection? Could she reach her phone?

The balaclava man twisted the gun against Taylor's head, sure to leave a bruise, but as he did, Jaz noticed a tattoo on his wrist. It looked familiar; she'd seen one like it before. She did what Ryan would expect her to do: she took mental notes. The guy's size, his voice, any other distinguishing features she could find, and even what type of shoes he wore.

'This is a warning. You got that, kid? This is your first and final warning.' The weapon-wielding maniac's voice was harsh and deep.

Jaz felt her chest twist at the fear in Taylor's eyes. She wanted to save him, but how? She wasn't sure if the pounding in her head was from the whack or the adrenaline in her blood. But just as she was trying to come up with some scrap of a plan, the bad guy lifted his arm and brought the gun down hard on Taylor. He fell towards her like a bag of sand.

She rolled over just in time to try to catch him, not thinking about faking anymore. But it didn't matter. The guy with the balaclava and gun was gone. She hadn't even seen him leave.

'Tay, are you okay?' she whispered to him, still fearful that the guy might change his mind and come back.

Jaz brushed at his hair, her hand coming away with blood. 'Oh no.' It wasn't much, but the gun had split his head. Jaz felt her own head. She had a massive lump but no blood. Jaz pulled off her school tie and used it to stop the bleeding. 'It's okay, Taylor. I'll call the ambulance and then your dad. You'll be okay.'

Jaz sat up, resting Taylor's head in her lap. Her own head protested at the move but she ignored it as she pulled out her mobile. Damn, she didn't know his dad's number.

She reached down into Taylor's pocket and got his phone. In seconds, she had called for an ambulance and then rang Mr Stewart.

'Taylor, what's up?'

'Mr Stewart, it's Jaz here. Taylor's been knocked out in a home invasion. The ambulance is on its way.'

'Oh my God. I'm on my way now. Is he okay?'

Jaz could hear the worry in his voice. He was telling people in his office he had to go and the ding of the elevator showed he was on his way to his car.

'He'll be fine. He got hit on the head with a gun and it's split his head open. I've stopped the bleeding. He might need stitches and he could be concussed.'

'Oh, thank God you were with him, Jaz. I'm so sorry. I'll be there soon.'

Jaz quickly called Anna and moments later Taylor stirred in her arms, letting out a croaky groan.

'It's okay, Tay. Just lie still. You have a bump on your head.' She watched as Taylor tried to focus on her.

'Jaz. What the hell just happened?'

'Wish I knew, Tay. I'm just so glad he left and didn't hurt us worse. The ambulance is on its way,' she said as she heard the sirens.

'What, no,' he said, trying to sit up.

'Tay. Your head's bleeding. Just sit still, will you.' Jaz was brushing his fringe back off his face and trying to ignore her blood-stained fingers.

Mr Stewart arrived five minutes after the ambulance and rushed straight in to Taylor. Jaz watched his face drain of colour when he saw the blood marks down Taylor's white school shirt.

'He's fine, Mr Stewart. Just a little split,' said Jaz.

The ambulance people stepped back to let Taylor's dad give him a hug. 'Dad.'

'Son. God, I was so worried.' Mr Stewart moved to the side to let the ambulance guy finish checking him over. 'Does he need to go to the hospital? Is he all right?'

'The split has stopped bleeding and will be fine, but he may have a slight concussion. He can stay home but make sure someone is with him the whole time, just in case. But I think he'll be okay,' said the ambulance officer as he began to pack up his things. 'I suggested to the kids that they call the police, but I can see that they already did,' he said, nodding to Mr Stewart's uniform.

'Thank you so much,' Mr Stewart said as they left. Then he turned to Taylor who was still sitting on the dining chair. 'Can I get you some water? How are you, Jaz? Were you hurt?' When they shook their heads, Mr Stewart took a seat beside Taylor. 'Tell me everything, from the start. I want both your versions.'

'I don't remember much, it all seems a little hazy now. But I remember seeing Jaz go down and this black blur grabbed me. I was held so tight and I remember the cold steel of the gun.' Taylor shivered and looked a little clammy.

'Jaz? What about you?' Mr Stewart asked.

'I walked in and remember it going black. Then I came to on the floor and I could see the guy holding Taylor with his gun to his head. I wanted to do something to save him but I wasn't sure.' Jaz had decided to keep the tattoo a secret for now, at least until she could figure out where she'd seen it.

Mr Stewart held up his hand. 'Oh Jaz, you did the right thing. Trying to take on an armed man is a no-no, and we don't know how stable he was either. Please, go on.'

'He was saying something to Taylor. Something about this being a warning.'

Taylor sat up straighter. 'That's right, I remember. He said it was my first and final warning. But what have I done?' he said, turning to his dad.

Mr Stewart tensed up and swallowed hard. Jaz suddenly wondered if maybe it wasn't Taylor but Mr Stewart who'd done something.

'Taylor! Oh my God, Tay.' The words were screamed from outside and continued inside as Anna came running through the door, the worry etched in her face bordering on panic. She flew straight into Taylor's arms muttering, 'Are you okay?' over and over.

Jaz could see the warmth spread through Taylor.

'Oh, you're covered in blood, oh my God.' Anna had only pulled back a fraction.

'It's just from a small cut on my head. I'm fine.'

Knowing she was now safe to hold him again, she flung herself back into his arms. 'Thank God. When Jaz rang, I just couldn't believe it. I heard "gun" and just about passed out. I had to know you were okay.'

Taylor glanced at Jaz and smiled as if to say thank you. She knew that a dose of Anna would cheer him up, and after the last few months of her being distracted with Ricky, this would feel like Christmas for Taylor.

'What did he want?' asked Anna. 'Was he robbing you?'

'We don't know. He didn't take anything with him, unless we got here before he had a chance to take the guns. They're the only things of real value. Maybe he came to get them, but they're all under lock and key, so he missed out. I don't know, it's all a bit weird. But Dad will sort it out, won't you?'

His dad had been staring off into space but jerked his head back. 'Sure will, son.'

Jaz felt a prickle of unease. Something about this whole event didn't sit right and she feared that Taylor could still be in danger. She was relieved that the man left without killing either of them – but would he be back?

Mr Stewart took the rest of the afternoon off work, which pleased Taylor. Jaz, however, couldn't help thinking his dad knew more about this home invasion, robbery or whatever it was. She also couldn't help thinking that she was holding onto a big chunk of the puzzle too. If only she could remember more about that tattoo.

CHAPTER 9

'Hey, it's my lucky shirt.'

Jaz walked towards Marcus, who was leaning on his BMW outside her house. She carried his T-shirt against her chest in one hand and her skateboard in the other. 'Here, thanks again for the loan.'

Marcus took the shirt, pulled off the one he was wearing and put on his lucky one. His hair was out today and he was wearing loose-fitting jeans and black Converse shoes. Jaz had gone with her cargo pants, to protect her skin from any skateboarding stacks, and a grey singlet. 'You feeling lucky?' she teased.

'Sure am. Is that your board? Nice.' He opened the boot and put it beside his, which was covered in scratches and chips. Hers looked obviously new.

'I got mine for Christmas last year,' she lied, 'but I've only just started to try to use it.'

'I hope you don't mind, but a few of my mates will probably be there as well,' he said, as they got in his car and drove off.

'No worries,' she replied. This afternoon would be a great diversion from her thoughts. It had been a few days since Taylor was attacked, but Jaz hadn't stopped thinking about that man. About why he was there, and his message to Taylor. She was exhausted from the worry and hadn't left Taylor's side. To the point he'd actually told her to go with Marcus. But Jaz had rung Anna and asked her to visit him today. She just didn't want him alone, and maybe it was a good excuse for Anna and Taylor to spend some time together. They'd organised to watch movies and hang out at Anna's place. Taylor hadn't liked being in his house since the break-in. Jaz didn't blame him.

At the park, it turned out that Marcus had three of his mates there hanging out. They were all doing tricks on their skateboards, but came over to fist bump Marcus when they spotted him.

'Guys, this is Jaz. Jaz, meet Kaino, Ben and Trent.'

Kaino was the shortest one, Ben had a shaved head and Trent wore a loose singlet that hardly covered his chest, which was probably the point.

Marcus didn't explain how they met or who she was, which led Jaz to believe that he'd already told his mates about her. She took that as a good sign.

'Come on, Jaz. I'll show you some stuff.' Marcus nudged her shoulder before jumping onto his board along the cement. 'Can you ollie?' he asked. He jumped on his board as if to show her what he was talking about.

'I've been trying.' Jaz tried to copy him on her board, unsuccessfully. But it didn't faze Marcus. He was patient and guided her through each trick. He even tried teaching her the backside noseslide along a step, without much luck.

'That's all right,' he said. 'Practice makes perfect.'

'Lots of practice,' said Trent with a chuckle.

'Hey! If you must know, I spend most of my time doing other things,' said Jaz.

'Like what? Girl stuff,' said Trent. He flipped his board up and held on to it.

Marcus laughed at him and shook his head. 'You shouldn't be provoking her, Trent, you'll come off second best.' Jaz shot Marcus a smile.

'You want me to show you the girly stuff I do?' Jaz asked Trent. 'Think you can handle it?'

Trent squared his shoulders, his cocky smile filling his square face. 'Bring it on.'

Jaz walked over to the grassed area and beckoned him to follow. Trent looked at his mates questioningly. Kaino and Ben shrugged while Marcus waved him on.

'You ready?' Jaz asked Trent as she stood in front of him. He nodded, and before he'd finished Jaz had him on the ground in a series of swift movements.

'What just happened?' he said from the ground, while his mates were bent over laughing.

'Man, that was awesome,' said Ben, as he gave Jaz a clap.

That was the start of the rough and tumble. All the boys wanted a go at taking her down. Jaz tried to be careful and not hurt them seriously, but being typical thrillseeking guys they bounced back. 'Let's go again,' said Ben as he got up from the grass.

'Dude, she's just going to lay your arse out on the ground again. Give it up,' said Marcus. 'Can you show me how you spun Kaino around and locked his arms up? That could come in handy if we ever get into trouble.' Marcus's green eyes were swimming with awe as he gazed at her.

'You planning on a few pub brawls later?' she teased.

'No, but you never know these days. I had a drunk guy want to fight me a few weeks back at a bar. Lucky the bouncers came. So, how did you do that?'

Jaz grabbed for his hand and spun him around so his body was pulled up against hers. She had his arm locked behind his back and one of her arms around his neck.

They stood like that for a while, it seemed. The warmth from his body was nice.

'So, what's my safe word?' he said. 'How do I get you to let me go? Not that I really want you to.'

Jaz noticed that his mates had gone back to the concrete area, leaving them all alone on the grass. 'I could let you go, or you could try to break out of my hold.'

'And how would I do that?'

'You could try to kick me. Your legs are still free.'

'I don't want to hurt you.'

'You won't,' she said. If only Marcus knew how much she was capable of taking. She'd had years of sparring with Tick and Bags, who managed to connect a punch from time to time. Then there was the knife attack in which she got cut and then had to sit through Ryan stitching her up. She was sure she could take anything Marcus was willing to throw at her.

She must have sounded a little cocky, because Marcus hooked his leg around hers and yanked it, pulling them off balance and they fell backwards onto the lawn. Jaz wasted no time, flipping over on top of Marcus and holding his hands against the grass by his head. 'Not bad, not bad at all.'

'I have my moments,' he said with a smile. 'Even though it didn't really come off like I'd hoped, I'm rather happy with the outcome.'

Marcus was cute when he smiled, and Jaz was enjoying herself. It was nice to have a guy generally interested in her, one who wanted to spend time with her. Why did Ryan keep floating back into her thoughts? Jaz moved to lie on the grass beside Marcus. She saw the disappointment in his eyes flash briefly.

'So,' he said, propping himself up on his elbow. 'I have this thing next Saturday night that I need a date for. Would you be interested?'

'I might.' She tilted her head to the side, watching Marcus watch her intently. He stretched out a finger and ran it along her cheek to move her hair from her face. It felt nice.

'It starts at eight, you'll have to wear a dress and I'll be in a suit.'

'Oh, one of *those* dates. Your school ball?'

He nodded. 'Wanna come? It might be fun but I can't promise you any wonderful dancing.'

Jaz laughed. 'Good, because I'm not sure I'm that good either. Just as long as there's no Sprinkler moves or Chicken Dance, I'm in.'

'Awesome. I'll come pick you up. Oh, um… actually my mum will want photos.' He pulled a face.

'Hey, that's okay. I get it. My mum's the same. I can catch a taxi to your place. Then we can go together from there?' Yes, a way to get closer to Marcus and his family.

'You sure?' A little line appeared on his temple.

Jaz raised her hand and pressed it away with her thumb. 'Yeah, I'd like to see where you live.' He caught her hand, drawing it away from his face but keeping it wrapped tightly between his fingers. It was sweet and his hand was warm.

'You know, I'm really glad you were having a bad day when we first met, but for me it was just more proof that my lucky shirt was doing its thing.'

Jaz laughed out loud.

He raised his eyebrow. 'Too corny?'

'No,' she said. 'It was nice.' Jaz leaned over and kissed him quickly on the lips before lying back on the grass. It felt right and would move along the friendship into something more. A proper girlfriend would get lots more access to his home and private life. 'So, tell me all about your folks. What's your mum do?'

Marcus smiledand squeezed her hand. They looked up at the sky as they talked. They were oblivious to the sound of the guys at the skate park, of time ticking by and the people walking past.

Even two hours later, when Jaz finally headed home, they continued to text questions to each other about themselves. The only thing that stopped it from being completely normal were the notes Jaz wrote down that she thought might be relevant for the Agency. She finished jotting down what Marcus had said and then sat staring at the photo she'd taken of him on her phone.

Jaz couldn't help but think of how Marcus had dropped her home but didn't try for a goodbye kiss. She could tell he was interested, he'd held her hand for most of their time together, but as for wanting to move things along – well, he was being really sweet and gentle. He was surprising her. He didn't fit any of her pre-drawn conclusions about how a son of a possible drug dealer would be. Maybe she had watched too many movies.

Jaz had an idea and sprang from her chair. Using her phone, she took a photo of their last family portrait and sent it to Marcus.

Here is my family. My half-brother Simon & stepdad Paul. Yes, I know I'm the odd one out.

His reply was quick.

Only because ur beautiful. Nice family.

And as she'd hoped, he followed that text with a family picture of his own. His dad and mum just looked like parents. Normal, well-dressed parents who loved their son. You could see it in their eyes and the way they each held a gentle hand on Marcus. Was it just his dad who was shifty or did his mum know about the business too? Did Marcus know? Kids are pretty clever, he'd have to know something was going on, wouldn't he? Maybe MTG had it wrong? It wouldn't be the first time someone had jumped to conclusions, right? But then, that was why Jaz was here, to make sure.

Jaz's mind buzzed with so many questions, her head felt heavy. She printed out the photos Marcus had texted and added them to the collection she would leave at the next cemetery drop.

She climbed into bed later that night, her head spinning with thoughts. What kind of dress to get for the date. The best time to deliver her info. Talking to Pax about a listening device for the Sinclairs' house. Missing Anna. Worrying about Taylor. Thinking of Marcus and how cute he was. She thought back to when he'd changed his shirt, his chest bare except for a silver circle on a black leather necklace. She'd been preoccupied with his tight stomach muscles but she remembered the silver circle had a dragon on it, but the way the dragon curled it looked like a snake. And then it hit Jaz. Finally, she remembered where she'd seen the tattoo on that black-clad guy who broke into Taylor's house. Reaching over to her bedside table she grabbed her phone. She needed to talk to Ryan urgently. She knew she shouldn't text him but she hoped something coded would be okay. Quickly she thought of what to say.

Hey u. I found ur lucky shirt. Will return it asap. x

If his phone was in the wrong hands, surely this wouldn't seem out of the ordinary. Jaz sent the text and lay back on her pillows, still holding her phone against her chest. Her heart was racing. She just hoped Ryan understood she needed to see him. And it was the thought of being near Ryan again that had her tossing and turning all night.

CHAPTER 10

I T   WAS   T HURSDAY afternoon and Jaz still hadn't heard from Ryan. It was killing her. Every time she got a text, she'd hold her breath hoping – and then exhale when it was from Marcus or Anna and Taylor. She was feeling so tightly wound that she'd snap at any moment.

'Hey, I'm here,' said Anna as she joined her at the table. They were at Molly's, their favourite coffee shop. It was a tiny, unassuming building among the other shops, and it was cosy, with a warm, rustic feel. Each chair was different, all wooden or old school. There was nothing new about this shop, except for the kitchen side of things. There were exposed old bricks and photo frames with vintage posters and black-and-white pictures. They had been coming here since Anna found it when they were thirteen. Mr and Mrs Marlette had owned and operated it since the girls could remember, and they always looked after their regulars.

Anna sat beside her and picked up the menu, even though she knew everything on it. 'Is Tay coming?' she asked.

'I'm here already,' he said, behind her. He had the biggest grin and Jaz got the feeling he liked Anna's question. He squeezed her shoulder before sitting down. 'I just ordered for us all.'

'Except there's going to be one more,' said Jaz. Then she sat back and waited for the question.

'Who's coming?'

'Is it him?' said Taylor, leaning forward on his elbows. He wore his favourite black AC/DC tour shirt and his slouch jeans. They were his casual clothes, but Taylor could still make them look great.

'It is,' said Jaz, before waving her finger at them. 'And I want you guys to be nice, okay.'

'Scout's honour,' said Taylor with a mischievous grin.

Anna's jaw dropped. 'Tay only just told me you had a possible guy. I didn't believe him, though. I was certain you weren't over Ryan.'

Jaz hoped they didn't see her flinch. Of course she wasn't over Ryan and she felt bad for lying to them, especially to Anna. Anna knew where Jaz's heart belonged, so it was no surprise she found this news about Marcus hard to swallow.

'Marcus is really nice and I want to see where this goes, okay?'

Anna squinted, and Jaz felt her interrogating eyes burn holes in her head. Sometimes Anna was just too clever. 'Has Ryan really gone? Are you really trying to move on?'

'I'm trying.' That was the only reply Jaz thought Anna would believe. But it wasn't the truth. She couldn't just try to get over Ryan. 'Oh, he's here,' Jaz said, pointing to the black car, glad for the distraction from her thoughts and from Anna's curious looks.

'Is that his car? Nice,' said Taylor.

They all watched as Marcus parked on the opposite side of the road. All eyes remained on him as he walked towards the cafe with a bag in his hand.

'Well, I must say he's no Ryan but he is cute,' said Anna. 'Nice clothes, and his hair is sexy.'

'Anna,' grumbled Taylor.

'Please be nice.' Jaz shot them a look as the door opened.

Jaz stood up and waved to Marcus, whose carefree smile lit up his face. His jeans hung low on his hips and he was wearing his rust-coloured lucky T-shirt again. Jaz bit her lip to stop herself from laughing. Did he own any others?

'Hey, Jaz.' He went and stood beside her and gently touched her arm. Jaz felt that if they weren't in front of her friends that he might have kissed her cheek. And she wouldn't have minded one bit.

'Marcus, I'd like you to meet my best friends.'

Marcus held out his hand. 'Nice to meet you, Taylor and Anna.' Her friends shook his hand with awed expressions.

'So, Jaz mentioned us, did she?' asked Anna as she watched him sit down. She also watched how Marcus tucked his hair behind his ear with his long fingers. Hard not to blame her, he made it look very sexy.

'Yes, of course. You guys are all she talks about.' Marcus turned and winked at Jaz. 'Here, which tie will suit your dress? You said it was a pale green?' he asked, handing over a bag.

Anna leaned across and pulled out a tie while Jaz got the other two. 'What do you think?' Jaz said to Anna.

The ties were soft greens. 'I think this one is closer to your dress colour,' said Anna, holding out a sage green with thin silver stripes through it.

'Yep, I agree, this one,' she said, taking it and handing it to Marcus.

'Sweet. So, do I get any hints on what it looks like?' he asked.

'Nope, it's a surprise,' said Jaz. She had thought about wearing her dress from her ball, but it was the dress she'd worn when Ryan had kissed her. Then she thought about borrowing her mum's red one, but that held memories of Ryan too. So, instead she went out and bought a new one in soft sage green.

'It's floaty and sexy and sweet all in one,' said Anna. Jaz rolled her eyes. 'What? You gotta give him *something*.'

Jaz ignored her friend, while thinking that the lilac T-shirt Anna was wearing – with Little Miss Blabbermouth splashed across the front – fitted her perfectly. They had both worn denim skirts today, something Taylor had certainly noticed when she caught him staring at Anna.

'Do you want a coffee?' Jaz asked Marcus as she started to rise.

He put his hand out to stop her. 'I can get it. Be back in a tick.'

Jaz watched his jean-clad butt as he walked to the counter. Hard not to, really. He was narrow and lean, young and firm. A hand squeezed at her arm and Jaz turned to see Anna smiling at her. She mouthed the words OH MY GOD.

'I know, right?' Jaz glanced at Taylor, who was shaking his head. 'Hey, why didn't you bring Ricky?' Taylor flinched and Jaz wished he'd do something about it. At least he could tell Anna how he felt and let her decide from there.

'I did ask him, but…' Anna's voice faded away.

'But?'

'He feels uncomfortable around Tay.'

'What?' That made Taylor sit up and take notice. 'What do you mean? I'm not scary!'

'He feels a little intimidated by you. I can see where he's coming from. You're gorgeous, Tay, you're good at everything and you're really sweet. That's a hard act to follow.'

God, if Taylor hadn't just turned into a beetroot. He was lost for words, staring at Anna, who was picking at her fingernails.

'And he said you seem a bit gruff towards him.'

Taylor's eyes dropped to the table and Jaz had to stifle a giggle behind her hand. Of course Taylor was gruff around Ricky. He had the girl he liked.

'I'm sure he just got Tay on a bad day. A lot has been going on with the break-in and his dad,' said Jaz, hoping to give Taylor a break.

'Oh yeah, true. I didn't think of that. Sorry, Tay. Is your dad any better? Have they got any leads?'

'Nope, nothing. Maybe that's what's got Dad so tense lately, knowing the guy is still out there. He's looking worn out. I told him he needs to take holidays, have a break.'

'That's a good idea, Tay,' said Jaz. Taylor probably needed one too. Surely there was nothing worse than not feeling safe in your own home, even after his dad had doubled the security on the house.

She looked for Marcus, who had made it to the front of the queue and was ordering. He must have felt her eyes on him because he turned to smile at her, which she returned.

'I'm here anytime if you need anything. Just call,' said Anna, reaching over to hold Taylor's hand.

Jaz wished she could give them some privacy. Poor Anna was so clueless about the effect she had on Taylor. But having years of people call you names because of your strawberry-red hair, freckles and intelligence had knocked her confidence. Jaz knew she didn't think she was worthy of Taylor's love apart from friendship. Anna didn't know just how perfectly beautiful she was. Flawless and sweet.

'I got us some chips to share too,' said Marcus as he sat back down. 'I missed lunch, so I'm starved.'

'So, you all ready for the ball? What time shall I get to your place?' asked Jaz.

'Eight-ish. I don't care if we arrive late. I want to get away from the folks as fast as possible so Mum doesn't fuss.' He rolled his eyes. 'I'm apologising in advance for my mum.'

'You haven't met Anna and Jaz's mums yet, so I wouldn't worry too much,' Taylor laughed. Then his smiled faded and he added quietly, 'You should just be lucky you have her.'

'Tay's mum passed away a few years ago,' Anna said softly.

'Oh, sorry, man. That's rough,' said Marcus. He picked up the salt-shaker and rolled it through his fingers. 'My sister died when she was young. Not as young as Jaz's sister, though. Rach was seven. She drowned in our pool. Since then, Mum's been more protective of me because I'm all they have now. Are you and your dad close?' he asked.

Jaz reached under the table and squeezed Marcus's leg to let him know she cared. He found her hand and laced his fingers through hers.

'Sort of. He works a lot.' Taylor shrugged.

Coffees arrived, giving them a break from the deep conversation. It went back to safer territory, like school and skateboarding.

'I prefer going to the range and having a shot. Clears the head,' said Taylor. 'And I don't end up with grazes or bruises.'

Marcus looked confused. Jaz watched him carefully for a reaction of any sort. 'Tay means shooting guns. He loves it,' she added.

'Wow, really? Guns?' Marcus screwed his face up. 'Isn't that weird?'

Jaz liked his reaction. It didn't look like he'd been around guns, so that was a plus.

'No, just something I've grown up with. My dad has a gun collection. It's no different to any other sport.'

'Yeah, dude. Whatever you say,' said Marcus with a chuckle. He shot Jaz a look as if to say, *Is this guy for real?*

All it did was confirm that Marcus's dad didn't walk around with guns or have guards with guns near his kid. And kids find stuff hidden in their parents' house, so if his dad had them around the house somewhere, it was more than likely Marcus would have found them by now. Jaz realised she kept basing her opinions on drug lords from TV shows. Ones with armoured cars, armed guards and vicious dogs. She had to remember that people didn't have to look like a bikie or the mafia to sell or import drugs.

After they had finished their coffees and eaten all the chips, they made a move.

'Jaz, you need a ride home?' Taylor asked.

She glanced at Marcus and he smiled. 'Na, I've got one. Just make sure Anna gets home safe,' she said with a wink.

Marcus reached for her hand as they left the coffee shop.

'I like your friends,' he said, pulling her close as they stood on the path while Taylor and Anna made their way to Taylor's Mustang. 'But I can't wait to have you to myself on Saturday.' He smiled at her, his green eyes swimming with suggestion.

'I'm looking forward to it too.'

He leaned across and gently brushed her lips in a fleeting kiss. It was sweet and it held a promise of what was to come.

'Let's go before I lose my control on a busy street,' he said with a cheeky grin.

'That I'd like to see,' she teased.

He groaned as he pulled her towards his car. 'Get in.'

All the way to her house, the car was filled with an emotional energy, the kind that spoke of his anticipation for their date and the guarantee of something more. Jaz felt the excitement herself but was unsure which part was greater: being with Marcus or meeting his parents, as per her job.

Outside her house, he walked her to her door. 'I'd get you to meet everyone, but no one is home. Do you want to come in anyway?'

He shook his head but pulled her close to him so their bodies touched. 'No, I'd better not. I have to go pick up Kaino from his place to meet up with the other guys. I'm already late.' But he made no move to leave. Instead he tightened his arms around her and smiled. 'But there is one thing.'

'Yes?'

'Can I call you my girlfriend?' he asked softly, his cheeks slightly flushed.

She could tell he was holding his breath as he waited for her answer. 'You can.'

His smile was large and catching. Marcus brought his hands up and gently caressed her face as he kissed her lips. This time it was longer. This time he parted his lips and the pressure was more urgent. This time Jaz felt herself torn between a terrible guilt and the enjoyment of being wanted.

Marcus pulled away. 'I so have to go. Talk to you soon.'

Jaz waved as he jogged back to his car. But her thoughts were still on that kiss as she tried to decipher her feelings towards it. And the kicker was, she had no one to talk it over with. No one to help her through the emotional rollercoaster of what she was doing. She felt like she was cheating on Ryan when they weren't even anything and she felt like she was deceiving Marcus even though she found herself enjoying his attention. With a frustrated breath, she spun on her heel and headed inside.

CHAPTER 11

SHE WAS BURNING in anger and frustration. A whole week and still no word from Ryan.

A pain burst from her chest as Tick connected a hit. She doubled over, catching her breath against the pain. But it was good pain, the sort that rendered her mind blank from thought. This fight with Tick was exactly what she needed.

Jaz glanced up at her opponent. His eyes watched her carefully, his tattooed body primed.

'You okay?' He never said sorry. They had a rule that you never apologised for connecting.

'Yep,' she said, trying to stand up as her breath came back. 'Don't bruise me too much, I have a dress to wear tonight, and purple and green is not a great colour combination.'

Tick laughed and flipped his dark fringe back with his hand. 'Well, you just better move your arse a bit quicker if you don't want bruises,' he teased. He reached out and gripped her shoulder, his brown eyes hinting concern. 'Nothing broken?'

'Nah, I'm okay. Just needed to get my breath back.' Tick was the best, he treated her like another fighter: even though he cared for her, he didn't take it easy on her. And that's what Jaz loved. She wanted to be pushed, she wanted to be treated like the others and she loved a fair, hard-worked fight. Tick gave her one every time.

'Ready?' he asked.

Jaz didn't reply. Instead she spun around, lifting her leg to hit him high. She'd caught him a little off guard, but not enough, as her foot brushed past him. He grinned, bright white teeth standing out against his tinted skin. Tick threw a punch, which she deflected. He tried two more consecutively, which she blocked before throwing her own. The hits came and went before the pain could register and Jaz thrived in the release it gave her. Arriving at The Ring this morning to find Tick keen for a fight was God sent. Pax had been away for the week on another mission, the details of which he wouldn't share with her, so she had been literally on her own waiting for Ryan to reply to her message. And because he hadn't got back to her she was imagining all sorts of horrible things. Was his mission dangerous? Was he captured? Was he hurt? Jaz was at the point where she thought maybe she should go to James with her information. But her gut instinct was to go to Ryan. She trusted him and, maybe, if she was true to herself, she was using this information to get to see him.

Tick's foot brushed through her hair, narrowly missing her head. Jaz laughed. 'Hey, no high stuff. I have a ball on tonight, remember. The swollen-face look is not currently in fashion,' she puffed, before aiming a punch to his abs, which connected. 'And on that note, I think we should finish up.' She shot Tick a winning smile while he rubbed his gut.

'God I love fighting with you, Jaz. Let's do it again soon,' he said, pulling her into a sweaty hug.

Even though Tick was covered with tattoos and scars from his days in street gangs, they didn't define him. When his mother had got sick with cancer and died, leaving him to raise his sister, his whole world had changed. He left the gang, got a serious job and moved his sister to a better area. He regretted his life as a teenager; the things he'd seen and done, and the turf wars they'd had, all seemed so trivial after losing his mum.

'Yes, soon. What are you doing this arvo?' she asked as they stood in the gym alone.

'I've gotta take Annaliese to her netball game. Just so you know for later, don't have girls. All the drama that comes with turning thirteen is nightmarish.'

Jaz laughed. At twenty-five Tick seemed like any normal parent, except he was much too young to have a teenager. One had to admire his devotion to his sister. 'I'm going to have a shower and hang around here for a bit.'

Tick nodded as he headed for the door. His house was only a block away, so he never used the gym showers. 'Righto. Have fun tonight, Jaz.'

Jaz followed him out, locked the front door and then went for her shower. She opened the door to her cubicle and started to undress. She turned to throw her clothes over the door and nearly dropped them. She had been so preoccupied with Tick and their fight she had forgotten about Ryan. But here he was. His handwriting was familiar and she felt as if he were standing in the shower cubicle with her. Jaz reached for the note. This time he hadn't bothered with a code. It simply said: *My place. 7.30pm.* Her heart was racing. Finally he'd contacted her. Finally she'd get to see him. Finally she felt the relief wash over her as the week's tension eased out of her limbs.

She felt like shouting with joy. The note clutched in her hand felt so precious, as if she were touching Ryan. She resisted the urge to hold the note against her heart in case she ruined it with her sweat from the fight. Reluctantly she put the note in her bag, after reading it another three times. While she showered she couldn't control the tingling in her skin and the nervous buzz like a million bees circling her body. He was finally home. Back at his house.

But his timing sucked as she realised she had to be at Marcus's at eight. She'd have to go to Ryan's on her way to the ball. It wasn't ideal. She wanted more time with him, not a rushed half-hour. *But it's better than nothing*, she reassured herself. *Any amount of time is better than nothing.*

Later in the day, as Jaz was getting dressed for Marcus's ball, she kept looking at Ryan's note. Only three words but they had kept her on edge all day, as if she were about to take flight with nervous energy. She had it stuck on her mirror after she got sick of pulling it out of her bag to look at every five minutes.

Jaz pulled her sage dress from her robe and hung it on the door.

Anna was with Ricky but had requested a photo of her in her dress. Taylor had got bored at home – more like didn't want to be there – and had insisted on helping her get ready. Luckily she knew he wasn't serious and he was actually downstairs playing games with Simon. But Jaz much preferred Taylor at her house than thinking of him alone at his home. She felt that he wasn't safe, that the man was still out there, lurking in the shadows waiting to come back and finish the job. That's why seeing Ryan tonight was important. Surely he could help.

Jaz slipped the dress on. She'd tied her hair back into a lose knot at the nape of her neck. Her make-up she'd left light, with a hint of green eye shadow, but thickened her long eyelashes with mascara. The dress said it all, really.

Sinking her feet into her silver heels, she grabbed her silver clutch purse. Before leaving her room, she took Ryan's note and hid it in her book on the desk.

'What do you think?' she asked Simon and Taylor.

Simon stared at her for a bit, then shrugged and went back to his game. Taylor, on the other hand, let his controller drop as he went to her.

'Wow.'

Jaz smiled. She hoped she would get the same reaction from Ryan. The dress was a soft sage green with a wide V-neck that went out to the edge of her shoulders, where short soft sleeves draped towards her elbows. Just under her bust was a soft wraparound belt in the same material, which knotted at the front and fell with the rest of the soft flowing material. The dress was almost backless, showing off her smooth skin and toned physique.

'Thanks. I'm just going to call a taxi and then I'm off. You gonna stay with Simon?' Jaz pulled out her phone from her clutch.

'Hey, no. I'll drive you.'

'No, don't do that. I can take a cab.'

'And sit in something sticky or end up smelling of incense or bad body odour? I don't think so. The 'Stang chariot awaits,' he said, with a stern look in his eye.

Damn it. Taylor wasn't going to let this go. She didn't want Taylor to see she was going to Ryan's. How could she get out of this?

'Whatever you are about to say, I don't care. I'm still driving you.'

Shit. 'Fine, but I need to go somewhere else first if that's okay.' Now she just had to figure out a story. Taylor already knew that Marcus lived in Cottesloe, so she couldn't pass Ryan's house off as his.

'Let's go,' he said as he pulled the car keys from his pocket. 'Si, I'll see you soon. I'll be back for another game.' Simon nodded but didn't turn away from his game.

'Your folks won't mind if I hang around here with Simon tonight, will they?' he asked as he held the car door open for her.

The sun had gone down; the night was pushing the last of the dying light with it. The air also had a cool crispness to it, making Jaz shiver. But most of that was from the turmoil of emotions raging inside her. She was about to see Ryan again.

Jaz tucked the soft material of her dress inside the Mustang so it wouldn't get caught in the door. It was full-length, and she didn't want it torn. 'Not at all, Tay,' she said when he got back in the driver's side. 'You can stay the night too, then I'll have someone to talk to when I get back,' she offered.

He pulled a face as he started the motor, the large engine rumbling into the quiet night. 'Jaz, I think you have me mixed up with Anna. I don't do intimate details,' he said with a laugh. 'Where did you have to go first?'

Jaz gave him Ryan's address as they pulled out onto the road.

'Why are we going here? Whose place is it?'

'Ryan's,' she said quietly.

Taylor glanced across the car. The only light came from the street lamps but it was enough to see he was a little confused.

She didn't reply. Hell, she hadn't really worked out what to say.

'Jaz?'

'I just found out he's back.'

'And… what – you thought you'd drop by while looking fabulous in this dress and see if you could make him jealous?'

Great. Taylor had come up with his own explanation. It was better than anything she could think of. 'Something like that,' she said, running with it. 'I just need to see him and see what's going on. You know, sort some stuff out.'

They rode the rest of the way in silence, both preoccupied with their thoughts. Jaz made every effort not to chew her nails, but began chewing her lip instead. And then her foot wouldn't stop jiggling. Before long Taylor had pulled up outside Ryan's place and Jaz felt faint. She looked down, but the low-cut V of the dress made her more nervous.

'Are you sure about this? Do you want me to wait?'

Jaz shook her head. She wasn't sure about either one. But she didn't think Taylor's Mustang sitting outside Ryan's house would be a good thing. Too easy to recognise and it always drew attention. She could easily call a taxi from here.

'No, you go back to Si. I'll be fine. Thanks, Tay.' Jaz made for the door but Taylor stopped her.

'You *are* going to the ball with Marcus, aren't you? Afterwards, I mean?'

Was he worried she wouldn't turn up? Marcus must have made an impression when they met at Molly's. 'Yeah, of course. I promised Marcus. I'm looking forward to it.' But the truth was she hadn't thought about it. She couldn't get past seeing Ryan. Her mind refused to think past this big event.

Jaz got out and thanked Taylor again, before shutting the door and watching him drive off. She was alone in the night with just the street-lights. Jaz turned and looked at the fence around Ryan's house. Her chest was rattling with a million bouncy balls. Her skin was prickling with anticipation and her breath was barely normal. She sucked in the night air and headed to the gate. Reaching over, she found the release button; if she hadn't been so nervous she would have smiled at the memory of the time she'd climbed over the fence and fallen into his daisy bush, hence he had shown her the button. Walking towards his house was familiar yet scary. Each step to his door seemed to match the pounding of blood in her ears. Her hand gripped at her purse so hard she was afraid she'd draw blood and stain her pretty dress.

With a deep breath, she raised her hand and knocked, then stood back and tried to smooth her dress and make sure it was sitting on her shoulders right.

'Come in!' she heard him yell. His voice: she had missed it but it was just how she remembered it. Deep and alluring.

Jaz turned the handle and entered his house. It was bright inside and she felt self-conscious out of the dark.

'I'm in the kitchen, hang on.'

She followed his voice as her mouth went dry. He stepped out, drying his hands on a tea towel, but paused when he saw her.

'Jaz.'

CHAPTER 12

HER NAME ON his lips sent tingles down her back as her eyes feasted on him. His hair was still clipped short and the shadow of stubble along his chin was neat but gave him that sexy rustic look she'd missed so much. She stumbled over his lips; feeling her pulse race, she moved upwards to his deep dark eyes. Still so mysterious and full of strength, but she saw something tender pass through them too.

'Hey, Ryan,' she replied.

He cleared his throat. 'You look nice. Going somewhere?'

Heat touched her skin as his eyes trailed paths over every inch of her dress, setting a fire alight deep in her belly. 'Yeah, I'm off to a ball. But I got your note.'

The mention of the note broke something as he cleared his throat again and threw the tea towel into the kitchen. 'Come,' he said gesturing to her. 'We'll go sit in the lounge and talk.'

Jaz walked down the passageway; as she went past Ryan, she heard a noise, almost a groan from deep in his throat. It was faint but she'd caught it. A smile grew as she remembered the backless part of her dress. Jaz went to the couch, sat carefully, and watched as Ryan paused between the couch and the single chair. Was he wondering which one was safer?

'I don't bite,' she said with a smile.

Ryan clenched his fists, but Jaz was more taken with the way his grey trackpants clung to his hips. His T-shirt was white with a circular print in the middle, but it was the way it snuggled against his chest and arm muscles that had Jaz swallowing hard.

He scratched at his chin. 'Can I get you anything? A drink?'

'No, I'm fine, thanks. But I do need to talk.'

'Right. Yes. I did get your text message.' The thought of work spurred Ryan on. He stepped towards the couch and sat beside her. 'I'm guessing you really needed to talk. Is it your mission? Has something gone wrong?'

The concern that sparked through the dark depths of his eyes warmed her heart. How was she going to be with Marcus tonight when her whole body and mind wanted to stay by Ryan's side?

'No, the mission is going fine. Marcus is great.' Ryan frowned, not what Jaz was expecting. Would he be jealous of Marcus? Jaz doubted it. Ryan probably didn't suffer those emotions. 'But it's Taylor. He was held at gunpoint.' Jaz went on to explain the events of that day.

'Jesus, Jaz. Trouble seems to follow you,' he said, but he wasn't laughing. 'Are you okay?'

'Yeah, I am, but I'm worried about Taylor. I don't think he feels safe at home anymore. The thing I really wanted to tell you about, Ryan, was this guy's tattoo. I only saw a part of it but it seemed familiar. I contacted you when I finally worked out what it was. Actually, I'd drawn you the picture of it once.' Jaz waited to see if Ryan remembered the time he'd asked her to spy on some guys at the club he was working in and she'd spotted the tattoo on one of them.

She knew she wouldn't have too wait long.

'The snake tattoo in the circle? Are you sure?' He looked less than impressed with this news.

'Yep. I am. Taylor's dad is really stressed at the moment, and with the things the guy said to Taylor as he held him at gunpoint...' Jaz faded off.

'You think something's going on? What are your thoughts?'

Jaz was thrilled that Ryan trusted her opinion and was taking this seriously. He believed in her.

'I'm wondering if this snake-tattoo guy belongs to the same drug mob you were looking into. Maybe they're trying to get Taylor's dad to spy for them by threatening Taylor. He's the Deputy Commissioner of Police Operations. What if they want Mr Stewart to help them by tipping off raids or other little bits of information from the inside? Who's going to argue with a mob like that, who can break into your house and threaten your only child? Something's definitely going on, because when I told Mr Stewart what the man had said to Taylor he went really pale. He knew what it meant, I'm sure of it.' She repeated the gunman's words as she remembered them.

Ryan sat back in the couch. Jaz watched him carefully.

'This isn't good, Jaz. That tattoo you found – we linked it to a large gang who call themselves the Shesha Serpents. They're like a bikie gang, but instead of wearing their colours on their leather jackets, these guys have it tattooed on their wrist or neck. They've been on our watch list as we gather more info. We've got someone working to get on the inside with them now, but it's not easy – they don't trust anyone but their own. I think what you said could be on the money. Why else would they go after Taylor's dad? Having a guy inside the police, especially one so high up, would save them a lot of trouble, and it's not the first time something like this has happened. There are leaks everywhere, Jaz. Guys held over a barrel by these unforgiving pricks.' Ryan turned away in frustration.

'So, what should I do?'

His hand shot out to hers. 'Nothing, Jaz. You do nothing. Leave this with me. I'll see what we can do from our side, but keep an eye on Taylor. There's a good chance the gunman could be back if his dad doesn't cooperate.'

'Don't worry, I am,' she said. Meanwhile her whole body was reacting to his touch. His strong calloused hand had zapped against hers like static but she couldn't deny how safe his grip felt. How much she had missed it and how much it felt like home. As if he'd read her thoughts, he withdrew his hand. It probably didn't help that she'd been staring at their hands like they were set in gold. 'I just can't believe how bad this all is and how it can affect people like Taylor.'

'Once you open your eyes to the world, you find so many dark hidden secrets. I'm really sorry you had to go through that with Taylor but I don't want you taking any unnecessary risks. We're working hard to bring the Shesha Serpents down.'

Jaz closed her eyes, taking comfort in Ryan's words.

'There's another reason I needed to see you,' he added, spiking her interest. 'I have another mission I could use your help with. It's not something I can do alone, and everyone else is tied up. You don't have to do it, though, if you're not comfortable.' He watched her carefully.

Jaz just about yelled out 'Yes!' Hell, she'd do anything for him. 'I'm keen.'

'Hmm, just wait till you know all the details,' he said with a hint of a smile.

A normal person might have missed it but Jaz knew Ryan, the shape of his face, the hidden emotions and the curve of his lips. He was happy with her eager response.

He sat forward on the couch, which brought his knees close to hers. 'It means coming to Pakistan with me, pretending to be my doting girlfriend while I play an invalid in a wheelchair. It's just a ruse to smuggle information out of the country, but eyes will be everywhere, so we have to play the game on the plane and in Pakistan. Do you think you could handle that?' He was deadly serious.

But so was she. 'Yes.'

'Good. Pax is due back tomorrow. I'll get him started on your fake passport.'

Jaz didn't even want to ask how Pax managed to make a fake passport but she was sure it would be realistic.

'Don't worry, Pax knows his job. He has all the same equipment the government uses, so it's a real passport, just a fake you.'

Jaz didn't understand how Ryan always seemed to know what she was thinking. Was she an open book? Should she be working on better controlling her expressions?

'When do we go?' she asked, suddenly feeling nervous. She'd been overseas before but to Italy and England. Not Pakistan. That wasn't exactly a holiday destination. It would be dangerous and scary, but she had faith that Ryan wouldn't have asked her if he didn't think she'd cope. She forced her thoughts to that and let her fear slide away for the time being.

Ryan ran her through the details. They would go next week and be gone for one night, and Pax would serve as her alibi. Just the thought of one night with Ryan made her tremble. Jaz knew she should be a little fearful of a trip to Pakistan. It would be a place full of trouble, unsafe and teeming with guns. Yet she was ready to go tomorrow. She hoped her eagerness didn't show on her face.

'Have you done something like this before?' she almost whispered. She longed to touch his face, to run her fingers across his stubble and to feel the shortness of his hair tickle her skin. She was losing focus. Gritting her teeth, she tried to concentrate on the words forming from his all-too-familiar lips. Oh, that didn't help either.

'I have. Don't worry. I'll walk you through it again before we go. I'll come to Pax's the night before we go to cover all the details. What to pack, what to say, how to act. I'll have the hard part of not speaking for the whole plane trip.'

'Somehow I think you'd cope better with that than me,' she said.

Ryan's deep chuckle just about made her melt into his lap. Their knees were now touching and she wondered if he'd noticed too.

'Will I need a gun?' she asked. Taking a big risk, she moved her hand to his leg. She felt his muscles spasm under her touch. But it still wasn't enough. She wanted his arms around her and his breath against her neck. Just as her fantasies were taking off, a knock at the door startled them both.

Ryan sprang up from the couch. 'Who could that be?' He looked at her and Jaz wondered if he was deciding whether to hide her in a cupboard.

'Do you want me to hide out in the spare room?' she asked. He raised his eyebrow as if contemplating it.

'Ryan, hurry up!'

Jaz knew that voice.

'Oh, it's Steph. She could be here for a while. I can't hide you. We'll just have to wing it,' he said, as he headed to the door Steph was knocking on again.

'Sis, what's up?'

As they greeted each other, Jaz fidgeted on the couch, not sure whether to stand or stay here. She felt like a robber in a jewellery store even though she hadn't done anything wrong.

'Come in. Jaz is here. You remember?' said Ryan, as he brought Steph into the lounge.

Steph's dark eyes found her and she smiled brightly, making her more beautiful than Jaz remembered. Her blonde hair was swept up into a high bun and she was dressed in skinny jeans and a cute olive jacket.

'Jaz. Hi. God, you look gorgeous.' Steph shot a curious glance to her brother.

Jaz stood up, realising now was her chance to escape. 'Hi Steph. Yeah, I'm on my way to a ball.'

'Oh, I loved them. The downside to growing up,' said Steph. She sat down and motioned for them to do the same. All that was left was the couch, so she shared it with Ryan again.

'So, to what do I owe this visit, sis? You got time to hang around for a while? I've got a roast in the oven.'

'Sure bro, I'd love to. I'm not interrupting anything, am I?' she asked.

'Nah, we were just catching up. I've only just got back from my trip,' he said with ease. Jaz wasn't so sure she could have pulled it off right now. Her heart was racing, wondering what Steph was thinking.

'Well, let me tell you why I'm here. It's Mum and Dad's anniversary in two weeks and they want us to come. Gazza's going to be there, so make sure you bring someone too,' said Steph.

'Like who? I'm not dating anyone,' said Ryan.

Jaz was relieved. One day she hoped it would be her but realistically, in their line of work, probably not.

'Bring Jaz,' said Steph brightly. 'Come on, Ry. You've never brought anyone home. Not even friends. We want to be included in your life, we want to get to know your friends.' Steph leaned forward on her knees and spoke to Jaz. 'You'll come, won't you Jaz? You're the only friend of Ryan's I've met in years.'

'You don't have to,' said Ryan, cutting in.

'Come on, your family's not *that* bad,' Steph replied.

'I don't mind,' said Jaz. Really, she didn't. If anything, she wanted to meet Ryan's parents and to see the house he grew up in.

'Wonderful,' said Steph clapping.

Jaz spotted the clock on Ryan's wall. 'Oh crap, it's eight-thirty already. I'll be late. Sorry,' she said jumping up and trying to pull out her phone. 'I need to call a taxi.'

'Don't worry, I can drop you off,' said Ryan. 'It'll be quicker than waiting for a cab. Where do you have to go?'

'Just to Cottesloe. But you don't have to. Steph is here. Stay. I'll be okay.'

Ryan stood and put his hand over her phone to stop her calling, then turned to Steph. 'You don't mind if I drop Jaz off, do you? There're some roasting vegies that could use some basting while you wait, and there's wine in the fridge. I'll only be ten minutes. Cott's close by.'

'No, it doesn't worry me. Go,' she said as she got up.

Jaz waited for Ryan's hand to leave hers before putting her phone away. She desperately hoped Steph hadn't noticed the blush she felt at Ryan's touch; she didn't need Ryan's sister reading into anything. 'Thanks, I appreciate it,' she said to both of them.

'I hope you have a great night, Jaz. Who's your date?' asked Steph as they made their way to the door. Ryan was two steps in front and grabbed his car keys off the hook on his way past.

'A guy called Marcus. It's his school ball.'

'Oh, is he anyone special?'

Oh God. Jaz wished she could leave now. Ryan was at the door but his head was slightly turned, listening to their conversation. 'Yeah, he's my boyfriend. We made it official just this week,' she said with a nervous smile.

'Sweet. Is he cute?'

'We better go,' said Ryan, opening the door. He was frowning.

Steph held her hand. 'You'll have to show me the photos of you guys at our dinner. Promise you'll still come. Ry will bring you.'

Jaz smiled. She really liked Steph. She was bright and friendly. And they were close in age – only three years between them. 'Sure. I'll see you then.'

Steph waved as she stood by the door. Ryan shook his head before shutting the door. 'Sorry about Steph,' he said as they went to his black SUV.

'That's okay. I like Steph. Makes me wish my sister was still alive,' she said softly.

Ryan held open the passenger door while she climbed in, and checked her dress was safely inside before he closed it. Inside Ryan's car she felt safe. It smelled like him, even more so when he sat beside her.

They didn't speak until he'd reversed out onto the road. Jaz couldn't think of anything to say. Tonight had been a real overload of the emotions and senses.

'You don't have to come to the dinner,' Ryan said.

'Why? Don't you want me to?'

'No. No, it's not that. It's just Steph can railroad people a bit and I didn't want you to feel pressured.'

Jaz pulled out her phone to check the time. Should she text Marcus? 'It's okay. If it's all right with you I'm happy to go.' Jaz turned to watch him. His arms were so sculpted, so beautiful – and so deadly. Just being alone with him made her feel like she was standing at the edge of a cliff with the fresh breeze in her face as the height made her fell alive and giddy. 'It is all right?'

'Yeah, sure. Actually, you would be doing me a favour. My family are always nagging me about my life. Same old stuff: they never see me, never meet any of my friends. It's a bit hard in this business. If I could take you, then that would ease things. I hope,' he added.

Jaz quickly typed out a message to Marcus. *Be there in 5!*

Ryan watched her. 'The mission going okay?' he asked softly.. He was pulling up to the side of the road. Jaz could see the beach on the left, the moon glistening along the waves. She hadn't even given Ryan the address but he obviously remembered. For all she knew, he could have been one of the people staking out the house early on.

'Yes.' She didn't know what else to say and there was no time to elaborate.

In true style, Ryan had stopped a house short so no one would notice the car.

'Thanks for the lift.' She leaned forward to peer at the Sinclair house. The lights were on and she saw something move by the fence. Oh, Marcus was waiting for her.

As she opened the door Ryan's voice made her pause. It was spoken so softly but held so much weight and warning. 'Be careful, Jaz. Just... be careful.'

She turned back, meeting his eye, and her pulse skipped a beat. He was so gorgeous it took the breath from her lungs. She couldn't reply, the nod of her head the only thing she managed before she climbed out of his car.

Quickly she stepped to the path, refusing to glance back, and headed straight to Marcus. 'I'm sorry I'm late,' she said, walking quickly.

He stepped out onto the path and held his arms out to her. 'Wow, I would wait another hour for you, Jaz. You look amazing.'

She stepped into his embrace and felt his hands spread over her bare back while he kissed her cheek. Jaz leaned back and brushed his suit jacket. 'You're pretty spiffy yourself.' His black suit hung from his lean frame, making him look like a model. His hair was pulled back into a neat pony-tail at the nape of his neck and he was wearing the tie that matched her dress. Any girl would die to have someone like Marcus as a boyfriend.

'Come on, let's get meeting my parents over with quickly so I can have you all to myself.' He leaned down and kissed her lips. 'I don't want to let you out of my sight.'

Marcus stepped away, and took her hand to lead her inside. Jaz glanced back to the road, expecting to find it empty, but Ryan's black SUV was only just leaving the kerb. He had waited and watched. What did he think? Did he feel anything as he watched Marcus kiss her? Did it churn him up like it would her if she saw him with someone else? She watched as Ryan drove past but she couldn't see into his car. Couldn't glimpse one last look at his face. Trying not to think of the great big chasm of distance growing between them, she followed Marcus into his home.

CHAPTER 13

MARCUS LED HER inside deep red double doors, into a wide, bright foyer. While the walls were white, the colours came from the collection of paintings and sculptures that led to the prominent wooden and wrought-iron staircase. 'Wow, I love your house. My folks have nothing like this,' she said reaching out to a stone statue but not touching it in case it was worth a fortune.

'This is Mum and Dad's business. They love all this art stuff. Just don't mention it or it's all we'll hear about. They'll probably try to sell you some,' he said with a smirk.

Tugging on her hand gently, he took her along the large marbled floor to a room off to the left. Jaz was trying hard to take everything in. She hadn't seen any personal photos yet, just the artworks.

'She's here,' said Marcus as he pulled her towards him, offering a safety buffer.

Jaz recognised his parents from the photos he'd texted and the file James showed her. But they seemed even warmer and more real in person. Diane Sinclair stood first, rushing towards them with her hands outstretched. 'Oh, welcome, Jaz. We've heard so much about you.' Diane was wearing a stunning white pantsuit accessorised to perfection, and had her hair pulled up into a high ponytail. 'Nice to meet you, Mrs Sinclair,' said Jaz.

'Oh no. It's Diane, please. Diane and Carl,' she said motioning to her husband.

Jaz could see Marcus in both of them. He had his mum's eyes and dark hair but he was his father in everything else.

Carl stepped forward and offered Jaz his hand. 'Hi, Jaz. You look lovely,' he said, before giving Marcus a wink. Carl's grin was wide, the same as his son's, and it was genuine. He wore a dark blue suit but was minus the jacket.

'Thank you. You have a lovely home.'

'I'll give you a tour next time,' said Marcus with a knowing grin. 'But now we should head off to the ball.'

'Oh wait. I need photos. Hang on, let me get the camera,' said Diane, rushing back to the coffee table by the cream leather couch where a large Canon camera sat.

'What did I tell you,' Marcus mumbled into her ear.

'You must come around for dinner, Jaz,' said Carl. 'Then we can get to meet you properly.'

'I'd like that. Thanks.' And Jaz really meant it. She felt as if this were all real, that Marcus was her boyfriend and this was the next step in their relationship. If only Ryan hadn't left her feeling a little shaken. Fancy telling her to be careful. This situation seemed anything but dangerous. But then she realised… maybe Ryan meant be careful with Marcus. Pax had already warned her about liking him too much.

'Marcus honey, smile,' said Diane as she took aim with the camera.

Jaz snuggled up beside him, pulled her shoulders straight and smiled.

'Just a few more.'

Marcus eventually held up his hand. 'Mum, enough already. We have to go.'

Jaz almost swore she could see tears in his mother's eyes when she came to hug them goodbye.

Both parents walked them to another door that went to the garage. Three expensive cars sat quietly inside, Marcus's BMW the closest.

Jaz couldn't help looking at everything. She wasn't sure what she was searching for, maybe a big sign saying 'drug importer' or maybe stacks of white powder or wads of money. She did know that she would be back and, if she could, she'd go straight for his dad's office. It seemed like the obvious place to start finding information. But for now she was going to take a deep breath and enjoy her night.

'Hey Pax, you're back!' said Jaz, as she walked through the gym to the office. Pax was shuffling through drawers looking for something. He paused to give her a hug.

'Sure am, kiddo. So, tell me, what's been happening?' he asked as he resumed his search.

'What are you looking for?'

'Scissors?'

Jaz plucked a pair from the canister by the computer screen. 'These do?' she said with a smirk.

Pax pushed his glasses back on his nose and sighed. 'Yep. Ta.'

'What do you want to know? Are we alone?' she whispered.

'Bags is down the back with a client, but we'll go into the house. I need you for something.' Pax scratched at his round belly while he spoke. Then he nodded towards the house and Jaz followed him.

She thought it was strange when he locked the door behind them. But it probably made sense because Anna had a habit of materialising from nowhere. She was so thin and whispy it was like she floated, unlike Jaz who made each footstep count.

Pax led her through the house to the spare room, which for as long as Jaz could remember had always been locked. He'd told them over the years that the roof had fallen down due to a leak and he just hadn't got around to fixing it. But now he pulled out his key set and unlocked the door. Jaz noticed the worn marks from turning a key. This room was used more than she realised.

When Pax pushed open the door, he shuffled her in and then shut it behind him, locking it.

Jaz's mouth dropped as she saw the expensive computer equipment. She thought what was in the office was good, but this stuff was fancy. There were three different printers. The computer screen was huge, the desk was covered with papers, there was a side desk with fancy paper on it and sheets of plastic. This was the hidden hub of Pax's MTG Agency work.

'Wow.'

'Here, stand against the door,' said Pax, now holding a camera. 'You need a passport photo.'

'Oh gee, hang on,' said Jaz as she tried to smooth out her hair. 'Do you do this stuff a lot, Pax?'

'Yep, sure do. Pakistan, hey? Are you sure?' He dropped the camera so he could see her properly. She knew the lines on his face as if they were the paths she'd travelled to her home and The Ring every day. The crinkles near his mouth were like miniature smiles and the little speckles in his eyes were what she searched for when she needed his comfort. And yet here he stood, with this whole side she had never known about. He was the man she knew but not. In a way, Jaz felt as if she'd grown up, that she was finally privy to the secrets of the adult world. And she was glad she could share this with Pax. She felt it brought them closer than ever.

'What's wrong?' he asked as he studied her. 'You having second thoughts?'

Jaz reached out and hugged him. 'I'm just so glad I have you, Pax. I love you, you know that?'

'Me too, sweetheart. I love you too. What's brought this on?'

She had him rattled, which wasn't her intention. 'It's not the trip, Pax. I'm excited about it, really. It's just seeing this room, this side of you. It makes it all real, you know. And I'm glad that this is something we share, that there are no secrets between us. You're the only one, besides Ryan, who I have that with now.' She swallowed the rising lump in her throat. She didn't want glassy eyes on her passport.

'Oh love, I know exactly what you mean.' He kissed her forehead. 'Come on, let's get this photo done so I can get to work on your passport. Especially when you need it by Tuesday. Love it how they spring this stuff on me,' he muttered to himself as he raised the camera.

Jaz smiled and the flash went off. Then she followed him to his desk, where he took out the SD card and put it in his computer.

Pax paused and then turned to Jaz.

'What?' she asked.

'I've never had anyone watch me work before. It's usually a job I do alone,' he said. 'It's just a bit weird.' He gave her a wink to know he still didn't want her to leave.

'Do you have to do a passport for Ryan or does he have a few others already?' she asked.

'No, I'll have to do him another one to suit. He needs a photo taken while in character, if you know what I mean.'

Jaz looked at the program on his computer, and the other bits, and shook her head. 'It's all double dutch to me, Pax. I never did get all this. Anna, on the other hand, takes after you in every way, even down to the pastry addiction,' she teased.

Jaz's phone vibrated. 'Oh, Anna's just left Ricky's and is on her way here. She has the *Auto Trader*. We were going to look for my car.'

'That's okay, I can finish this later. I have a few errands to run. We better lock up.'

Jaz had just finished making a cuppa when Anna came into Pax's kitchen. She looked so fresh in denim shorts and a black *Big Bang Theory* T-shirt. Her fair skin was bright, the freckles along her nose alive and her delicate features making her unassumingly beautiful.

'Hey ya. Where's Pax?'

'Just gone off to do some errands. Did you bring the paper?'

Anna held up a plastic bag and gave it a shake. 'Got some choc biscuits too.' She laid it all out on the table. 'Can't gossip about boys without chocolate,' she said.

Before she'd even got her bum to the chair she started. 'So, did you kiss Marcus last night?'

Jaz frowned. 'I haven't even put our cups down yet.' As she handed Anna her large red mug, she remembered back to the ball. She hadn't known anyone except for Marcus's three friends, who were there with their dates. But Marcus had taken her away from them and onto the dance floor, in the dimmed light, to hold her close. She remembered the gentle touch of his hands as he held her tightly. They had gazed at each other. She tried not to compare it to the night of her own ball, when Ryan had held her and kissed her. It wasn't fair to compare them, but being with Marcus was still sweet. And he had kissed her too. Not the normal little sweet kisses they had shared before. They had been dancing close, her head on his shoulder. She had enjoyed being held in his arms and feeling wanted. He smelled nice, a sandalwood scent, and his hands had moved over her skin like silk. He'd whispered against her ear how much he was enjoying himself, his breath had been warm. Then he kissed the spot below her ear, moving along her chin until he reached her mouth. By then she was ready. Ready to be wanted. She could remember the taste of his lips, which were smooth and soft like his skin. He'd opened his mouth and she'd taken advantage. He'd trembled and it had excited her. She had certainly got lost in the moment, or moments.

'Oh, I can tell by the way you're blushing that you did. Was it good?' Anna asked as she watched her.

Jaz took her time, reached for the biscuits and opened them. 'Yeah, it was great,' she said. 'He's really great.'

'You say that like you're surprised. Did you not think you'd get over Ryan?'

Jaz felt her frown form before she could stop it.

'Oh, Jaz,' said Anna when she realised.

Jaz could only shrug. 'I really like Marcus. But he's not Ryan.' And that was the truth. 'It's just going to take time.'

Anna nodded. 'You got over Taylor, remember.'

'Yeah, but I love Tay differently. It took me a while to figure that out, but with Ryan…' Jaz glanced off to the wall with its faded yellow cupboards. How did she explain what she felt for Ryan? There was nothing else like it. Jaz turned back to Anna and shrugged. 'What's it like with Ricky? Is he…?'

'The one? Hell no,' said Anna. 'I like him, and he's smart, which is nice, but that's only one side of me. The other side likes hanging out with you and Taylor and going to the range to shoot and all those things Ricky doesn't like. I'm feeling like this is just a bus trip to somewhere, you know? He's just someone until the right one comes along.' Anna frowned. 'That makes me sound bitchy, but what I'm trying to say is that it's not serious. I'm just enjoying the ride at the moment. Isn't that what you're doing with Marcus? Seeing where it goes? The more time you spend with him, you might end up really liking him.'

And that right there would be a problem. Having a thing for Ryan was also a problem. Nothing was ever clear-cut. Jaz pulled a face and grabbed a biscuit. 'Wow, this guy stuff's hard work. Think I'll need two.' And she took another biscuit. Anna laughed and took another one as well. If only chocolate could really fix all their problems.

CHAPTER 14

Jaz was almost at The Ring when her phone rang, stirring her from her thoughts. School had been a total write-off, especially when she was leaving for Pakistan in two days. She couldn't think about anything else except seeing Ryan tomorrow and finding out all the details of their operation. Not even Minka found her radar today. Just some conversation with Anna and Taylor and texts with Marcus was all she could remember.

'Hey, Pax,' she said, answering his call. But the line was silent. 'Pax? You there?'

She stopped walking and squished her phone closer to her ear. Then she heard short breaths. 'Pax! Can you hear me?'

'Help, Jaz.' It was only just a whisper, so close to nothing.

Jaz sprinted the last hundred metres to The Ring while yelling into the phone. 'I'm coming, Pax! I'm just here! I'm coming!' But she had no idea what she was going to find. Was he being held hostage too? Was he injured?

She flung open the door of the gym and ran inside calling his name but there was no answer, just the emptiness that echoed back Pax's name.

She ran to the empty office, and then continued into the house calling for him. Her eyes bounced off walls, searching for him like lasers. Heading down the passage, she checked the rooms; only his special room was left. 'Pax, you in here?' she yelled while rattling the door.

A painful groan leached through the door, confirming her fears. Grabbing the handle, she tried to open it, but it was locked. He always locked it. *Damn.*

'Pax, do you have a spare key?'

'Bathroom,' she heard faintly, followed by, 'toilet.'

Jaz darted into his small bathroom, square yellow tiles around the sink and shower, mould growing on the ceiling in one corner. She went straight to the toilet and pulled off the top of the cistern. Sure enough, a tiny key sat inside on top of the float.

'I've got it, Pax. I'm coming,' she said as she got back to the door and unlocked it. She opened it carefully in case Pax was behind it, but he was near his desk on the floor, clearly having dragged half the stuff on his desk down with him. His mobile phone was in his hand and his glasses had fallen from the top of his head. Jaz went to his side, using her phone to call an ambulance. Her fingers shook, making her glad it was only a three-digit number. 'What is it, Pax?' she asked as she touched his face lightly. 'What's going on?' He was clammy and held his hand to his chest. She hated seeing him lying there like this. This shouldn't be happening to Pax.

'Hello, yes, I need an ambulance. My friend has collapsed.' She gave his address. 'He's fifty-five. Yes, he's conscious but he's struggling for breath… Yes, he's very pale and sweaty. No, no heart problems that I know of.'

'Was dizzy,' said Pax breathlessly. She passed this on to the man on the phone.

'Pax, do you have medication?' she relayed to him. Pax shook his head. 'No to medication,' she said into the phone. 'Okay, I will. Thank you.'

'Ambulance is on its way, Pax. Hang in there. I just need to sit you up a bit, make you comfortable.'

'Not here,' he said.

Jaz looked around and understood now why Pax had called her and not the ambulance. No one could see what was in here. She had to move him. She didn't have time to call Ryan for help, the ambulance would be here soon.

'I'm going to try to move you to the hallway, okay, Pax. Just bear with me.'

He nodded and squeezed her hand.

Jaz got behind him and lifted him up under his arms. 'You just relax; let me do all the work. I don't want you doing anything,' she said through gritted teeth.

It was only a few metres to the hallway. Once Jaz got him out, she grabbed two pillows from the bedroom and made him comfortable. Then she got his glasses, quickly checking for anything else he might need from the room, before pulling the door shut. Jaz tucked the key deep in her jeans.

'You'll be fine, Pax,' she said, holding his hand. He had to be. Pax was indestructible. He was not allowed to get sick. He was going to be here forever. Life wouldn't be the same without him. She could feel the tears building and didn't want to upset him further. Jaz kissed his hand, a lingering scent of coffee and cinnamon. The sirens were making their way closer, and she stood up.

'Are you okay here if I go and meet the ambulance?'

He nodded, and she tried not to run from the house as a tear escaped.

When she was satisfied that the ambulance officers had him well looked after, Jaz called her mum and then Anna, and rode in the back of the ambulance with Pax to the hospital. It was so surreal. Jaz had never seen anyone sick before. She'd never been this close to losing someone she loved. Her dad had died before she was born, and she was too young to remember her sister. She found herself trembling, her eyes fixed on Pax the whole way.

At the hospital, Jaz sat in the stark white waiting room. It gave her chills and it was with stiff cold fingers she sent Ryan a text.

Royal Perth Hospital. Now.

Anna and her family came a few minutes later, followed by Jaz's mum with Simon. It was a madhouse as they quizzed her.

'A heart attack?' asked Tasha, as she reached out to hug Jaz. Pax had been like Tasha's father, taking care of her and Jaz when she was first born. 'I should catch up with him more, I've been so self-absorbed.' Tasha was pale. Jaz hadn't seen her mum this scared in ages, if ever.

'I bet it was all those pastries he loves,' said Anna. Her eyes were red and glassy. She held Jaz's hand. 'How awful to find him like that, but I'm glad you were there, Jaz. I can't imagine life…' Anna couldn't finish.

Anna's mum, Lenore, motioned to Tasha. 'Lets go find a doctor.' She brushed her hair back from her face as they headed down the corridor. Simon went with them, walking between the two mums. Lenore was tall and twiggy, like Anna, and they shared similar green eyes and freckles.

'Anna, you okay?' Taylor asked as he came rushing to their side. He hugged Anna before turning to Jaz. 'Hey, Jaz. Is he okay?' He reached out to draw her into the hug.

'I'm not sure. Our mums have gone to find a doctor and check. It's Pax, he's as strong as an ox, he'll be fine,' she said chewing on a fingernail. Jaz looked back out the doors of the hospital, hoping Ryan came soon.

'Shall we go find out too?' said Taylor. Anna nodded as she hugged him close. Her head rested in the crook of his neck, and Taylor had his lips pressed to the top of her head.

'You guys go, I need to find the toilet.'

'We can wait?' he asked.

'I'm fine. You go. I'll catch up.' Jaz felt the relief wash over her as they left, still arm in arm. They really did make a sweet couple. Jaz moved over to the other side of the room so she would be out of sight if they looked back. She sunk down into a chair and buried her face in her hands while she waited for Ryan.

She was oblivious to the sounds of the hospital and didn't even hear the door, or know Ryan had come in, until she heard him call her name.

Before she could lift her head, his hands were on her shoulders as he crouched down to her level. 'Jaz, what's happened? Are you okay?'

His voice washed over her like a warm safety blanket. She hadn't realised how cold she felt, how frozen with fear. Meeting his eyes was hard to do with so many emotions at breaking point.

Ryan moved his hand, bringing it to her face. His warm caress sent more warmth flooding through her, but it was the tenderness in his dark eyes that stilled her breath. It took all her strength to remember where she was. Ryan had a way of making her forget the world. Which was funny, because he was the one who opened her eyes to it.

'Pax had a heart attack. He was *working* when it happened. That's why he called me. Lucky I was just about at The Ring. Ryan, it could have been much worse.'

Ryan was quiet but his hands left her face and now his thumb rubbed circles on her shoulder. 'Let's not worry until we know how he's going. Shall we go and see?'

He stood up and Jaz followed. They found everyone gathered by Pax's door. Tasha was beside Pax helping him answer a questions for the doctor.

They had put an oxygen mask on him in the ambulance, but now he had tubes in his nose.

'Hey Ryan,' said Taylor. Jaz glanced back to her friends who had just spotted them. Anna was wearily watching them both. 'Did you just get here?'

'Yeah, I turned up at The Ring just as the ambulance was leaving,' said Ryan, the lie coming easily. 'Not what you want to see.'

Jaz introduced Anna's mum to Ryan, then Tasha joined them. 'Mum, this is Ryan, a friend of Pax's from The Ring. He arrived as the ambulance was leaving.' Jaz watched her mum give Ryan the once over. It would be hard not to when he was sexy in his stone-washed jeans, black belt and fitted black T-shirt. His was face shadowed by stubble, set stern, and his body hard with muscles. She could just see her mum quizzing her about the hot guy at the hospital later and making sure Jaz didn't know him too well.

Eventually Tasha held out her hand. 'Nice to meet you, Ryan. Shame it's under these circumstances. Are you one of his Ring crew?' she asked.

That's what her mum called the regulars like Tick and Bags. Pax's mates who helped him keep it going.

Ryan nodded, letting her believe that. 'How is he?'

Tasha sighed as she glanced at them all huddled around her in a circle. 'It was a heart attack. They have him hooked up to an ECG to screen for arrhythmias and they'll keep him here for a few days so they can check if he sustained any damage to his heart. He'll need medication and he'll have to watch his diet from now on.'

'No more pastries,' they all said together with a smile.

'Can we see him?' Jaz asked her mum.

'Yes, just not for long.'

Anna, Lenore and Taylor walked into Pax's room while they waited outside. 'I'm going to go pack him some things. Do you want a lift or are you all right?' asked Tasha.

'I'll be right, thanks Mum. I'll wait here till you get back.'

Tasha pulled her into a hug. 'He's going to be fine. Nice meeting you, Ryan.' Then she motioned for Simon to follow her. Simon gave Jaz a half-wave goodbye. He didn't know Pax like she did. Simon hated The Ring, thought it was too smelly and silly. But Pax was over for dinner at least once a month when he was home, so Simon was fond of him, like anyone who met the gentle teddy bear.

'Are you going to hang around?' she asked Ryan. He'd been standing by her side the whole time, but it wasn't near enough for her liking. He stepped closer now her mum had gone and lowered his voice.

'I need to talk to Pax. If he hasn't finished our passports we might have to cancel our trip,' he said. His eyes held her spellbound.

Jaz frowned. 'Isn't there someone else who can do it?'

'No. Our other guy is in Sydney at the moment. Did you notice if they were on his desk?'

Jaz put her hand to her head and rubbed her temple. There had been loose papers but no passport books. 'I didn't see any, sorry.'

They waited outside until Anna, Taylor and Lenore left. 'See you guys later,' called Jaz, as Ryan put his hand on her lower back and guided her into Pax's room. Anna's eyes widened at the gesture. *Great.* That would be another chocolate biscuit conversation for later.

'Pax, mate. What are you doing in here?' said Ryan teasingly, as he sat down beside the bed.

'Ha ha,' he replied before shifting his eyes to Jaz. 'Thanks, honey, for saving me.'

'Gah, just don't do that to me again. You are going on a diet.' Jaz chuckled at the look of disdain on his face. She reached out to hold his hand, to feel some comfort that he was alive and okay.

'Diet sounds like death,' he said rolling his eyes. 'I guess I know what you want to know,' he said to Ryan. 'And you aren't going to like the answer.'

Ryan's face gave away no emotion. 'Damn, I was afraid of that. How far did you get?' Ryan dropped his voice as a nurse passed the door.

'I got Jaz's done; it's in the drawer in the desk. But I haven't printed yours yet. Is Mick in WA?'

'No, Sydney. We're out of luck there,' said Ryan.

'I could talk you through the program from here? I know how important this trip is. I don't want all that planning to go up in smoke because of me. You've been after this bastard for years. This is your chance to nail him.'

'I know, you don't have to tell me.' Ryan nudged Jaz. 'You any good with computer programs?'

'Nope. Simon got all that.' Jaz glanced at Pax. 'What about Anna? She could do it in her sleep and you know it. We could ask her to do it, it's only Ryan's so she doesn't need to know much more than that, right?'

'I don't like you involved, Jaz, let alone Anna,' said Pax, who'd started to get his colour back, but the mention of Anna made it fade again.

'She won't be in harm's way, Pax. Maybe we should go and let you get some rest,' she said worriedly.

'Probably a good idea,' agreed Ryan. 'I need to talk to my commander and see what we can do. But if it's cancelled, it's going to be hard to get word to our guy in Pakistan. He'll end up taking a big risk for nothing if we don't show,' he said more to himself. 'All right, Pax, you just focus on getting better.'

Jaz gave him a kiss. 'Love you. I'll be just outside waiting for Mum.'

Pax closed his eyes, resting, and Jaz felt better. He looked so fragile in the room, with all the cords and machines.

'What are you thinking?' Jaz whispered to Ryan as they walked down the corridor. Their shoulders rubbed and Jaz itched to reach for his hand. To feel the comfort there in his grasp, while her mind raced with thoughts of Pax, of some faceless man risking his life in Pakistan, of Anna and Ryan.

'I'll go make some calls. Are you sure Anna could do this?' he asked.

'I'd bet my left lung,' said Jaz. 'But Pax?'

'Maybe Pax doesn't need to know, at least not right now.'

'I read you loud and clear,' she said as they shared a smile.

Then Ryan turned and walked away, leaving Jaz all alone in the wide sterile corridor.

Jaz and Anna headed straight to Pax's house the next day after school. They told their parents they were going to tidy up the place and check over The Ring before he came home from hospital. Both parents thought it was a sweet gesture, especially as they both worked till late and couldn't do it themselves. If only they knew the real reason.

At least, Anna thought they were going there to clean. But Jaz had other plans.

'Oh, someone's here,' said Anna as they stepped inside The Ring. 'Hey Bags,' she said, giving him a wave.

The big, muscled guy came straight over, leaving a fifty-something-year-old man in the back corner to pull off his gloves after a hard workout.

'Did you wear him out?' asked Jaz, seeing the sweat marks down the older guy's back.

Bags laughed. 'No, only half-pace. I think he's just a sweater,' he added quietly. 'So, how's the boss going?'

'Pax is fine. They might release him tomorrow if he's good. They're sorting out some medication for him,' said Anna. 'We're here to help tidy up. Are you hanging around?'

Bags shook his head. His singlet was not even damp. 'I've had two sessions today. This guy was the last. I'd be closing up in five if you two hadn't come along. Do you want me to stay and help out?'

'Nah, Bags. Us girls got this,' said Jaz with a laugh. 'Can you lock up as you go? We'll be in the house.'

'Sure. See you later.' He gave them a wink and went back to his client.

Jaz unlocked the door to Pax's house but locked it behind her again, ignoring Anna's curious glance as they headed for the spare room that had always remained a mystery to them.

Jaz pulled out the key from her pocket and unlocked the door.

'What are we doing here?' asked Anna, finally no longer able to hold her curiosity.

They entered the room and Anna hardly glanced around. It was as if she didn't have to.

'Oh my God – you've been in here before!' she hissed at Anna.

Going a shade of red, Anna nodded.

'When?'

'A few months back. How else do you think I managed those fake IDs?'

Jaz sucked in a breath. 'No way. I thought you just used the gym computers.'

'No, you need special stuff, not normal computers.'

'But how did you get in? Did you find the key or did Pax—'

'No. Pax hasn't shown me this room. He always told us it was damaged.' Anna closed the door and grabbed a seat. Jaz sat on the second chair, where Pax had last been working before his heart attack. She waited for Anna to continue her story. 'Okay, so remember the time you and I stayed here a few nights during the school holidays and then Pax had to go away for the night? Well, you were out like a light in seconds and I couldn't sleep. So, I got up and made a Milo. Then I got to thinking about this door. Why was it the only room in this house with an actual door lock that needed a key? None of the others are like it and there are worn marks on it. You know how I hate mysteries, and I've often thought about this room. And there have been times when we've come to visit and I've seen Pax coming from this end of the house. It all spiked my curiosity… and I was bored.'

'Wow, I can't believe I was asleep while you were having this great epiphany.'

Anna rolled her eyes but continued. 'Anyway, I managed to pick the lock with the stuff from his toolbox. I can tell you I was shocked to find this.' She waved a hand vaguely in the direction of various pieces of equipment. 'I mean, this is government-level stuff. Straight off, I went to the computer. It was password-protected and I tried a few things, mainly your name, mine, and then a few combinations. Then I thought of the one thing that Pax loves nearly more than us.'

Anna paused while automatically the answer formed in Jaz's mind. 'Muhammad Ali.'

Anna smiled. 'Yep.'

Pax had brought them up on stories of Muhammad Ali and his great fights. How he stood up for what he believed in and, after years in jail for refusing to fight in Vietnam, came back out to be a champion yet again. The Ring had four photos of Muhammad Ali on the walls, along with some of his sayings.

'Bingo. So, when that opened up the computer I found all sorts of stuff. One of them being a program for IDs. And it wasn't like a fake, pirated copy. Jaz, it was the real deal. I couldn't believe it. Anyway, seeing as I was wide awake I thought I may as well make good use of what I'd found.'

Jaz just shook her head, her mouth open in disbelief. *Go, Anna.*

'I loaded our photos off my phone onto the computer to use as our ID photos and managed to figure out how to work the rest of the stuff. Then I tried to put everything back the way it was and hoped Pax would never notice.'

'Why didn't you tell me this?'

'Shit, Jaz. If I didn't admit to it then maybe what I'd done wasn't so wrong,' she said with a funny expression. 'And maybe I was also a little worried about what Pax was doing in here. I shouldn't have broken in.' Anna chewed on her lip for a moment before her eyes snapped up to meet Jaz's. 'Hey, how come you have a key to this room and none of this is worrying you?' Anna waved her arm across the room.

'This is where Pax collapsed. He had me move him so no one saw this room. He told me he works for the government doing special IDs and passports and that no one could ever know because this stuff would be dangerous in the wrong hands.'

Anna laughed a little crazily. 'Like in the hands of seventeen year olds!'

'Actually, it's those seventeen-year-old hands that he needs right now.

He never got to finish a passport and it's needed tomorrow. So, we thought you were the best person to figure out the program and get one made.'

Big green eyes stared at her, dumbfounded. 'Say what?'

'Pax needs your help. Can you do it? All the stuff is here.'

'Is this why you suggested we come clean up? Was this the plan all along? Jaz?' Anna saw a sheet by the computer and picked it up. It listed a man's name, along with the date and place of his birth.

'Maybe I should put the kettle on and find some chocolate, yeah?' Jaz would try anything to bring Anna around.

Anna nodded. 'I'll go put the kettle on. I need a moment.' She walked from the room on autopilot.

Jaz took the opportunity to find her passport and reached for the drawer Pax had mentioned. Quietly she pulled it open and found a few passports stacked there. She tried for the top one and opened it. There was her picture Pax had taken the other day, but it was weird seeing her new name and details. It said she was twenty-three, her name was Yasmeen Chadhar and that she was Australian. Jaz was curious about the name. Were they trying to pass her off as a Pakistani descendent? She guessed Ryan would fill her in soon when he came over to talk about tomorrow's mission. That's if Anna could finish his passport.

Quickly she hid her new passport in her back pocket and shut the drawer before Anna came back.

'Here, I've put extra sugar in mine. I think I'll need it,' she joked weakly as she passed a full cup to Jaz. Anna sat at the computer and looked back at her, her fingers wrapped around her hot Milo like she was in Antarctica. 'So, what is it that Pax needed? I don't know why he didn't just talk to me.' She seemed a little put out, but Jaz knew she'd have to tell her eventually that they'd kept Pax in the dark.

'See if you can find the passport program. He said he already had the photo loaded, just needed to enter the rest of the information on that sheet.'

Anna mumbled as she put down her cup and let her fingers do the walking.

It didn't take her long to suss it out. 'What the hell. Is that Ryan?'

asked Anna as she put her face closer to the screen. 'Oh my God. Why does he look disabled?' Anna swung around. 'What's going on?'

Jaz gave a nervous giggle and smiled. It so didn't help. Anna's face contorted.

'Jaz,' she growled.

'Okay, my turn to fess up.' She took a big gulp of her Milo. Anna would need some information, but not all so Jaz went with the little story Ryan had suggested. It scalded her throat on the way down, but that was the least of her problems. 'You know how Ryan is never around? Well, he also works for the government, undercover.' Jaz kept it basic; the less Anna knew about the finer points of MTG, the better. 'And he needs this passport for a mission tomorrow. Without it, years of planning will go down the gurgler and bad guys will walk. You feel me?' said Jaz.

'Is he like a secret-agent guy? Oh, he just got ten times hotter. He totally fits the bill.'

Jaz put her head in her hands. Anna was not helping at all.

'How come you know about Ryan? Is this why you and he aren't together?'

Oh, trust Anna to come away with that out of this whole explanation.

'Kind of,' Jaz said truthfully.

'Wow. Makes sense now, how he disappears and why he wouldn't date you. How long have you known about him and Pax?' said Anna softly. Jaz didn't miss the betrayal in her voice.

'Not long at all. I wanted to tell you but you're safer not knowing. Pax didn't even want me to know, let alone you. *Actually*, while we're telling truths here, um…' Jaz looked down at her torn jeans. She'd paid good money to have those holes. 'Pax didn't want you involved but we went behind his back anyway,' she said with a rush.

'What? Really?'

'Yep. Ryan really needs this passport and no one else in the Agency can do it. I knew you could but Pax didn't want you involved. So, we kind of went against his wishes. We'll have to tell him eventually, but not while he's still recovering.'

'Right. You really thought I could do this?' Jaz nodded enthusiastically. 'Aw, thanks, Jaz.'

'Hey, even Ryan knew you could do it after seeing our fake IDs.' That made her face light up. 'Ryan is coming here soon, to see how you're getting on. Also, can you cover for me for the next two days?'

'Oh my God, anything else you wanna throw on me?' Her eyebrows rose up to her hairline.

Jaz didn't want to lie to her best friend, but telling Anna about Pakistan would be too much too soon. 'Marcus's parents are away for a few days and he's asked me to stay with him. He's planned a trip down south, just the two of us, for a romantic couple of days. Could you cover for me with Mum, tell her I'm on a fencing camp? I've already written a letter for the school excusing me for two days. And I'm hoping you can make me up a school letter about a fake camp?'

'Jesus, Jaz. Anything else you'd like me to do?' Anna's face was a ball of mixed emotions. 'I feel like I need to scold you for forging and wagging school yet again,' she stressed. 'And for running off with a boy you've only just met. But the other part of me is honoured to be your sidekick. And, well, I'm a little flattered you assume I can do all those things.'

Jaz laughed at her best friend. 'I know it's a piece of cake for you. Please?'

'Of course. You know I'll always have your back. We can draft up a fake letter later. It shouldn't be hard to get what I need off the school's website.' Anna pushed out her lips in thought. 'So, you really are trying to make it work with Marcus? You don't want me to drop his name when Ryan gets here and see if we can make him jealous?'

Got to love Anna for trying. 'Thanks, but I don't think he'd care.' That and Ryan knew damned well she wouldn't be with Marcus. 'I think I imagined whatever we had. Whatever it was, it wasn't strong enough to make him go against his job values. So, I guess I'll see where Marcus takes me.'

Anna was searching her face for any signs of a lie. She knew how hung up on Ryan Jaz had been. Still was, which was why Jaz had to work hard at hiding her emotions from her best friend.

'All right.' Anna turned back to the screen, took another sip of her Milo and then cracked her fingers. 'Let's get started on this baby.' After five seconds she turned back to Jaz. 'You think Pax would mind if I made myself a passport? Nah, never mind. Maybe later,' she said, chuckling to herself.

Anna went to work, mumbling to herself from time to time. Jaz finished her Milo and began to tidy Pax's desk. It didn't take long, and soon after, she heard a voice call out.

'Oh, that could be Ryan. I'll be back,' said Jaz, but Anna hardly acknowledged her. She was in computer mode.

Sure enough, Ryan had been banging on The Ring door and calling out.

'Hey, sorry. You been here long?' she asked, letting him in. She locked it behind him while trying to remain calm in his presence. But boy, did he smell good. Getting control of her legs, she led him to the side wall, under one of the photos of Muhammad Ali. 'We can sit here to talk – that way we can see Anna coming before she can hear us.'

'Yep, good idea. How is she going?' He'd put his sunglasses on top of his head, leaving his dark eyes to study her.

Jaz tried hard not to shiver from their contact. She sat on one of the mats and watched as he joined her. He was wearing cargo pants, his combat boots and a black singlet. His upper body was so well sculpted Jaz itched to reach out and touch him. *Focus*, she warned herself.

'Anna's onto it. I've kept it simple, just that you and Pax work for the government. At the moment she's preoccupied with the challenge of doing your passport, so she hasn't asked too many questions. But they may come later.'

He agreed. 'We'll cross that bridge when it comes.' He lifted up a bag she only now noticed. 'There's a *Niqab* and a *Jilbab* in here for you to pack in your bag. You'll need it when we go out for the rendezvous. Make sure you pack full-length clothes, no skimpy stuff. We'll try to mask ourselves as tourists. You're taking me back to see the place your father came from.'

'Hence my new name?' she said pulling out her passport.

Ryan nodded his approval. 'Yes, this is good.' He gave it back and handed over the bag. They sat for what seemed like ages, discussing the mission in great detail.

'I won't be able to talk to you, so we must go over everything now, you understand,' he said, nudging her knee to check she was listening.

Of course she was listening. She was about to have her first trip to Pakistan. The Australian travel advice said strongly advised against travelling to Pakistan due to the threat of terrorist activity, kidnapping and sectarian violence. She knew, she'd checked. They also recommended she take out kidnapping insurance. *Shit.*

'Hey, you two,' said Anna as she walked towards them. 'I'm finished.' She threw the passport at Ryan. 'Took me a while but I got there in the end. Wanna tell me why you took such a bad photo? Because it so doesn't do you justice,' she said with a smirk, as she openly admired Ryan's physique.

Damn, Anna had no shame. Jaz rubbed her face and realised how numb her bum was. How long had they been sitting here talking? Hours. Outside it was getting dark.

'Thanks, Anna, this is brilliant.' Ryan checked the passport, clearly impressed. He smiled up at Anna. 'You're very good.' Anna blushed at his praise.

'Nah, it's all in the program. I just had to press a few buttons. But you didn't tell me about your photo?'

Ryan gave his best cheeky smile. 'I could, but then I'd have to kill you.' He laughed. 'It's all a part of my job. Anyway, I best be going. Lots more to get done.' He stood up and kissed Anna's cheek. 'Thanks, Anna. You have no idea what you've done. I appreciate it.' Then he walked out without a backwards glance. Jaz was a little disappointed she didn't get a kiss. Hey, she was the one who got Anna to do it, after all. Did that not count for something?

'Did you see that?' said Anna, rubbing it in.

'You are shocking.' Jaz got up and looped her arm around her friend. 'Come on, let's get this fake letter done. I need to get my story straight.' She had so many stories to get straight she hoped she didn't slip up.

Jaz was feeling the overload of information and nerves. Tomorrow she would be flying to Pakistan. With Ryan. God help her.

CHAPTER 16

Jaz had gone with jeans, boots and a long-sleeved T-shirt. She assumed it would be hot in Pakistan, so trying to stay covered but cool meant wearing her white-and-blue cotton baseball-style shirt. They were taking only carry-on bags, so her backpack was full with a change of clothes, a hat and the muslim clothingRyan had given her. Just the basics he'd said, they weren't going for a holiday. He'd also given her his bag, which now hung from the back of the wheelchair she was pushing through Perth Airport. Ryan had shocked her this morning wearing baggy trackpants and an extra-large long-sleeved shirt. His hair looked almost greasy and he wore running shoes.

They had met at a random house, one used by the Agency, at eight in the morning. They had gone over the mission again, Ryan drumming in all the things she needed to be mindful of and how to play her part. She'd even practised lifting him in and out of the chair. By eleven they got a taxi and started acting. Ryan was slumped in the wheelchair, a fake colostomy bag tucked into the side. He certainly looked the part. There was no way he could have pulled it off with fitted clothes; his lean, muscled body would have given the game away.

The taxi ride to the airport had been the end of the conversation. Ryan wouldn't speak, and the quiet was eerie. It made her feel like she was in this thing alone, but she had to reassure herself that if trouble struck Ryan would jump in if need be.

As she pushed the wheelchair towards the Emirates counter, she was amazed at how many people glanced away upon seeing Ryan. Except for the little kids, who openly stared with curiosity.

For Jaz the whole process was rather scary. They had to swap Ryan over to an airline wheelchair while his other one went with the luggage. Jaz played the part of the doting girlfriend who helped lift him as if she'd been doing it for years. Then they were whisked through a side gate straight to the plane.

The flight attendants were very helpful, and she got Ryan settled into his seat.

'You seem so young to be coping with this,' said the attendant as Jaz pulled out a tissue to wipe drool from Ryan's lips. It was the weirdest thing, especially knowing how capable he was, but Jaz knew they had to act. They had to play their parts, because it would be the only thing to save them on the way back with the important intel. If they got caught, they wouldn't make it home. Simple as that, Ryan had said. Eyes were everywhere and spies were everywhere. It was not a concept that made Jaz feel particularly comfortable.

Jaz smiled up at the attendant, who was perfectly polished in her Emirates uniform. 'We were engaged before his accident. I was only twenty then. You just can't walk away from someone you love. He's still in there and he knows me.' Jaz sat beside Ryan and held his hand.

The attendant smiled warmly, her eyes glassy. 'Well, if you need anything, just let me know. My name's Sandra.'

'Thanks, Sandra. We should be fine.'

Jaz put on a movie for Ryan. Teasingly, she selected a romantic comedy and watched for a reaction. Besides the odd grunt, he gave no outward sign of his disdain.

'Don't worry, I wouldn't do that to you,' she said, gently patting his hand before changing his movie to something more his style. It had guns and fast cars; at least, she assumed it was his style. He was a man of action, after all.

The flight was long, with a stopover in Dubai, so Jaz tried to sleep after the movie. They changed flights in Dubai to Lahore in Pakistan. This one was only a short flight and they'd had to rush to catch it. Jaz found out that trying to move quickly and efficiently with a wheelchair was hard to master.

'Next time, I think I'll let you do all the work,' she said, as they settled into their last flight. She watched Ryan, whose eyes were closed. Probably easier to pretend he was asleep. She was now so used to playing the part of the doting girlfriend that she had to stop herself from reaching out to hold his hand. Heck, who was she trying to kid. She was always having to stop herself from touching him. At least now she had a legitimate excuse. One she was probably enjoying too much. With his eyes shut she could study him, all those details she loved and yearned for.

She realised she in turn was being watched and turned to see Sandra smiling at her.

'I can see how much you love him,' she said. 'You're an inspiration.'

Jaz tried not to tense and hoped to God that Ryan really was asleep. Then she remembered she was supposed to 'love' him. She gave Sandra a nod and turned back to Ryan and caressed his arm. 'He's my inspiration,' she said softly. And it wasn't a lie or a part of the act. Sandra had moved on, but Jaz kept her hand on Ryan. She felt so much safer and less nervous if she could hold onto him. Closing her own eyes, she relaxed enough to get some sleep.

It seemed like only moments later that she felt Ryan's arm move, jolting her awake. He hadn't moved it far, just enough to stir her from her sleep. Stretching, she realised everyone was getting ready to land. She glanced out the window and watched the unfamiliar landscape below them. Different rooftops, buildings with dome tops, and the frantic movement of traffic. It was close to lunchtime in Pakistan. They'd been travelling for many hours, and she couldn't wait to stretch her legs.

'We're here,' she said to Ryan. 'I can't believe it.' But now her nerves came back full force. They were off sightseeing first, keeping up the appearance of tourists. Then they would head to the hotel, change, get the motorbike and head off to meet the other agent. It could be a late night. Their flight home was the next morning at six.

Outside, Jaz got a taxi while the noise, smell, dust and humidity assaulted her. Instantly she was clammy and sticky.

She didn't know the language, but Ryan had told her to negotiate with the taxi driver before they left. In the taxi, Jaz passed the note forward that listed the things they wanted to see. The driver nodded and drove them back out into the mayhem of traffic. Jaz took this time to soak up Pakistan. Who knew if she would ever be back? It was still sweltering hot, humidity at an all-time high.

Jaz was fascinated with the huge piles of flowers and petals in the road-side markets, including garlands for necks and wrists. Boys at the road tolls, street corners and lights generally sold these, and sometimes they sold bread or sweets. She tried to imagine the children stripping the petals off through the night, ready for the morning trade.

They passed slums, homes made from bits of iron, cardboard, wood or even junk, and with no water or septic facilities. Jaz understood why the women wore such heavy, clinging perfumes. The driver took them past the Badshahi Mosque. Rows of tall archways made up the building, the largest in the middle, and the brickwork made it seem like it was topped with lace. Three big pointy domes also protruded from the roof. Jaz wished she had her phone to take photos but it had to remain home to not compromise them if it fell into the wrong hands. Instead, all this would have to stay alive in her memories.

Jaz also wished she could buy something, anything, to bring home, even if it was one of the beautiful *salwar kameez* outfits she'd seen the women wearing.

When they'd spent sufficient time touring, she gave the driver the address of their hotel. Jaz felt a deep appreciation for carers and what they went through, as she lifted Ryan into and out of the taxi. It was backbreaking, time-consuming work, and she would never take getting into a car for granted again.

She also thought Ryan was enjoying it a little too much when she caught a hint of a smile after she'd groaned at how heavy he was. 'When we get home, look out,' she said as they rode to the Marvel Hotel. Ryan had said it was in Military Zone 19, he'd mentioned all the checkpoints before they'd left.

The taxi driver kept glancing back at her, and Jaz was starting to wish she could hide under her Muslim clothes she'd packed. She would rather the taxi driver watch the road. It was bloody chaos out there. Motorbikes whizzed past, drivers without helmets. Sometimes a whole family crammed onto a Honda or Yamaha, some women sat side-saddle. Little cars and three-wheeled contraptions – half-motorbike, half-cart – jostled for position. And then there were carts, pulled by a horse or donkey, once even a buffalo. There were mini-vans too, and buses, brightly painted. It was so noisy. Hundreds of horns tooting different sounds, the revving of motorbikes and the squeal of brakes as the traffic merged. Traffic police were everywhere with their whistles, causing more chaos and noise. Jaz watched out the window in horror, amazed there were no accidents. People were also walking through the traffic, men in long loose pants with big dress like shirts, some with a scarf around their head, women in full burka. The colours were khaki, brown, white and blue. What a different kind of world. The smell of the slums permeated the car as they passed, and then came the large billboards advertising Coke that edged the road like a fence. She glanced back to Ryan to see what he made of it all, but he was watching her. 'I suppose this isn't new to you.' Yep, he was having more fun watching her reactions.

The taxi slowed as cars were split into very narrow lanes that zigzagged with witches' hats. As the cars came to a halt, two soldiers in khaki uniforms with red berets, armed to the teeth, walked along the lanes. Another vehicle further up was surrounded by six guys inspecting it. The boot and bonnet were up, and a guard was scrutinising the driver and passengers, checking passports and IDs. Another carried a mirror on a stick, putting it under the car. Jaz felt her pulse race. One of the soldiers glanced inside. Ryan had told her that the soliders mainly stopped cars with people who looked like terrorists. She wished she could ask Ryan right now exactly what did terrorists look like. The soldier waved them through, Jaz had never felt so relieved. Obviously they didn't fit the terrorist profile. What was most frightening was seeing the two soldiers on either side of the lane with AKs at the ready. Behind them was a Land Rover with a machine gun perched on the roof with a soldier who aimed it at the lane, and not far from them was another pair of Land Rovers with matching machine guns mounted on the roof. Guess they weren't planning on letting anyone get away. Jaz didn't stop gripping the seat until they were long gone from the checkpoint.

After more crazy traffic, they arrived at their hotel before they became a road statistic. Imagine if she'd died here or was badly injured. How would she explain that to her family? The thought had popped up once or twice, but she'd pushed it away. Ryan had said it wasn't a dangerous mission so she was not going to think about anything going wrong. Besides, thinking about that just made her feel bad for lying so much to her parents.

As they entered the hotel, Jaz passed an armed guard. She didn't know if she should be relieved or worried about the two other guards she saw out the front of the hotel.

Inside was less frantic, and Jaz felt herself relax a bit. This was all so new but the hotel reception was nice, like a hotel back home. Only, she was struggling with communication and money side of things. At least the man at the desk knew enough English to check them in.

After booking in, they went to their room along passages of cream walls with wooden doors and a floor that followed the colour scheme in the tiles. Their room was also similar in colour and was spacious enough for a wheelchair.

The moment Jaz shut the door, Ryan got up out of the chair.

'Oh my God, it's a miracle,' she said. It actually felt like one, considering she'd hauled his butt everywhere today. It had got to the point where it had begun to feel very real.

'Ha ha,' said Ryan, turning to her as he stretched. Hearing his voice was sweet pleasure. 'Get your stuff ready. We need to change and be out of here soon.' Then he ducked into the bathroom.

Jaz went to the double bed and flopped down on it, stretching out. She felt like crap, which was probably jetlag. She wished she had her phone. Had Anna texted? Or Taylor? Or Marcus? She'd left her phone with Pax and was going to pretend she'd lost it for a while. Hopefully that would satisfy everyone until she got back.

'Ah, that's better,' said Ryan as he reappeared. He pulled his bag off the wheelchair and threw it on the bed, then began to pull apart the wheelchair.

Jaz sat up with interest. Within seconds, Ryan was holding a knife.

'Was that hidden in the chair?' she said with awe, as she watched Ryan flip it around. Was it wrong to think it was sexy watching him play with a dangerous weapon? It got better when he pulled off his big shirt, revealing the chest she dreamed about. He was all bumps and lumps of formed muscles, tight caramel skin and a scattering of hair leading down into the trackpants. Jaz swallowed hard. She knew she was staring but she couldn't stop, couldn't rip her eyes away.

It wasn't until he pulled out one of those nightshirts and pants called shalwar kameez that he looked up. There was something warm in his eyes, like a purple swirl of passion. Or maybe she was dreaming it; it was probably just the reflection from her own eyes.

'You'd better get ready.'

If he'd seen her gawking he didn't say, but his words moved her into action.

She pulled her bag closer and unzipped it just as Ryan kicked off his shoes and dropped his trackpants. *Holy cow.* His black trunks were fitted, to the point Jaz forgot to breathe. Ryan sat on the bed to pull off his pants and Jaz started fumbling for her *Jilbab* and head cover. Her eyes kept flicking back over Ryan's wide shoulders, across his skin and scars. Oh boy, the outside heat was now in their room, temperature nearing boiling point.

Well, two can play at this game, she thought. She didn't want to be the only one floundering. Jaz took her boots off, then her shirt and jeans, until she was standing in her black bra and briefs. She was reaching for the *Jilbab* when she saw Ryan pull up his trousers, turn and fumble as he caught sight of her. She was deliberately slow pulling it on, while Ryan remained motionless. Frozen.

Jaz took great delight in feeling his eyes roam over her, but when he met her eyes, he turned so she missed reading him. But his shoulders moved with each breath and his fist bunched tightly at his side as he faced the other way. He seemed uncertain of what to do next. Jaz had her *Jilbab* in place when he finally ducked back into the bathroom. Obviously he left to give her some privacy, but Jaz wasn't fussed. Seeing the way he'd stared at her had given her courage. She realised that, for once, she was holding the power in that moment. Maybe there was something there between them still.

By the time Ryan came out of the bathroom, Jaz was all dressed except for the headdress.

'Can you help me with this?' she asked.

'Sure.'

Jaz felt like the world had gone quiet with the black *Niqab* on. It was as if she were hiding and no one could see her. It reminded her of school when she seemed invisible. Or when she was younger and would hide in a box with a hole cut out to look through.

Ryan gave her the once over, this time with her clothes on, and nodded his approval before turning to use the mirror. He was applying dark foundation to his face. Jaz realised it didn't matter what her face looked like but Ryan needed help to disguise his. By the time he'd finished, Jaz reckoned she wouldn't have recognised him on the street.

'How's it look?' he asked.

'Perfect,' she said.

He grabbed her arms, giving her a gentle shake. 'You ready?' He was watching her eyes intently; after all, it was the only part of her he could see.

'Ready as I'll ever be,' she replied.

CHAPTER 17

'THE KNIFE'S IN my right boot if you need it,' Ryan said before he opened the door and quickly checked the hallway.

That was reassuring of him. Just what her nerves needed.

He slipped the door key into his pants and led her out of the hotel. She was to remain just behind him, he'd briefed her before leaving.

He was heading somewhere specific, he'd told Jaz the whole plan. Her main reason for coming was to help disguse them as a couple on holiday and to use the wheelchair to get the knife and information through the airports. She wasn't needed for this next step but was tagging along to the drop off point to see how it worked and gain some experience. It would be another notch on her belt, of course she wanted to tag along, even if she was freaking out a little. It should be straight forward, he'd said. But if something happened he'd made sure she remembered the hotel address.

They crossed a dual-lane road beside the hotel and went into a housing area. Jaz felt a little restricted looking through the slit in her headwear. It was scary enough being in a different place, let alone it was nearly dark. Foreign sounds and smells assaulted her, keeping her nerves on edge. She wanted to reach for Ryan's hand, but in this country she would likely be put in prison for it.

Jaz felt hot and sticky beneath the full weight of the niqab and black jilbab they walked a few blocks, until they came to a house, of sorts, and Ryan knocked on a door. 'Stay back here,' he said, pointing to a spot by the road. She watched as a man came to the door and spoke with Ryan in his native language. Ryan handed over some money, and the man disappeared into his house then returned and pushed out a newish motorbike.

It was a prearranged pick up point. Ryan pushed the bike to the road and started it. 'Get on.'

She sat on the back, choosing to hang onto the bike and not Ryan. Partly because she thought she'd get arrested if she held onto him and the other part was because she didn't need to feel his hard abs right now. All focus was needed on the mission.

They moved along the street until they hit the main road. The rush of air was refreshing, cooling her off, the bit that flowed through the small slit over her face even more so. The traffic wasn't so bad out here as they left the yellow-and-black painted curbed areas and lights and headed out towards more open country. Jaz would have much preferred they did this during the day, so she could at least see some of Pakistan.

The big bike had a light on the front, which they needed when Ryan turned off the main road and weaved his way to a place Jaz could never get back from. To start with, she tried to remember landmarks, lefts and rights, just in case something happened and she had to get them out of there. But something told her unless she had been writing this down she'd never remember her way out. The best she could do was hope the things she saw, like the broken cart or the dead mule, would be enough to get them back.

The bike lurched as Ryan found a pothole. Jaz grabbed for his waist and latched on. She couldn't stop the little smile that appeared at the touch of his warm body.

The road was now gravel and full of unseeable holes, making it rough riding. She kept her arms around Ryan, sure no one would see them out here and in the dark. Besides, it was a chance to hold Ryan and calm her heightened senses. She could smell water in the warm night air, almost musty.

Ryan slowed and turned them onto a smaller track. In the light from the bike she could see an old-looking building. Maybe a disused farmhouse. Ryan parked the bike next to it in the grass. Jaz got off, her body sore from all the unfamiliar jarring and bumping. It went quiet as Ryan killed the bike, and as the light went off they were encased in darkness.

'That was my first time on a bike,' she said, keeping her voice at a whisper, unsure whether she should be talking.

'Really? I've got a Harley at home. I'll have to take you for a ride on a real bike.' He wasn't whispering but he wasn't speaking loudly either. His hand found hers and he gently tugged it. 'This way, we'll wait inside.'

Jaz was glad he could see because she still couldn't. Her foot tripped over something and Ryan stopped to catch her.

'Careful.'

Finally, her eyes were adjusting and she could make out the building. It was only a five-by-five space, dirt floor and a single hole for a window. Ryan stood by the door, staring out into the darkness. Jaz sat on the ground.

'How long do we wait?' she asked and then regretted it. She didn't want to sound so green and impatient. Especially when Ryan was probably used to waiting all night.

'Not long. Half-hour maybe.'

They settled into silence, which suited Jaz because she was too scared to talk and her ears were too busy listening for sounds of car tyres, voices or footsteps. Even the sounds of the night seemed creepy. Ryan would move his weight to his other foot and Jaz would just about jump through the roof from listening so intently.

Jaz was starting to get a numb bum when they heard a vehicle approaching. She jumped up and Ryan moved, hiding behind the wall near the doorway. She saw a gleam from the moon, it was a blade edge, Ryan's knife held at the ready.

Now was not the time to panic, but she could feel the fear and adrenaline coursing through her, building up momentum as footsteps came their way.

'Fletch?' came an unknown voice, but Jaz relaxed when she realised the accent was Australian.

'Tilly, you made it,' said Ryan with a hint of relief.

A torch came on and Jaz watched as the two men shook hands and gripped each other's shoulders.

'Only just. I was followed but I think I lost them. But let's do this quickly.' In the torchlight Jaz could see 'Tilly'. He looked to be in his thirties but it was hard to tell, with the shadowed lines on his face. He looked drawn, thin and a little wired. But she wouldn't hold that against him if he was undercover in a drug operation. Tension would be high, sleep would be minimal and trust would be unobtainable. Tilly also had a gun sticking out of his pants.

'Who's this?' asked Tilly. He almost moved to get his gun. Jaz tried not to feel offended. He shone the light in her eyes.

'This is Jaz, one of our newest,' said Ryan. 'Jaz, this is Matt Tilby.'

Jaz felt it was safe to pull off her headwear. 'Hey,' she said, unsure how she should greet him.

'Damn,' said Tilly. He was still pointing the torch at her, so she couldn't really see him, but she could hear him. 'Fletch, how did you scam that? I haven't seen a pretty face like that in a long time.' He put the light down a fraction. 'Nice to meet you, Jaz. I hope you're enjoying your introduction to Pakistan. I'd like to show you around the poppy fields where I've been working but I think we'd probably get shot.' The beam of light now went to his hand and the stuff in it. 'I think they know this stuff is missing by now. And don't lose the USB either. Just about lost a leg getting some of those pictures.'

Ryan took the small bag from him and tucked it into his pants. 'Thanks Tilly. You look like shit.'

'Worse than you did after Afghanistan?' he asked.

'Close,' replied Ryan.

Jaz didn't find their humorous banter funny. It brought home just how hard it must be and the sacrifices they made, the bad things they might have to do to infiltrate the gangs and prove their loyalty. She couldn't imagine the horrors they'd seen.

'How bad is bad?' asked Jaz. She wanted to understand.

Tilly glanced at her, then to Ryan. Seeing as Ryan didn't stop him, he looked back to Jaz and began a story. 'You really wanna know?'

She nodded, but was starting to regret her decision.

'One of the things I saw down at the fields after I got word we were moving on was the slaughter of all the workers. People they had tending to the fields, mothers, fathers, even kids. They shot them all into a mass grave so no one would talk. And the only thing I could think was that I was glad I hadn't been one of the guys who'd been given the order to kill.

But standing by, watching the blood, the faces of the ones waiting to die like the others, the screaming, the crying kids. That will never leave.' He put a finger to his brain like he was going to shoot himself. 'It's burned in here, forever.'

Jaz shivered even though she was hot. Ryan was watching her but Jaz didn't move or say anything. What the hell could she say after that? *Sorry you had to see that?* It would never be enough.

Lights flicked across her face, but this time they came from outside the doorway. The torch went off in a heartbeat but light still came in from a vehicle outside. The rumble of its motor now audible.

Both the guys moved so quickly. Tilly's gun was cocked and ready, Ryan's knife was unsheathed and Jaz was still standing there like a statue. Quickly she put her headwear back on and squatted down against the wall.

She could hear voices, but these ones were not Australian, they were not even English-speaking. *Crap.*

Ryan silently held up two fingers, indicating to Tilly.

One of the approaching men yelled out something, maybe a command to come out. Nobody moved. Then Jaz almost screamed as shots were fired in through the door.

Ryan flung his hand out to her and indicated for her to stay low. Jaz wanted to inch forward the few metres so she could touch him, but remained where she was, petrified.

While one guy remained out the front, Jaz could hear another moving around the building. How long till he reached the window? Shots went off again and an explosion went off, red light flooded the doorway and small window. Jaz could see Tilly and Ryan with serious faces as they pressed back hard against the wall still armed. The men outside must have blown up the bike. Jaz could feel the heat through the building. Was that a warning? On the bright side, it made access through the window a no-go.

Jaz watched the door and saw the muzzle of a gun enter and fire. Suddenly, bullets were going everywhere, and the gunman fell through the door. Tilly had shot him. Ryan reached out for the gunman, probably hoping to take his gun, but his body was dragged away and more shouting voices came near.

Ryan held up three fingers. *Ah hell*, thought Jaz. This mess was a long way off being over.

More bullets flew through the door, but the shooter wasn't going to get them from his angle and he probably knew it. He came towards the door, but it was two men at once and only Tilly had a gun. While Tilly fired at the guy on his side, Ryan pulled on the other man's muzzle of his rifle, pulling him further in and then wrapping his arm around him. Jaz saw the glint of his blade in the light from the vehicle's headlights as Ryan slit his throat. It was probably quick, but to Jaz time slowed as she tracked the blades path across his neck. She covered her mouth as the man's body went limp and blood poured from the gash. She'd never seen so much blood. Now she wished the vehicle's lights weren't so bright.

Her eyes were glued to the man who was now lying face down in the dirt. He blinked a few times before his glassy eyes stayed open, unseeing. A dead man. Killed right in front of her. Her stomach churned as the metallic scent reached her nose. She focused on breathing – she didn't want to vomit inside her headwear – and suddenly Ryan was pulling her up.

'Jaz, are you okay? Are you hit?'

He was holding her at arm's-length, watching her face while touching her arms, checking for bullet holes. 'I'm so sorry you had to see that.' He pulled her into his arms and it was Ryan's body that calmed her belly. She tucked her head into his chest, preferring the smell of his sweat to the blood.

'Is she okay?' said Tilly.

'I think so.'

Ryan let her go and Jaz caught the expression on Tilly's face. They probably didn't hug while on a mission. He lifted an eyebrow at Ryan questioningly. But he didn't get any answers. Ryan wasn't big on sharing. Her mind was rambling but anything was better than thinking of that dead man and his open neck wound. Not to mention the other two dead men, shot by Tilly. A prickly sweat came over her; she was close to being sick again but forced it away. Hell, she wanted this, she'd said yes to this so, she had better try to get used to it.

Beside the throat guy, the other gunman lay sprawled out. Jaz could see blood pooling at his back from bullet holes. Three precisely. Tilly was a good shot. More absent rambling. She felt detached, as if this were a dream. Maybe they were dummies? Was this just an episode of *CSI* or *Bones*? Fake blood and gore?

She wished.

'Let's get the hell out of here,' said Tilly.

They went to his ute first, only to discover it had been shot to bits. 'We'll have to take theirs. Get in. Someone would have seen the bike explosion or heard the guns.'

They climbed into the open jeep. Ryan was still holding Jaz's hand, probably because Jaz was holding him so tightly he couldn't let go.

'Tilly, you're shot,' said Ryan, his voice raising in concern.

Jaz noticed the blood on Tilly's arm.

'It's okay, just a straight through.' He found a shirt on the floor and gave it to Ryan to tie up his wound.

Ryan needed his other hand and had to pry it away from Jaz. 'I just need to fix Tilly's arm, okay?' he said, trying to reassure her.

'You sure she'll be all right? Is this her first mission?' asked Tilly as Ryan wrapped his arm. 'She looks young.'

'Don't know. Jaz is not yet eighteen. This wasn't supposed to go bad.' Ryan's voice was thick with emotion. Jaz could hear it but couldn't feel it. She felt nothing.

She was nearly going to tell them she was fine but felt like she'd erupt in giggles. A little hysterical? A little crazy? She was feeling all those things at once and decided keeping quite was best for them all.

'Well, now she knows what she's said yes to. We all have to see it eventually, she'll get stronger from here,' said Tilly.

'I feel awful,' Ryan whispered, as he finished the bandage.

'She's still alive.'

Tilly started the jeep and headed back out the way they came.

It had felt so long on the bike, but in the jeep they seemed to arrive at the hotel in seconds. Jaz had sat frozen in the same position the whole way back, unable to lean against Ryan and too scared to let herself sleep.

'See you, mate. Good luck,' said Ryan.

'Thanks. You too. Until next time.' Tilly shook his hand. 'Nice meeting you, Jaz.'

She wanted to say something or at least nod but she couldn't do either.

They got out of the jeep and Tilly drove off as thoughts jumbled through Jaz's mind. Would he get out of the country safely? Would there be a bounty on his head and people looking everywhere for him? Surely Tilly had an exit strategy. She wished she'd said something to him now. Even if it was 'Good luck'.

Ryan tucked his hands into his pockets; it was a must, especially since one hand was covered with dry blood.

They snuck back to their room, not passing anyone that late at night. Ryan shut the door and Jaz went and sat on the end of the bed. She just sat there, staring at nothing. Ryan was moving about the room and said something about a shower and then he was gone and she was alone. For the first time since she was little, she wanted her mum's arms to hold her tight and for her to whisper that everything was going to be all right.

CHAPTER 18

Jaz didn't realise time had passed, but Ryan was crouched in front of her, his hands on her knees and he was talking to her. She tried hard to hear his words, as she stared at the black head cover with the small slit beside her on the bed.

'Jaz, go and have a shower, you'll feel better.' The concern in his voice tugged at her heart. She could smell him, fresh from the shower, no metallic blood tainting him. Ryan's thumbs massaged her knees but she couldn't raise her eyes to his face. She was scared that if she saw him, she'd see the dead man too.

'Come on, shower.'

Jaz nodded and collected her toilet bag and items. She undressed, not really remembering how it happened, and stepped under the water. It was scalding hot but she still didn't really feel it. She put her head under the water, soaking her hair and trying to wash away the night's images. She didn't even know what time it was; probably well after midnight.

Looking down, she watched as the water drained away. A flash of blood running like the water assaulted her mind and Jaz felt her stomach flip. Bending over, she dry-retched, then again before the tears fell. Visions came flooding back as her stomach continued to churn. Ryan was banging on the door calling out to her but she couldn't reply. Sobs were coming faster than the water from the shower as she clung to the side of the wall. She couldn't control it anymore.

'Jaz, I'm coming in.'

She didn't care. She was beyond any thought as her emotions took over. The water stopped and a big white towel came around her shoulders. When she was covered, Ryan turned her around and hugged her tightly. Strong but gentle arms held her. It was just what she needed and she fell against him like a dead weight and cried.

'I'm so sorry,' Ryan kept saying over and over as she drowned his shirt with her tears.

When her sobs slowed, Ryan took another towel and dried some of her hair. It was tender and sweet and, had she not been having a meltdown, it would have been romantic.

She wanted to get dressed but she felt so drained and weak. Ryan must have known this because he picked her up and carried her to the bed. Its covers were pulled back and he laid her down before moving to turn off the main light. He climbed in alongside her and pulled her into his arms so her back was pressed against his chest.

'How're you feeling?' he asked softly.

With his arms holding her tightly, she felt safe. Not even lying there in just a towel fazed her. She'd seen a man die; nothing compared to that.

'Better,' she said. She knew he was waiting for her to talk. That he needed to know she would be okay.

'Do you want to talk about it?' His words were gentle against her ear.

But she shook her head. What was there to talk about? She saw Ryan kill a man. How did that make her feel? She wasn't yet sure. It was a them-or-us moment. Live-or-die, and Ryan chose to live. She couldn't fault him for wanting to live, and to save her. It was just going to take time to adjust.

'Do you remember your first?' she asked curiously. Her eyes were sore and would no doubt be puffy and pink. She was glad Ryan was behind her and it was dark enough, even with the bathroom light on. Thankfully, her nose had stopped running but she wished she hadn't used Ryan's shirt as a tissue. Luckily it hadn't bothered him. Had girls cried all over him before?

'Yes, I do. I was nearly nineteen. Funnily enough, I was with Tilly and another guy. We were still in Perth and I was just an extra to help out. Turns out the guys they were trying to do a deal with smelled a rat and pulled guns. I just remember bullets and people flying everywhere. When it came quiet, the three guys were dead, and Tilly was shot.'

'He must get that a lot,' she said.

Ryan chuckled. 'He does. I was also shot in the leg and I was lying next to a guy with a bullet hole in his head. I can still picture it. First time I'd seen a dead guy and he was staring at me lifelessly as a small trail of blood ran down his face.' She tensed. 'Sorry, probably too much information, but that's how I remember it. Lucky for us Tilly's a bloody great shot. So was Tim, the other guy, but he had all the luck because he came away unscathed.'

'Did it stay with you? Did you get past it?' She felt sleepy as his heart beat rhythmically against her back.

'It's still kind of with me, in the deep recess of my mind, but I moved on. Figured out how to deal with it, which really came down to kill-or-be-killed.' A pause. 'Jaz, I wish you hadn't seen that. Hadn't seen me—' He stopped and took a few shaky breaths.

Jaz turned around in his arms and rested her hand against his face. The light from the bathroom glowed enough so she could see his eyes. The pain in his voice was so raw that she had the courage to face him. He was so blindingly handsome, even when his eyes were filled with so much regret. 'I wish I could have saved you from seeing that.' His voice trembled. 'It was supposed to be a simple intel pick-up. I'm sorry. I hope you don't hate me.'

Jaz forgot everything as she traced her finger over his face, her thumb across his lips. 'It was going to happen one day, Ryan. And I could never hate you.' Far from it.

Her words eased some tension from him, his eyes clearing. 'Really?'

'Yep.' With a smile she said the first thing that popped into her mind. 'If anything, you were really bad-arse.' And he had been. She thought back to what Tilly has said, how those men had killed all those innocent people. Now there were three fewer killers out there.

Ryan opened his mouth as her thumb crossed his lip again and she felt the heat spread through her. This close to Ryan, her emotions shot to bits and all she could think about were his lips. She wanted him, wanted to erase the bad memories and put new ones in their place. Leaning across, she kissed him. It was soft and gentle, and he didn't reciprocate at first. She brushed her tongue against his lip, urging him to play.

A growl rumbled up inside him as she stretched her hands over his short hair, pulling him closer. And like that, Ryan was won over. His mouth opened, drawing her in. Jaz was no longer sleepy, instead her nerve endings buzzed and her toes curled. He was better than she remembered. His tongue brought red-hot fire to her lower belly as she tried to drink him in.

Jaz moaned when his hand gripped her barely covered backside, drawing her closer to him and against his hard erection. She'd never wanted him so much as she did right now. She wanted to touch, taste and explore all of him. Her towel and his clothes were in the way.

Jaz shimmied the towel down, letting her breasts free. Pushing her hard nipples against his chest brought her tremors of pleasure. Ryan must have felt them too, for his hand found a soft mound. He pulled away from her mouth, breathing heavily as his finger rolled over her nipple, sending her body into shock with each brush. That animal growl came again as Ryan kissed her then moved his lips down her neck. He traced his lips along her collarbone, then down until he found her hard nipple and took her in his mouth. The wet roughness of his tongue was even more torturous than his fingers. Jaz was burning with the need for him, everything was hot, wet, wanting. She pushed herself against his arousal, gently rocking back and forth, sending her close to the edge.

'Ryan, I want you,' she said huskily.

He stopped abruptly. Slowly he pulled away from her, his breathing heavy. The next thing he did hurt. He pulled her towel up, unwrapped himself from her and skittled off the bed.

'Jaz, this can't happen.' He stood there, his hand over his mouth, but he was still aroused. 'This was wrong. *So* wrong.'

If she thought him jumping away from her hurt, it was nothing compared to his words. 'Ryan?' She sqeaked out his name like the tiny afraid mouse she felt like.

As he headed to the bathroom, his voice was gruff. 'Get some sleep, Jaz. We still have to get home yet, and I have to hide the documents.' Then he was gone, shutting the bathroom door and encasing her in the dark.

She heard the shower start up. A cold one this time? She wanted desperately to join him but she was scared he would reject her again. He was in there a long time, and the events of the night quickly sent her to sleep.

It felt like moments later that she awoke. Ryan had boiled the kettle.

Could it be morning already? She was under the covers but it looked like she'd been in the bed alone, although faint memories of nightmares lingered. Had she screamed out? Were there tears and had Ryan really held her? Was it his voice softly telling her it was okay and to go back to sleep? If he'd been there, he wasn't there long; the bed looked unslept in on his side. Jaz turned to the other side, watching Ryan make coffee. The wheelchair was ready and he was in his baggy clothes.

Jaz sat up in the bed. 'What time is it?' she asked as she held the cover to her breasts. The towel felt like it had moved to the bottom of the bed. Had she been thrashing about in her sleep? It was gone and she was naked.

'It's nearly six. We have to head to the airport, so get ready.' He only glanced at her before turning his back.

Jaz dug around in the bed until she found the towel and pulled it back around her before she got out. She tingled with the thought of last night, of Ryan's mouth and his hands all over her. Did that really happen? Right now it seemed as if it was a figment of her imagination. Only Ryan's refusal to meet her gaze made her think otherwise. Then she felt the anger and shame at how he'd left her.

Now that she was fully awake and upset, she got her clothes and headed into the bathroom to change.

When she came out, dressed in her jeans and olive long-sleeved shirt, Ryan handed her a coffee. 'Eat up.' Without facing her, he waved to a breakfast tray on the small table.

They ate in silence and then it was time to pack up and check out. As Ryan set himself up in the chair, Jaz asked him where the documents were.

'Hidden in here,' he said shaking the colostomy bag.

Jaz screwed her face up at the brown muck in the bag. Not even she could see the documents hidden inside. Great hiding spot, she sure wouldn't think to look there. The drug lords had people in high places, Ryan had told her, and they owned soldiers that would be on the lookout for people like them, nervous and sweating, at the airport, knowing incriminating information could be on them. It had to be hidden well in case they were caught. If it was found then they wouldn't make it out alive.

Thanks to Ryan's little story, he seemed really good at telling them, she was now rather nervous for the trip home which only made her want to sweat more. How obvious was she going to look now?

'It will be okay Jaz. You've got this,' he said reassuringly.

With a deep breath she opened the door and their acting was back in place as they went about checking out and heading to the airport.

She was glad that Ryan could no longer speak. She didn't have to worry about making conversation. Words would have escaped her. What did one say after what they'd just been through and done? How did one move on from that? And she wasn't just thinking about the deaths. She'd given herself up to Ryan and he'd turned away from her. Now what?

Jaz was so preoccupied with her own thoughts, she spent most of the plane flights staring off into space and avoiding Ryan unless she had to pretend she was the doting girlfriend. She even forgot about putting a movie on for him. Funnily enough, she didn't feel bad about that. Jaz wanted him to suffer because she was suffering. It was only fair, right?

When they arrived back in Perth later that night, due to the time difference Jaz felt exhausted, mentally and physically. But it was so good to be home. Taking a taxi back to their original meeting point, she couldn't help but take in the familiar sights of home. There was no place like it.

CHAPTER 19

'Watch where you're going, bitch,' said Minka, as her shoulder collided with Jaz.

Jaz had been watching where she was going, sort of. She glanced at Minka with her perfect hair and nails and couldn't even bother with a retort. Minka was nothing in this world. She should be sent to Pakistan so she could see some real stuff. With a sigh, Jaz continued on her way.

It was Friday. Jaz could hardly believe she had been overseas yesterday. She had walked around school in a daze, really struggling with the jetlag as well as what she had seen over there, and the fact that people like Minka took this way of life for granted.

'Hey, there you are. Man, am I so glad you got your phone back. Talk about feeling like I'd had my arm cut off, not being able to talk to you,' said Anna as she joined Jaz on the way to class. They had their end-of-year exams coming up, so most classes were just revision and study.

'I know. I can't believe I lost it before my trip with Marcus. Pax's bathroom of all places.' It was almost the truth.

After leaving Ryan, Jaz had gone to The Ring and found Pax home from the hospital.

'I've already called your mum and said you're staying with me,' he'd said. 'I told her you were in the shower after your camp so she didn't bother talking with you.'

Lies. Lies. Everywhere. She could build a bridge with the lies they'd all told between them. Pax, Anna, and Jaz. Were her pants on fire?

He'd looked much better but he didn't let her get a word in about him and how he was feeling. Instead he'd bombarded her with questions about the trip, but Jaz kept it brief. A simple operation, she'd said. 'We got the documents and got out.' She was never in danger, never saw death, never nearly gave herself up to Ryan. The version she gave Pax seemed so perfect and he didn't seem to detect her lies. He just seemed relieved that she was okay, and then went on to quiz her about how they got the passport done.

'Did you do it yourself?'

She'd told him another lie. 'Yes, I managed to figure it out.' More lies. How many more until she drowned under the weight of them all.

Anna stepped into rhythm beside her down the school corridor. 'So, how many texts did you have when you found it?' asked Anna, snapping her back into the present.

'Lots,' said Jaz, laughing. She couldn't tell Anna but plenty were from Marcus. She'd rung him that night to explain how she'd lost her phone briefly. He'd been worried she'd changed her mind about him.

'So, what else happened with Marcus? I got all the scenery details, the romantic dinners, but anything else I should know about?' Anna was twisting her hair through her fingers as they paused by the door to their classroom. She'd bugged Jaz all morning about her two days with Marcus. But Jaz kept it all minimal and knew she was going to have to keep Anna away from Marcus so she didn't quiz him too and unravel all Jaz's lies.

'You've got it all, Anna. I told you. I'm not ready to go there yet. Our relationship is still new.'

Jaz just about groaned when she saw the look Anna gave her. Even though it was filled with compassion, her *You're not over Ryan* sad smile irked her.

'You can't rush these things. What about you and Ricky?' Jaz said quickly.

That changed Anna's attitude. 'Hmm. What you said. You can't rush these things.' She laughed as they went in to their seats.

Jaz pulled out her phone and found a message from Marcus.

I am so glad u have ur phone back. Can u come to dinner on Sat? Mum's been buggin me about meeting u again

Sure. Time?

7.30. I can't wait to c u

Me 2

Jaz smiled. At least Marcus couldn't wait to see her. Ryan had left her with nothing more than a, 'Thanks, Jaz. I'm sorry it didn't go as planned but we got the documents and photos we needed to put this bastard away, and that's what really matters.'

Was that his way of saying the stuff between them didn't matter? Or was she just reading too much into it? It was hard to know. Ryan confused her; one minute he was all over her and she was sure he felt the same way, and then he switched back to distant professionalism. He ran hot and cold, worse than a faulty hot-water system. The worst thing was, she couldn't really move on with Marcus either, because that relationship was a total lie too. At times it felt real and normal, though, and maybe that's what Jaz liked so much. What she had with Ryan wasn't real or normal, but he could ignite her body with a smile or a simple smouldering look. And to add to that, she now had hot memories of his touch to torment her at all sorts of random moments. Her head was so messed up. Bloody Ryan, she should send him her psychologist's bill.

Jaz put her phone away and got out her books. She would try to lose herself in studying for her exams. The little kids she'd seen in Pakistan would never get this chance, and it made her want to make the most of the opportunity.

*

'Jaz, I feel like I never see you,' said Tasha as Jaz came down to the kitchen.

'I'm a teenager, Mum, you're not meant to see much of me.' Jaz gave her a smile.

'I miss the days when you loved spending time with me. Before your friends were more important,' her mum teased.

Jaz hugged her mum. 'Aw, Mum, I still love you. Is that better?'

'Thanks darling.' Tasha's mobile beeped and she jumped up and down when she read it.

'You okay, Mum? You totally reminded me of Anna then.'

'Yes, I'm great,' she said excitedly. 'Your dad's home. Let's go see him.'

Jaz raised an eyebrow. Her mum was far too perky for a late Saturday afternoon. Something was going on.

Tasha grabbed her hand and led her outside just as a black jeep pulled into the driveway. Paul got out with a massive grin. 'Taadaaa,' he said, waving his arms over the car.

'Happy birthday, Jasmine,' said Tasha. 'I hope you like it.'

Jaz's jaw dropped. It was the coolest-looking Jeep Wrangler she'd ever seen. *Rubicon* was written on the side of the bonnet in white but that was all, the rest was black.

'It's a two-door but there are four seats in it, so you can take your friends or Simon to school,' said Tasha.

But Jaz was already walking towards it, her mum's words hardly registering. She was speechless. The Jeep had a black bull bar and a roof rack, tinted windows and awesome tyres.

'Well?' said Paul. His hands sat on his hips, as he waited. He was wearing his favourite yellow Big Bang Theory shirt.

'Oh my God, I love it! It's amazing. Is it really mine?' She threw herself into her dad's arms, hugging him tightly. She did the same to Tasha, who'd joined them.

'Thank you so much. I can even help pay for it with my wages,' she said as she gazed at her vehicle.

'It's second-hand but well looked after. We've worked out a repayment plan for half of the cost, the rest is your eighteenth birthday present, even though we're early,' said Tasha. 'Wanna take it for a spin around the block? I'll just get Simon.'

Jaz got in, still in shock. 'How did you get such a cool car?' she asked Paul. This was a car she didn't think her parents would ever think of. She'd imagined they'd come home with a safe, sturdy Volvo. 'I couldn't imagine you guys ever letting me have something like this.'

'We've had some help. We wanted something reliable, but Taylor said it had to be something you'd love, and this is what we ended up agreeing on. If it wasn't for Taylor, we probably would still be refusing to get you a car, but you are nearly eighteen and we have to let you go at some stage. It's hard to watch your little girl grow up,' said Paul with a sad expression. He leaned in on the open window.

Jaz put her hands over his. 'Thanks, Dad. I love you. And I'll always be your girl.' He may not have been her flesh and blood, but Paul was her dad in every way that mattered. They had no similar features, but the love she saw in his eyes was the exact same look her mum gave her.

'So, you love it?' he asked.

'Totally.' This was the best day ever.

Her family climbed in and they drove around the block, testing out everything inside the car. Then she dropped them home and headed for Anna's house. She pulled into the driveway and tooted the horn until Anna came out.

'You are so lucky,' said Anna as they cruised the suburb.

'I know. I thought I was gonna get a Volvo for sure.'

'I probably will,' said Anna screwing up her face. 'I know it.'

They had the windows wound down as they drove around, feeling the freedom.

'So, have you heard from Ryan? Do you know if the passport worked?' said Anna carefully, as she played with the radio.

Jaz nodded. 'As far as I know all was good. I haven't heard from him since Thursday. Probably won't for a while now. Except I did get an invite to his house next Friday for his parents' anniversary dinner,' she said without thinking.

'What! Really? Why didn't you mention this before? So, you have two dinner dates: one with Marcus's parents and the other with Ryan's parents. Man, you get everything.'

Jaz didn't see Anna's side at all. 'I wouldn't say that. I'm only going to Ryan's because his sister asked me to, because he's never brought friends home before.' Jaz stopped at a stoplight and turned to Anna. 'Makes me feel a little sad for him and his family if that's the case. I guess it's hard in his line of work to have friends you can mix with and bring home. Sounds like they miss him a lot. To invite me, they must be desperate.'

'Do they think you two are going out?'

Jaz laughed and shook her head. 'Steph, his sister, knows I'm just a friend, so I hope they don't get the wrong idea. His parents would probably freak, knowing he's friends with a schoolgirl,' said Jaz, trying not to think about how the dinner would go.

'You're nearly finished with school, and then it won't even be a problem. They'll see that you're just friends,' said Anna. 'Because you are, aren't you?'

Jaz ignored that question. She hoped his parents wouldn't see anything but friendship between them. If Anna still could tell she had something for Ryan, then would they?

'I've got dinner with Marcus's parents tonight to get through first,' she said.

Anna cleared her throat loudly, obviously annoyed she didn't reply to her earlier question. 'Well, at least you can drive yourself there, and if it all turns to shit you can drive yourself home,' she teased, as she flipped open the glove box as if looking for hidden secrets.

'I'm so glad I can count on you for the wonderful advice and direction, Anna. Cheers.'

But Jaz was nervous. That evening she changed her outfit three times, from jeans to pants to a dress and then back to jeans. Marcus's mum had looked so classy when they'd met, and Jaz initially thought she should wear a dress, but then… maybe she was better off going casual and being comfortable. In the end she went with her black leggings, a flowing white top her mum had bought her and some jewellery to accentuate it. It was a happy medium.

'See you guys later,' she said as she grabbed her Jeep keys; still a wonderful novelty. Probably would be for months.

'I guess we'll have to have Marcus over here so we can meet him too,' said Tasha with that mum look on her face. No doubt she was already planning the night in her head.

'I'll think about it,' said Jaz. 'Bye, Mum.'

'Be back before it's too late, please. Or at least let me know when you're coming home so we don't worry.'

'Yes, my overprotective worrier. I'll be fine.' Jaz pulled on her black jacket, kissed Paul on the cheek and headed outside. Her new Jeep sat on the driveway, waiting for her like an old friend. She couldn't wait to show Marcus. She couldn't wait to see him. Right now she craved some attention, even just the touch of his hand, and a moment without Ryan creeping into her thoughts.

CHAPTER 20

SHE PULLED INTO Marcus's driveway and smiled when she saw him waiting for her. He was so sweet. He stood up and was looking at her Jeep as she got out.

'Not bad, hey?'

'It's very cool, Jaz. It suits you. Have you named it yet?' he teased.

Jaz walked straight over to him and melted into his arms. 'Not yet. I missed you,' she said. She really had.

'I missed you too.' He nuzzled her neck, kissing her softly.

Jaz didn't let him go, instead she held on tightly, enjoying the firm circle of his arms and the fresh scent of his skin and the hint of aftershave. It was dark outside, except for the lights from the houses. Across the road, the last hint of glow from the missing sun glistened on the water.

Meanwhile, his hands worked their way up to her face and cupped her chin so he could kiss her. The waves crashed on the beach behind them, making her feel as if they were alone on an island.

But the front door opening dissolved that. Marcus stepped back and took her hand. 'I better take you inside or I may just forgo dinner completely,' he whispered.

'Your mum wouldn't like that,' she said, following him inside where Marcus's dad held open the door.

'Jaz, so nice of Marcus to actually let you get inside the house,' said Carl.

'Hi Mr Sincl— Carl,' she added when she saw the look he gave her.

'Mr Sinclair was my dad, and he wasn't a nice man.' He smiled. Jaz knew that Marcus was going to age really well if he took after his dad. 'Come in. Diane is in the kitchen, she's just finishing up with the risotto.'

'So glad you came,' said Diane upon seeing Jaz. 'How did you find such a natural beauty, Marcus?' she teased.

It made Jaz blush. Marcus still had her hand, which was nice and made her feel more relaxed. It also helped that Carl seemed just like Paul but in a less geeky way. Carl walked like a man of importance but could flirt with his wife and stir up his son. He was probably once a school leader or captain of a sports team. He just oozed likability.

Watching him kiss his wife's cheek and whisper something to her, causing her to laugh, made Jaz feel right at home. It was just like watching her mum and dad: disturbing to watch but also nice to see how much they loved each other.

'I'm sorry. I wish they would behave,' said Marcus.

'Hey, you'd get the same at my house.'

'Come, I'll give you the tour before we sit down to eat. Be back in a tick, Mum,' he said to Diane, who was wearing soft blue pants and an expensive-looking cream blouse.

First he showed her the lower floor: the theatre room, games room, downstairs bathroom and the office. All the rooms were spotless and well designed, very sparse with the focus on the art pieces. Next was upstairs to the bedrooms. 'This is my mum's office, that was Dad's downstairs. Here's my room.' He pushed open a door to a room much like Jaz's: large, with a window and its own ensuite. The carpet was a soft grey, with wooden furniture throughout. She tried not to stare at the double bed with its blue cover. Ryan's room would fit into this one twice. Damn, she couldn't believe she'd thought of that. *No Ryan thoughts*, she'd promised herself.

'It's cool. I like it.' She went to the far wall and touched some of his skateboards, he had four, before moving to his desk. A large pad and some pencils sat like they'd not long ago been used, and the drawings stuck up on the wall grabbed her attention. One looked like it was of his mate Kaino on his skateboard. 'Did you draw this?' she asked, turning to him.

Marcus glanced at the floor as he sat on the edge of his bed. 'Yeah.'

'These are great. Do you take art at school? Can I?' she asked motioning to the drawing pad.

'Sure. Yeah, I'm doing art. Dad doesn't like the idea, but Mum is real arty, you know. You can't grow up around art and not absorb some of it.'

Jaz was only half-listening, as the fourth drawing had taken her breath. He'd drawn her, from their first afternoon having coffee at the beach. He'd captured her so well, with her hair blowing across her face. 'Wow.' Then the next few were also of her. 'I'm detecting a theme,' she teased. 'They are amazing, though. Can I have this one?'

He came up behind her, his hand automatically snaking around her waist as he looked over her shoulder. 'Sure. Why that one?'

It was Jaz, drawn from the chest up, dressed up for his ball but she was looking off into the distance as if deep in thought. The funny thing was, that night she had been. It was after she'd seen Ryan. She could see it on her face.

So, that's what Anna saw all the time.

'I don't know. I think you really captured me. It's quite confronting seeing it, but still I'd like to have something you've drawn. You have real talent.'

Marcus tore the picture from his book and gave it to her. 'Well, you can tell that to my dad,' he said with a laugh.

Jaz detected the pain in his voice. Everyone had family dramas, parents who had preconceived ideas of what their kids would do and grow up to be. Her mum used to try and get Jaz excited about being a lawyer or a doctor, she soon gave up on those pipe dreams when Jaz shot her down with fits of laughter. And Paul had Simon following in his footsteps so he was happy and left Jaz's future to herself. Which is just how she liked it. Didn't seem like Marcus was as lucky.

'Dinner's ready,' came Carl's voice from near the foot of the stairs.

They headed to the dining room, where Jaz sat beside Marcus and put his picture by the empty seat next to him.

'What you got there, Jaz?' said Diane as she put a plate in front of Jaz.

Jaz thanked Diane for her meal before replying. 'I asked Marcus for one of his drawings. He's amazing. I wish I had that much talent,' she said brightly.

'Yes, he is gifted.' Diane glanced to Carl before she walked back to the kitchen for more plates.

They talked for a while about Marcus's drawings and then the art Diane liked to collect. 'I know nothing about art,' Jaz confessed, quietly wondering whether any of those art pieces were hollow and filled with drugs.

'No, unless it's martial arts,' said Marcus, who then went on to tell them of Jaz's karate skills in between mouthfuls.

'But you seem too pretty for that,' said Diane, just as Carl's mobile phone rang.

'Oh, sorry. Sorry Diane, I really have to take this,' said Carl getting up from the table with a third of his meal left. His face was hard to read but he seemed very serious, tense almost. 'I've been waiting for this call. I'll make it as short as I can.' He left in the direction of his office.

This could be something important, Jaz thought, and she counted to three before casually turning to Marcus. 'I just need to go to the ladies, sorry. When I'm nervous, my throat goes dry and I end up drinking heaps of water and then pay for it later.'

'You were nervous?' he said, smiling as she stood up.

Jaz put her fingers together. 'Just a little bit,' she said shyly. 'I'll be back.' She gave him a wink and headed off to the bathroom past Carl's office.

How long could she string this out? As she walked past his open door she glanced in. Carl was leaning over his desk writing something on a notepad.

'Yes, I can meet you tomorrow. It's all arranged. Yes. You have nothing to worry about. Okay, yep.'

It sounded like he was wrapping up the call, so Jaz quickly stepped towards the bathroom and hid behind the door, leaving it ajar just enough to see through.

Carl left his office and she could hear him heading back to the table. Quickly she came out and stepped into his office, figuring she had at least half a minute up her sleeve. She knew what she was looking for and went straight to his desk. Frantically her eyes searched for the notepad he had been writing on. Her heart was racing, blood pounding in her head at the thought of being caught.

She saw an open day planner and in one corner was written: *8pm Cicerello's*.

She immediately thought of Cicerello's, the fish-and-chip shop in

Fremantle, but she didn't have time to ponder it further. Quickly she left Carl's office and casually walked back to the dining room, even though her body was pumping with adrenaline. Could they see her pulse racing?

It could mean nothing, but her gut told her that this was something important. Could this be a drug boss further up the chain? Or maybe one of his sellers? This could be the proof MTG needed. Or it could just be his mate, wanting to catch up over fish and beer and Jaz would look like a fool. But at least only she would know. But again her gut felt Carl's reaction to the call was serious and that was enough to set her alarm bells ringing.

'Jaz, what are you planning to do after school?' asked Diane as she watched Jaz take her seat.

'You sound just like my mum,' she said trying to give herself a few seconds to calm down and compose herself. She scooped up the last bit of her dinner then pushed her empty plate away from her as she tried to think of a reply. 'You know, I'm still not really sure. I haven't ruled uni out. I wish I had a talent like Marcus that I could follow, it would help with my choices.'

'I'm sure you'll find something,' Diane said.

'Marcus is going to uni, aren't you, son?' said Carl.

'Yep, just not sure which courses I want to take.' Marcus gave Jaz a look, which said it depended on what Carl let him take.

'Who's for dessert?' said Diane brightly. 'I have a chocolate cheesecake.'

'Yes, please,' said Jaz, standing to collect the empty plates, happy to do something. Also glad her nerves had settled down.

'Oh, you're the guest, Jaz, you shouldn't be helping,' said Diane. Her hair was up in a tight bun and Jaz wondered if she ever let it out.

'I don't mind.'

The rest of the night went smoothly. The Sinclairs were no different from her own family. After dinner, Marcus finally snuck her back up to his room.

'God, I thought I'd never get you away from their endless questions.' He shut his door and pulled her towards his bed.

Warning lights began to flash in her head.

'Come and lie with me for a bit. I want to be able to pretend you're beside me tonight when I go to sleep.' He released his hair from its ponytail and moved over on the bed, making room for her.

He wasn't undressing, so she figured she was safe. After all, this was Marcus, who never rushed anything, and his folks were downstairs, so it was unlikely things would get out of hand.

'Okay.'

Jaz climbed onto his bed and sunk down into his arms.

'See, isn't this nice,' he said.

Jaz's hand rested against his chest. The rise and fall of his breathing was normal, but his heart rate wasn't. It made her smile, knowing he was nervous.

'What are you smiling about?' he asked as he looked down at her.

'Nothing, just enjoying this.' Jaz tucked herself closer to his body, wrapping a leg over his so that the full length of their bodies touched. She felt warm and comfortable, as if she were lying here with Taylor. Happy and contented with someone she cared about. Lying next to Ryan, on the other hand, was never this easy.

Jaz lifted her head from his shoulder so she could see him. Big mistake. Marcus was watching her with heat-filled eyes. His lips came towards her and she readied herself.

His kisses were nice, very nice. His hand moved up to her waist as they moved to lie on their sides, facing each other. She felt his fingers slide under her top, gentle and almost unsure. Jaz couldn't help compare him to Ryan, whose fingers had moved with precision and great understanding of where to touch. How many more women had Ryan slept with than Marcus? That thought almost sent her cold but she took comfort in Marcus's fumbling fingers. She doubted he was new to this game either, but Ryan had five years on Marcus. You could do a lot in five years.

Marcus's hand brushed over her breast, and that's when Jaz knew. Ryan only had to lie beside her and she'd be burning with need for him. He just had some sort of magnetic pull that stole her thoughts and willpower. Was it because she loved him? Jaz could remember back to when she'd first met Ryan, before she cared for him. They just had a spark that would crackle whenever they saw each other. At least, she had felt it. But all this thinking wasn't getting her anywhere, not when Ryan had pushed her away. That hurt and embarrassment still lingered. Still caused her sleepless nights and still made her angry with him, or herself for not being what he wanted. And it wasn't helping this make-out session with Marcus either.

Determined to shove Ryan away, she moved her hand down Marcus's chest towards his low-sitting jeans. Marcus tensed and pulled away from her just a fraction, so he could talk.

'Jaz, I think we better stop there before I can't stop. I don't plan on doing this with my parents downstairs,' he said with a chuckle.

'No, me neither.'

He kissed her again, deep and filled with promise.

'Okay, let's go downstairs where I can't take advantage of you,' he said teasingly.

'Good plan.'

As they left his room, Jaz glanced back to his bed. Would she have gone through with it if it had come to it? There was probably no point saving herself for Ryan when he clearly didn't want her. But then, if by some chance he'd change his mind, shouldn't she be a bit more experienced anyway? Jaz was torn by her last thought. Maybe she was dreaming like the typical schoolgirl she was. What chance did she have with Ryan? None.

CHAPTER 21

Jaz spent Sunday with Taylor. She'd been worried about him while she was away, and time together was long overdue. It started with a late breakfast at Molly's, and that's where she first noticed a black Nissan X-Trail parked opposite the cafe. It was nothing unusual, except she saw another black Nissan X-Trail when they went to the shopping centre to watch a movie. Maybe they were the latest car trend, but since the attack on Taylor, Ryan had warned Jaz to be on the lookout for anything abnormal.

After they left the cinema and went for a drive, Jaz kept an eye on the side mirror as she chatted to Taylor. She couldn't shake the weird feeling that she'd noticed this car for a reason.

'It's a real bummer Anna couldn't come. Fancy not liking movies – Ricky's just weird,' said Taylor.

'Really? Maybe Ricky doesn't like the monotonous regurgitated plots lines that have all been done before. Maybe he doesn't like how the actors are idolised when they are no more special than you and me. Maybe he just has better things to do with his time,' said Jaz. *Maybe you just don't like him because he has Anna*, she thought.

Taylor raised his eyebrows. 'What? Are you his best friend now?'

'Hey, I'm just trying to figure out why you dislike the guy so much,' she asked.

'Ha ha, very funny. But you're right. I shouldn't diss him because he doesn't like movies. I just think Anna would have loved seeing this with us.' He sounded sad, and it made Jaz miss Anna too.

'Yeah, I wish she could have been here. No one laughs like she does. She makes the movies funnier,' she said.

'I know, right? You end up laughing because she is. She's contagious.'

'That she is,' said Jaz as he stopped at a light. She studied Taylor for a moment, the way his face lit up talking about Anna. Was she like that when she talked to Ryan? *There goes Ryan, invading my mind again*, she thought sadly.

Jaz checked the side mirror, a habit she was fast acquiring, and spotted another black Nissan X-Trail. What were the chances? Her gut was warning her to take notice. Ryan would say there are no chances and that you should check everything. So, Jaz noted the number plate: she was sure the one at the cinema had those same letters. This time she locked away the number plate more securely in her phone: 1EAM740.

'Let's take the long way home,' she said, gesturing to a left-hand turn coming up.

'Righto,' said Taylor as he indicated and switched across a lane.

The Nissan was two cars back but it also indicated to turn. It never got close, always a car or two between them. The guy she'd seen outside school so often drove the same car. Maybe she'd been right thinking he'd been watching Taylor. She shivered, appalled at the thought.

There was a park coming up and public toilets. Jaz quickly hatched a plan. 'Hey Tay, can you pull over here, I need to go to the toilet.'

'Ha, it was that super-sized Coke, wasn't it. That's what you get for hogging it,' he teased, but pulled over. Jaz held her hand on the door, trying to get out slowly so she could watch what the Nissan did.

'I thought you were busting?' said Taylor.

Jaz ignored him and got out just at the car passed. She thought it might have stopped back further if it was tailing them. As she headed around the block of toilets, she watched the car but lost sight after the bend in the road. She almost felt relieved but at the same time, she'd wanted to be right. Her gut was still churning. Maybe she was just overcautious?

'You okay?' asked Taylor when she got back in the car. 'You seem a little vague.'

'Sorry, I'm just away with the fairies, I guess.' Still feeling that sensation in the pit of her stomach, Jaz continued to search for the Nissan as Taylor drove home.

A black shape sitting in a driveway around the bend caught her eye as they went past. Was it the same one? She leaned forward watching the side mirror. 'Damn,' she muttered as the black vehicle reversed onto the road behind them. It was only minutes later she saw it again, nestled behind two cars. 'Turn left here,' she asked Taylor.

'Why? Jaz?'

She didn't answer him but he obeyed and turned, giving her the chance to see the Nissan turn behind them. Its plates were the same, she was sure of it. Jaz turned to Taylor.

'Don't panic, but I think we're being followed.'

Automatically Taylor looked into his rear-vision mirror. 'Really? Where? What makes you say that?' he asked.

Jaz shared her suspicions, watching Taylor's eyes grow big and his hands grip the steering wheel tighter.

'What would make you think we would be followed, anyway? Do you think they want my Mustang? Do you think this has something to do with the home invasion? The guy with the gun.' He grimaced at the thought.

Jaz checked the mirror again and sighed. 'That's what I was thinking. Tay, what if this is the same guy? Maybe he's still keeping watch for some reason. What if…' She let her words fall away, not really sure what it could all mean. 'Is your dad home?'

'Yeah, he is.'

'Let's just go back to your place and see if they keep following,' she said. What else could they do?

'What do you think they want with me?' Taylor's voice was shaky now, and he'd paled a fraction. The memories of the attack probably refreshed in his mind. It certainly had for Jaz.

'I don't know. Maybe they're just keeping an eye on us? They haven't made any moves. I got the number plate; do you think we could run it?'

Taylor was now watching the mirrors as much as she was as he headed for home. 'What? Ask my dad?'

'Well, I don't really want to worry your dad.' How could Jaz tell Taylor that she thought his dad might be victim to extortion? 'Is there anyone else who could help you out at the station?'

'I could try Meg. She has access to the vehicle database. But Dad could do it easily. I'm sure he won't mind.'

Jaz saw the Nissan fall back as they came up to Taylor's street. Obviously they already knew where he lived. 'Stop here, Tay. I need to run something by you.'

He pulled up short of his driveway, two houses down, but they could see Taylor's dad's car at home.

'What's going on?' Taylor turned in his seat to face her. He even lifted his sunglasses to his head, his face full of questions.

'I'm worried that this car and the attack are linked.' Jaz realised the best way to take care of her best friend was to make him aware, make him cautious. 'Look, I've been thinking about the attack and what the man said and about how your dad reacted.'

His brows met, creasing up his forehead. 'What do you mean about how my dad reacted? He was worried sick.'

'I know. But when I told him what the attacker said, about how this was your last warning – well, your dad looked as though he knew exactly what it meant.'

Taylor pulled a face, and Jaz felt sure he was going to defend his dad. Who wouldn't. 'Jaz, you don't—'

'Taylor, just hear me out. Your dad has been out of sorts lately and I think that maybe he's being made to help out some bad guys.'

'No, he wouldn't do that. Dad's as straight as they come, and he's a Deputy Commissioner,' said Taylor proudly.

'Not even if they threatened his son's life?' Jaz reached over and grabbed his hand. 'Tay, what if they attacked you to send a warning to your dad? To let him know just how easily they could get to you. It's the only thing that makes sense about what the attacker said. Unless your dad owes money for something and they want him to pay up.'

'Dad's got heaps of money, it wouldn't be that.' He rubbed his face with his hand. 'What if you're right? Dad *is* in the best spot for information.'

'I know. He could warn the bad guys about raids, and keep them in the loop about what the cops are targeting next. I'm sure some cops have no choice when their family is threatened. There are so many big bikie gangs and drug lords who would kill for the information your dad has access to.'

Taylor was quiet for a long time. They both just sat, milling over their thoughts. It was starting to get darker and the streetlights were all coming on.

'What do we do, Jaz? Do I confront my dad?' he asked softly.

'Not yet. Let's call Meg tomorrow and see who owns this car. Then we might have something to bring to your dad.' Or Jaz would have something to take to Ryan and MTG could look into it.

'Okay. Tomorrow at recess, we'll ring Meg. You wanna come in?' he asked as he started his car.

'No, actually, can you drop me off home? I told Mum I'd be home early tonight.'

Her house was only up and around the corner, so she was home in a minute. 'Thanks Tay. Just be careful. Watch for the Nissan. Watch for everything and tell me,' she said. She didn't want to scare him, but she didn't want him complacent either.

As Taylor drove away, Jaz felt fear grip her body. She couldn't lose him. She could only hope the number plate turned up a lead tomorrow. But right now she had to get ready to see who was meeting Carl Sinclair tonight at eight. Adrenaline was already running through Jaz's body from being followed, and now she was about to conduct her first stake-out. With jelly legs, she headed into the house.

The first thing she did was tell her family that she was going out for fish and chips with Taylor. 'I'll be back around nine, Mum.'

Tasha gave her an exasperated look. She wanted to be able to tell Jaz what to do, but she knew she was nearly old enough to do her own thing. 'Thanks for letting me know,' she said with a sigh.

Jaz ran up the stairs to her room before her mum changed her mind. She threw on Ryan's big hoodie that she'd kept and grabbed her Danny Green cap that Bags had signed for her. With her jeans and black Doc Martins, she was hoping to pass as just another guy. Ryan's jumper was baggy enough to hide her chest, and she tucked her hair up under the cap.

She was about to leave when she had another thought. Opening her cupboard, she pulled out her black camera bag and checked over her

Canon EOS. Both lenses were in there, and everything was ready should she have a chance to get photos from the safety of her Jeep.

Happy that she had everything, she snuck back downstairs and outside to her Jeep. Nervously, she drove south to Fremantle and found a park just off Mews Road so she could see the front of Cicerello's. Did she wait here and chance missing them? Or did she go inside and risk being detected?

Jaz felt ill as she tried to run each scenario through in her mind but then realised this was a walk in the park compared to Pakistan. Some of her nerves eased. Then she saw it: the perfect vantage spot. Just outside the shop was a bricked-up square, and in the middle of that stretched a large tree, from which she would be able to see the eatery as well as across the lawn to the boat harbour.

Jaz put the small lens on her camera so it fitted under her jumper easily; she hoped to get pictures of them inside by the light. Reaching across to her glove box, she pulled out a packet of cigarettes and a lighter she'd bought earlier.

She looked at the plain packaging, remembering when she'd first seen Ryan smoking and he'd explained how it was a great cover. Smoking would give her a reason to be sitting out the front of the shop in the first place; she could easily be waiting for her order or a friend. As long as she didn't actually drag from it she'd be okay. Her fits of coughing would ruin her attempts to blend in.

She'd have to wash her clothes soon too. If her mum caught a whiff of smoke on her she'd go ballistic.

It was 7.45; just enough time to get into position. She fumbled with the door and cursed her own nerves. She had faced worse in Pakistan, a night in Fremantle should be a breeze.

Jaz locked her Jeep and walked across the road towards Cicerello's. Her camera banged against her chest under the jumper as she tried to walk slowly.

Every person she passed scared her. What if it was Carl? She kept her cap low and eventually made it to the brickwork by the steps to the lawn. The tree behind would provide cover her while she tried to get some photos.

The bricks were cold on her bum and her leg began to shake. She stopped it but then it started right back up again. She pulled a cigarette from the box and lit it. Jaz tried not to screw her face up at the smoke. It had been three years since she'd tried smoking. She, Anna and Taylor had tried it together and had decided quite quickly that it wasn't for them after coughing their throats raw. But they had felt cool for five seconds before that.

Jaz put the smoke to her lips, took a small drag and quickly blew it out again. She was able to stifle a cough as she glanced at her watch again. It was getting close to time. Jaz began to watch for cars and the faces of men arriving alone. Would Carl be first?

It was a minute to eight when she saw the familiar dark hair of Carl. He was wearing his black suit pants and a white shirt without a tie. Jaz kept her cap down as low as she could without losing sight of Carl as he headed towards the shop door.

Jaz put out the cigarette and pulled out her phone, pretending to make a call while watching her surroundings.

She could only just see Carl through the glass, placing an order. As she watched him, she saw another man in a suit enter the shop and stand beside him at the counter, seemingly placing an order too. Jaz checked her watch: it was after eight. That must be him. Glancing around her, she couldn't see anyone coming or going. She stood up and quickly lifted her jumper and brought her camera up to her eye as she stood beside the pine tree, trying to blend in with its branches. Using her zoom, she found Carl and clicked off a few shots. She could see his face clearly. If only the other man would turn around.

They looked like they were just two people waiting for their order and chatting. Except the facial expression on Carl was the same one he had when he took that phone call at dinner.

'Come on, turn around,' Jaz begged quietly. She quickly checked no one was coming and went back to looking through the camera. She hoped like hell the lens didn't catch the light and give her away.

The man didn't turn around, even when Carl took his order and left. Jaz was just about having heart palpitations as she hid behind the tree while Carl went to his car. If this kept up, she'd be dead before the guy in the shop ever turned around.

Finally he stepped towards the counter for his order and turned to leave. Jaz almost screamed when his face became visible. She was so shocked she didn't take any photos; instead, she sat down and hid the camera as quickly as she could and then went about getting a cigarette out.

As the man walked back past her she tried not to shake as she attempted to light her cigarette. The smell of fish and chips followed him as he headed to the car park. He was in a silver Mercedes, an expensive-looking one. Did she risk using the camera to get his number plate or just hope he came back this way?

She decided she couldn't risk the camera, and had her phone ready to take photos while she tried to memorise the plate.

He pulled out onto the road, heading back towards Jaz. She started taking photos with her phone while pretending to look at it, when in fact her eyes were reading the plates. Jaz entered it into her phone with trembling hands.

She'd seen him before. She knew him. And it was worse than she could have possibly imagined.

CHAPTER 22

Jaz hardly slept a wink. Tossing and turning over what to do. Should she tell Ryan what she'd seen? Should she send word to MTG first? It was awful because all she could think about was Marcus. Surely he knew nothing of his dad's dodgy dealings. What would this do to him eventually? Break up his family, hurting him in the process. None of it was his fault. It sucked.

It had taken all her effort to get to school on time. Even Simon had asked if she was okay.

'You look like crap, sis,' he'd said as she drove him to school.

'I feel like it too,' she'd replied.

Hopefully school would keep her mind occupied.

'You ready to do this?' asked Taylor, as he found her after their last class before recess.

'Yep, you?'

Taylor nodded and grabbed her arm. Together they went outside to find a quiet spot where they wouldn't be overheard or interrupted.

'Wait for me!' shouted Anna who was racing along the corridor behind them, waving frantically like a two-armed octopus. 'Sorry I'm late. I just had to tell Ricky I couldn't catch up at all today.'

'Okay, got the number plate ready?' he asked as they lay down beside a tree, heads together in a close circle.

Jaz pulled out her phone and brought up both number plates. Taylor frowned when he saw two numbers there. 'The other one was another car that seemed a bit suss,' she said. 'Thought it wouldn't hurt to see if both were connected.'

'Good idea,' said Taylor as he dialled the number. 'Hi, can you put me through to Megan Stiller, please. It's Taylor Stewart. Cheers.' He shot them a nervous smile as he put it on loudspeaker, placing the phone on the ground in front of him.

'Taylor?'

'Hi Meg, how are you?' said Taylor.

'I'm fine. How come I haven't seen you around the office lately? We miss you around here,' she said. Her voice was young and peppy, but also carried a hint of importance. Her fondness for Taylor was clear.

'I know. I will one day soon. But hey, I need to ask you a huge favour.'

'Go ahead,' she said curiously.

'I took down the number plates of some cars I think have been following me, and since the assault I've been worried they might come back. Any chance you can bring up the owners for me? I don't want to worry Dad with this just yet.'

Meg inhaled sharply. 'Mmm. I'm sorry about that. Your dad's been a bit out of sorts lately. I can't believe that happened to you, Tay. I know he's got a task force trying to catch the bugger.'

'Until then I'm taking my own precautions. So, will you help me and check these plates? Please,' he begged.

'I can put you through to the task force if you want?'

'No, they'll only tell Dad, and I want to double-check they're still following me first before I pass on the info. Can you help?'

The line went silent as Meg thought over his request. 'Okay, but I never said anything, all right?'

'Promise. I'll owe ya, Meg,' said Taylor. They heard some tapping on a computer.

'First number?' she asked.

Jaz gave Taylor her phone so he could read the first plate.

'That belongs to a Mallinya Party Limited,' she said. 'I don't know if I should give the address in case you do something silly,' she added.

'No, I swear I won't do anything, Meg. Here's the other one,' said Taylor.

'That one belongs to a De Luca Industries. Now, is that all?' said Meg worriedly.

'Yep, that's it. Thanks,' he said before saying goodbye.

Anna put her hand on Taylor. 'Did any of that mean anything to you two?'

Taylor shook his head and looked to Jaz as she Googled Mallinya Party Limited. 'Let me see what I can find. Okay, it's a Perth company run by…' Jaz tapped through a few links. 'A Mr Nicko Serv…' Her voice trailed away. 'Nicko Serveyous,' she said again as her own mind registered the name.

Jaz could tell the name meant nothing to Taylor and Anna but it meant a lot to her. Nicko was the man she and Ryan had followed from the casino. Did that mean he was the one involved with the tattooed guy? Was he the one controlling the Shesha Serpents? Or were they controlling him? And what did they want with Taylor and his dad?

'Jaz, do you know something? Are you thinking Ryan could help with this?' said Anna leaning in close, causing her long plait to fall over her shoulder.

But Jaz was too caught up in her thoughts to answer Anna.

'Why would Ryan be able to help?' Taylor glanced between the both of them, and Jaz just about cursed at Anna for letting the cat out of the bag.

'We've just found out that Ryan works for the government doing… well, covert stuff,' said Jaz, keeping the details loose. 'I heard him mention a Nicko Serveyous once. Seemed like a bad dude.'

'You're just telling me this now.' His eyes grew wide and he looked hurt.

'None of us are meant to know, so you have to keep it a secret. You can't tell anyone about Ryan.' She waited until they both nodded. 'What I will do is tell Ryan about Nicko's guys following us and he'll do something about it. He's separate from the police, so he might be able to get to them without compromising your dad or you.' Jaz reached out and took Taylor's other hand, the one Anna didn't have in a death grip. 'You can't tell your dad. If he *is* feeding information to this Nicko guy to save your life, then we can't trust him. Ryan can help. Trust me on this. Ryan's a good guy.'

Taylor was thinking hard, she could see the vein lines protruding in his neck. 'So, that's why he's great with a gun and can fight? He's like a secret SAS soldier or something? Does he work for ASIO?'

'No, not ASIO. He doesn't work with national security. He's more focused on keeping the drug dealers and terrorists to a minimum.' Jaz probably shouldn't be telling them anything but she trusted these two and Anna knew most of this anyway. None of this would leave the two of them, she trusted her friends more than she trusted Ryan.

'Look, I'm going to get word to him about this, okay. I'm also seeing him on the weekend.' Jaz chose to ignore the pointed look Anna gave her. 'Just keep watching your back, Tay.' She couldn't believe it was one of Nicko's cars that had been following them. Was it him or someone else in the car? So many questions and not enough answers.

And De Luca Industries, was that company related to the guy she saw meeting Carl? Jaz shivered as she remembered the man's eyes. She hadn't got a close look at them that well last night but she remembered them as clear as a bell from when she ran into him at the casino. If Ryan hadn't have told her that Sal was the biggest bad guy around, then she wouldn't have thought him anything but a nice guy. She'd thought the same about Carl. Was he also capable of murder, like Sal? Again, so many questions and not enough answers. That was beginning to be her new motto.

'I trust you, Jaz,' said Taylor, bringing her back to the present.

'And so do I. Ryan will know what to do,' said Anna. 'And we will never speak a word of this outside this circle.'

'Thanks. We really need to be careful.'

The siren went, so they headed back to class but met up again at lunchtime. They had serious stuff to discuss and when they had exhausted all possibilities, they sat around wondering what would happen next. It was a horrible feeling not being able to take action. Being stuck in school made it even worse.

On Wednesday after school Marcus asked her to meet at his place, so after dropping Simon at home she headed straight over to Cottesloe. She also had a note hidden inside a flower, ready for the cemetery. This time she would take Marcus with her to meet Becky. The last two days had been hell, waiting until she could see Ryan and hopefully get some answers. Anna had been spending more time with them and even made a roster so one of them was with Taylor at all times. Her theory was that whoever was stalking Taylor wouldn't go near him if he was never alone. And Jaz agreed. Now the three of them were more inseparable than ever.

'Hey, you.' Marcus met her at the car, eager to hug her. His hair was out and blowing in the offshore breeze.

Jaz put her hand up, letting it sift through the strands as they moved. 'Hey, yourself,' she said, giving him a kiss.

'Wanna come inside for a bit or walk along the beach?' he asked.

'Inside for a bit. Are your folks home?' she asked.

'No, not at the moment. Can you stay for a while? You're not meeting up with Anna or Taylor?'

'No, those two have plans.' The range was their destination, but Taylor looked as if they were heading on a trip to the moon. He was loving every moment of his time with Anna. 'I did want to go to the cemetery and visit my sister, though. Did you want to come with me?' she asked hopefully.

Marcus's face softened and she touched his cheek, fascinated by how smooth it was. Nothing like Ryan's stubble.

'Of course, I'll go. I'll introduce you to my sister while we're there,' he said.

They had talked about their sisters before and found they were at the same cemetery. Jaz felt a little sad that Marcus was sharing his life with her and caring for her so much. Especially when she knew, at some stage, she would have to let him go. It would be hard. He'd become a wonderful friend.

'Let's go inside and I'll get you a drink. What do you feel like?'

'I feel like a coffee, actually,' said Jaz as she headed to his kitchen. 'Want me to whip us up one? Anna has the same coffee machine at her house,' she said pointing to the fancy silver box.

'Cool, thanks. Everything is in that top drawer.'

Jaz turned on the machine and waited for it to warm up.

'I've um, drawn another picture. Do you want to see it?' asked Marcus. He'd let his hair drop across his face like a curtain. Jaz went over and tucked it back.

'I'd love to see it. You should know that. I'm your biggest fan, other than your mum,' she said with a smile.

'I'll go get it,' he said and headed to his room.

Jaz knew this was a chance to snoop, so as soon as he disappeared up the stairs she snuck into Carl's office and went straight for his desk. Just the usual bits and pieces, plus a notice for a shipping container sale in South Fremantle. At the bottom of the page he'd written SCWA6519924 in red pen. Quickly she took a photo of it, and the desk in case she'd missed something. Heavy footsteps clucked back down the steps and Jaz knew she was going to be caught.

Oh hell. How would she get out of this one?

CHAPTER 23

'Jaz?'

SHE NEARLY DIDN'T hear him, her heart was pounding so loudly in her ears.

Jaz stepped to the wall and looked at a photo. She could feel sweat starting to gather at the back of her neck. She'd realised it would look worse if she was caught sprinting from the room with a guilty look on her face. 'In here. Look what I found,' she said turning. 'I like this photo of you. Very cute.' She turned back to it.

'Um, well, let's get back to the kitchen. Dad hates anyone in his office, even me,' said Marcus, steering her out and shutting the door

Now this was juicy news. Carl was protective of his office. *Doesn't sound like a normal art dealer to me*, thought Jaz. Especially the way Marcus herded her out, afraid of being caught.

'Here's the drawing,' he said, handing it over when they reached the kitchen.

'Oh wow. I love it. You and me,' she said smiling at him. 'Is this the first time you've drawn yourself?'

He nodded. Jaz compared the likeness. She could see the passion in his eyes, even on paper. Marcus was someone who would love deeply, and Jaz just hoped she wouldn't break his heart.

'How come the only photo I can find of you is in your dad's office?' she asked, trying to sound normal while she still vibrated with adrenaline.

'Mum took most of them down when Rachael died. She couldn't stand seeing Rach but she also hated the photos of us without her. So, she replaced them all with art pieces. Dad still has ones of us in his office, out of Mum's way.'

'Yeah, it's hard. My mum was a bit the same to start with.' Jaz moved to the drawers. 'Okay, how do you like it, Mr Sinclair?' she said, pulling open the drawer and getting the cups.

Marcus came up behind her, pushing her against the bench with his body after she'd shut the drawer. 'You really want to know?' he asked huskily.

She could feel the outline of his body pressed into her back; one part in particular caused her to stumble on her words. 'Well… um… now?' No. She hadn't prepared herself for anything like this today.

Marcus laughed. 'No, not when my parents could arrive home at any minute. They sometimes do. But I was thinking that Sunday night, my mum'll be away and Dad works late. Wanna stay for a while?'

His words were heavily laced with innuendo. Jaz could easily read between the lines and what she read scared her.

'Sounds like a plan,' she said, trying to keep the fear from her voice. She hoped to come up with a good excuse by then. Or would she go through with it? As far as first times went, at least she knew Marcus cared and he would be gentle. She couldn't imagine him any other way.

'So,' she asked, getting back to the coffees, 'do both your parents work at the gallery?'

'No, Mum runs it most days, unless Dad takes over to give her a break. But Dad does most of the shipping and delivery stuff. He's usually at the warehouse.'

'You'll have to show me. I've never been to a gallery before. My folks have boring office jobs.'

Marcus laughed. 'There's nothing boring about what your dad does. Computers are where the future's at.' He tilted his head. 'What's that face for?'

'I was just wondering what my real father did for work. Mum has never said. Guess it's no point if he's dead.' The noise of the coffee machine drowned out any more conversation, but Jaz was somewhat relieved. It gave her time to her thoughts. She was nearly eighteen. She had a right to know more about her father, even if it was bad. Jaz felt for the medallion around her neck, hidden under her shirt. She'd gone searching for her birth certificate once, even requested a copy, but there was nothing of her real father. Just 'unknown', and Paul listed as her adoptive father. Without anything else, Jaz had given up. The medallion was all she had left. All the rest was locked away in her mum's head and she wasn't going to give anything up anytime soon. But Jaz was hoping when she turned eighteen that her mum would change her mind. She had to.

After their coffee they headed to the cemetery; a few gardeners were out raking as Marcus and Jaz made their way to Becky first. Jaz carried the flower, rolling it through her fingers as she thought of her coded message inside. It was short and simple.

Target met with another known target.

Other than that, she didn't know what else to tell them. She'd decided that the rest she should tell Ryan in person. He was dealing with Nicko and Sal, so in a way she was cutting out the middleman. But nonetheless, she followed protocol and left her message. She knew they'd understand it.

'Here she is. I'll just put this down,' she said, stepping towards Becky's grave and lifting up the vase. Inside was tiny slip of paper wrapped in gladwrap, which she slipped out and hid in her pocket before putting the flower in and setting it back against the headstone.

She had her first reply. Her fingers itched to pull it out and read it, but she knew it would be in code and now was not the time. But her body was tingling with excitement. She had to try hard to hold herself together as they stood for a moment in silence. 'I never know what to say,' she said. 'Bye Becky,' she said before Marcus took her to his sister's grave.

'I haven't been here in a while. Sorry Rach,' he said as he faced the headstone.

The sun dipped behind a cloud and Jaz's skin prickled; not just from the sudden drop in temperature but the feeling someone was watching them. Without the sun, the cemetery felt dark and gloomy. Marcus crouched down and touched the little photos of his sister on the headstone.

'Wow, I can see the resemblance. You know, you're lucky. I bet you have some great memories with her. I wish I could remember Becky.' Her voice faded away on the gentle breeze that floated through the cemetery like lost souls.

Marcus stood up and put his arms around Jaz. 'Life works in funny ways, hey. At least you still have Simon. It's harder being an only kid. Mum and Dad are so focused on my life because I'm all they have.'

They talked for a while by the grave before finally heading back to her Jeep.

'Come on, I'll take you down to Mum's gallery in Freo. There's a great coffee shop next door, and on the way I'll show you the warehouse.'

Marcus gave her directions to an industrial kind of area, lots of space and surrounded by trees. He got her to pull into a large yard surrounded by a high fence topped with barbed wire and a massive shed-like building in the centre. There was a medium-sized delivery truck parked by the shed. Sea containers, six of them, lined up against the back fence, and wooden boxes and pallets were stacked beside the shed. On the nearest end of the shed was an office area, and maybe the toilets, by the look of the small windows. There was a dog kennel beside the big sliding door in the warehouse part of the shed. Lots of protection but, Jaz rationalised, they did work with expensive art.

'Can we go in for a look?' she asked.

'Nothing much to see. It's just a big shed where they pack up the sculptures and stuff. Lots of bubble wrap, though. I remember going in when I was little and I spent the whole time popping the plastic bubbles. I don't visit nowadays in case Dad tries to get me to work there. He wants me to take over the family business, and as much as I like art, I'd prefer to be the one making it, not selling it.'

Jaz let out her breath slowly, not trying to show she'd been holding it ever since Marcus said 'family business'. For a moment, she wondered if his dad had actually spelled out the business he was into. Even though Jaz had seen him with Sal, she still was struggling to think that Carl was into drugs of Sal's magnitude.

'But I can't see his car, so we might be safe. Park over there,' said Marcus pointing to a spot by the office section. 'Tommy is usually here,' he said.

Jaz was going to make the most of this opportunity to look for clues. As Ryan always said, *See, don't just look.*

The moment Jaz stepped out of the car a vicious dog bark started up.

A German Shepherd was straining at its chain upon seeing them, growling like it was ready to chew them up like a juicy steak.

'That's Cujo. Don't go near him if you value your legs. Dad got him a few years ago, but said he was never a pet and no one was to be trusted around him. Apparently they'd had a break-in, so Dad thought this would help deter graffiti kids and stuff. Don't know about you, but I don't trust the look in his eyes at all. Although he's fine with Tommy.'

Marcus grabbed her hand and pulled her towards the open shed door.

'Hey Tommy,' he said to a big man standing by a wooden box.

Tommy turned, his tattoos and bulk making him look scary, until Jaz saw the smile he had for Marcus.

'Marky mate, what are you doing here?' Tommy came over, shook his hand, and then glanced at Jaz.

'Tommy, this is my girlfriend Jaz. Jaz, this is Tommy, he's been working for Dad for years. There's another bloke, Rich, who works on occasion too.'

Jaz shook his hand. Tommy's grip was gentle and he grinned like a proud mate.

'She's a looker, Marky. Nice to meet you, Jaz. You getting the tour?' he asked. He wore blue work clothes, and his goatee was dark and thick, while the hair on his head was none.

'Yep, we're off to the gallery next. So, you wrap all the stuff up and deliver it?' she asked.

'Sure do.' He walked back to the box he'd been standing beside and picked up a clipboard. 'This one here is off to Margaret River as a show-piece in a winery. I've got those two left to get wrapped.' He motioned to a large picture on canvas, which was leaning against a proper frame rail, and a nearby sculpture made of wire and wood.

Jaz walked over to them, taking the time to check out the rest of the shed. A sea container was at the opposite end sitting under a great big con-traption that looked like a car hoist, but in this case probably lifted the sea containers on and off a truck.

'Do you ship stuff overseas?' she asked, turning to walk to the sea container.

Tommy didn't move or flinch. Because there were no drugs left around here, or because he was cool under pressure? 'Not much. Mainly we get the pieces in from overseas. Diane spends a lot of time overseas looking for new things.'

'I've never really seen a sea container before. Cool.' The rest of the shed was full of bubble wrap rolls, just like Marcus had said. Also lots of cardboard and packing straps; everything you would need to safely transport delicate items.

Jaz turned towards the office end of the shed. There were two doors.

'That's just the office part,' said Marcus, watching her. 'Sometimes Karen, Mum's assistant, comes here to keep the delivery paperwork up to date.' Marcus shot Tommy a look, and Jaz laughed as Tommy glanced away as if he had no idea why Karen would be needed. 'Tommy's more the muscle, aren't you?' he teased.

'Too right, kid. I'm lucky if I can sign my name,' he joked. 'I'm just going to back the truck in,' he said. 'Nice meeting you, Jaz.'

'You too, Tommy,' she said as he walked off outside. Jaz turned to Marcus. 'You know, if your dad is having trouble with break-ins, my dad could set you up with a good alarm system. His company make fully intergrated systems.'

'No need. Dad has one set up in the office and he has big locks on the doors, so no one could get in here without a big oxy torch.' He pointed out the bolts. 'But they try not to keep much in here anyway. The good stuff is kept under better security at the gallery. Dad has this place insured anyway.'

'Good to know. I can't imagine anyone would want to come and steal art pieces anyway. It's not like it would be easy to sell or hide.' Jaz turned back to the sea container. There was a link here, she could feel it, between this sea container and the sea container sale notice she'd seen on Carl's desk. There had to be. Why would he need to buy more when he already had an abundance in his yard?

Marcus agreed. 'Yeah, I know. But some people do anything for money.'

The beeping of a truck reversing had them moving out of the shed. They waved goodbye to Tommy in the truck and then got in the Jeep.

Jaz couldn't see anything funny at all in there, not even Tommy seemed out of place. But maybe during daylight hours it was supposed to seem like that? If they were going to put drugs in art to ship to clients, then Jaz guessed this would be the most likely spot to do it. It was out of the way, in an unimposing area.

Maybe she'd have to come back at another time to check the place out. If she did, she'd have to bring the biggest steak she could find.

CHAPTER 24

Jaz was nervous. As she sat by her computer she couldn't stop her leg from bouncing, nor could she stop chewing on her fingernail. Tonight she would see Ryan.

That thought alone made her leg pick up speed. Taylor was at Anna's, but he was going to drop her off at Ryan's tonight so her car wasn't left outside his place. They were all eager to find out what Ryan could do about Nicko.

She straightened out the note she'd received from the cemetery. Already deciphered and locked away in her brain, it informed her that Ryan would make contact soon to discuss her target and any findings. Did the Agency know she was going out to dinner with him tonight or was their private life none of the Agency's business?

Jaz glanced at her watch. She still had fifteen minutes before Taylor would be here. Thank God she'd already found something to wear. Mind you, she'd had most of the morning to sort it, and Anna had helped. Well, if you could call it help. Anna wanted her to wear a dress and go sexy. Jaz was sure Anna harboured a little crush on Ryan, or maybe she thought Jaz still did too and was hoping for some action. But Jaz had won the clothing battle, almost.

She wore skinny leg jeanswith a body-hugging long greyshirt. A little black jacket over the top, some silver jewellery and a pair of knee-high black boots and she was good to go.

She was ready. Except for her nerves. If only they would go.

While she was waiting, she'd Googled De Luca Industries and found a heap of businesses with the De Luca Industries label. She clicked on the link to the Perth-based one, which turned out to be a flight charter company. Did Sal own it? Is this how he shipped his drugs around to different places? Seemed very useful.

'Jaz, Taylor's here!' called Tasha as she neared the top of the stairs.

Jaz flicked off her computer, grabbed her small handbag and met her mum on the stairs. 'Thanks, Mum.'

'You look gorgeous. Hot date with Marcus?'

'Maybe,' said Jaz. Let her think whatever she wanted.

Tasha touched her arm, causing her to stop midway down the stairs. 'You remember about birth control, right?'

'Oh my God, Mum. *Please*,' Jaz begged, as she felt her face burn.

'I wouldn't be a very good mum if I didn't remind you about it. Even though you are old enough to know…' Tasha faded away as she gazed at Jaz. Raising her hand she smoothed out Jaz's ponytail as if taking a last moment to remember her little girl.

'I don't plan on that, Mum, but if I do decide to do that… well, I know what to do. Now, is that it? Tay's waiting,' she said, raising an eyebrow at her mum.

Tasha sighed. 'Yes, off you go. Have fun. But not too much fun,' she added hastily.

Jaz was still laughing when she still climbed into Taylor's car.

'What's so funny?' he asked.

'Yeah?' said Anna, popping up in the back seat.

Jaz jumped a little, but she should have expected Anna wouldn't miss out on this.

'Nothing. Just my mum. So, you both need to drop me off, hey?' Jaz asked.

'Of course,' said Anna, as she played with her hair. She was wearing jeans and a Hello Kitty T-shirt; a big kid at heart.

'You're just dropping me out the front and then leaving, right? I can't have Ryan knowing you know stuff. Okay?'

'You're such a party pooper, Jaz,' said Anna.

But they respected her wishes, and as she stood on the side of the road in the dark watching the Mustage drive away, Jaz was a little scared without her friends and suddenly wanted them back. Could she really face Ryan on her own, especially with what had happened between them? Or lack of. There was only one way to find out and Jaz was all for facing her fears head on.

She let herself into his yard and headed to the door, rapping her knuckles on the wood. There was nothing. What if the dinner had been cancelled? What if he didn't want her to come anymore? Was he even home? Dread and humiliation began to trickle through her before the door finally opened.

Ryan stood there in stone-washed jeans and a button-up dress shirt in dark grey. The sexy fresh scent of him hit her like a bucket of cold water, causing her skin to prickle with goose bumps. He almost smelled better than he looked. Almost. Those dark mysterious eyes won her over every time, especially when he gazed over her as if checking her out. Was he interested? Or was that just her hope and imagination running wild?

Tonight he was clean-shaven. Her fingers itched to reach out and feel the smoothness of his skin. But that wouldn't be enough; she would want her lips to touch the softness of his cheek down to his firm jaw. Jaz wasn't sure why her thoughts were torturing her. This was only the first five seconds, she still had a whole night to go yet!

'Jaz, you made it,' he said. His voice shook her core like a vibrating bell.

She forced herself to concentrate. 'Of course. I promised Steph.'

He reached back and flicked off the inside light and then pulled the door shut, making sure it was locked tight.

'Let's go, shall we.'

Jaz nodded and followed him to the car.

Inside she was quiet, not really sure what to say or do. How did she behave with him now? Professionally? Maybe that was her answer.

'I have lots to tell you,' she said turning in her seat to face him.

Ryan put his finger to his lips, shushing her. 'That's nice,' he said coldly. She might have taken offence had it been anyone else. So, she remained quiet. A few minutes later, he pulled over. 'Come on.'

They were stopped on the edge of a road; cars were passing them, their lights blinding Jaz as she got out. She felt Ryan's hand pull her to the front of the car.

'We couldn't talk in the car; I haven't checked it for bugs lately.' He let her hand go and she missed the contact. 'What is it you wanted to say? Is something wrong with the mission?'

Jaz had to lean in close to hear Ryan over the night traffic. She guessed at least no one could listen into their conversation.

'Okay, well, remember Sal from the casino? Well, Carl met with him last weekend,' she said.

'What, when? How do you know?'

Ryan stood wide-eyed while she told him how she overheard Carl's phone call and then followed him to see who he was meeting.

'Jaz, you should have told me about this before going off on your own. I can't believe you did that,' he almost yelled. His voice louder than the traffic.

That made Jaz angry. What an arse. She pushed her hands to her hips. 'Aren't you the one who wanted me to be a part of this stuff? Doesn't that mean getting information and taking risks? I thought you'd be happy. Isn't this what it's all about?' Jaz spat.

Ryan stepped back and brushed his hands over his head.

To the passing traffic, they probably looked like a couple having a fight.

'Jaz, you're new, you shouldn't be putting yourself in danger. What if they'd seen you? You could have blown everything, or got killed.'

Jaz felt the hairs on her neck prickle. He'd pushed her away, so he wasn't allowed to care for her. He couldn't have it both ways. It was doing her head in.

'Well, they didn't,' she growled back. 'I'm not stupid, I was disguised well. I did everything you taught me.' She felt like kicking him in the shins. 'I guess you don't want to hear what else I—'

Ryan grabbed her arms, bringing her closer. 'Jaz. What else have you done?'

Jaz wrestled out of his grip, her arms still tingling from where he'd held her. His condescending tone made her clench her fists. 'Just shut up and listen, will you. Taylor and I were followed by a car; it belonged to Mallinya Party Limited, which is owned by Nicko Serveyous.'

Jaz almost smiled at Ryan's reaction. He looked like she'd just slapped him across the face. For once it was nice to see him on the back foot.

'How…' he began but then shook his head as if it wasn't important now. 'So, the Shesha Serpents are working under Nicko?' he said more to himself than to her.

'That's what I think, or vice versa. So, would it be Nicko pressuring Taylor's dad? Is there anyway you can stop it?' Jaz asked.

'Soon. Those documents and photos we brought back all tie Nicko to the poppy fields in Pakistan. It's ironclad evidence, so the authorities have to take notice, he can't pay his way out of this one. He's going down, but the only problem is: what happens to the Serpents? We have nothing on them.'

'If Nicko is put away, will they forget about threatening Taylor?' she asked hopefully. Jaz had relaxed her stance, her anger melting away into concern.

'I don't know, Jaz. Depends what kind of deal was struck. Did Nicko pay them to do this job or is he at the head of the Serpents? Maybe he was owed a favour, or they both went in on it as a joint venture. Putting Nicko away won't solve this problem, Jaz. I think we'll need to infiltrate the Serpents.' Ryan pressed his hand to his forehead. 'Come on, we'd better go, we're late as it is.'

Jaz felt a tinge of pity for him. He looked stressed, which was probably from the combination of this news and the approaching dinner with his parents.

'Um.' Jaz still had one more question before they got into the car. 'Does Sal own De Luca Industries?' she asked.

Ryan's body froze at the mention of the name. Helooked her squarely in the eyes. 'Jaz, he *is* De Luca Industries. Salvatore De Luca is his name. De Luca Industries is the national company his father began.' He cocked his head to the side. 'Why do you ask?'

'That's who was listed under his car registration. I was just making sure they both fit.'

'Car rego? How did you get that?' Ryan paused and then sighed. 'Taylor?'

Funny how Ryan didn't need any more details to know exactly what they'd done.

'Just don't get caught,' he added gruffly.

Jaz was trying hard to focus on his words but the breeze was wafting his manly scent straight at her.

'Is that all?' he asked, challenging her.

When she didn't reply, he turned and got back in the car and waited for her.

It was only another twenty minutes before they reached his parents' place north of the city, and the whole time they remained silent. Jaz was trying hard just to keep the images from the hotel room in Pakistan at bay. But being near Ryan unearthed her guarded memories. Why could she not control her body around him? It wasn't fair.

Ryan's parents' place was a lot like his house. Single-storey, quaint, but instead of the big fence, his parents' front yard was open and had a big lawn. The front lights were on, waiting for them. A car was already parked in the narrow driveway.

'That's Steph's Holden,' said Ryan. He turned to Jaz. 'I'm sorry for the interrogation you're about to receive. Just answer the best you can, and if it's something touchy, then just ask to go to the bathroom or something.'

'Right. Got it,' Jaz nodded, unsure exactly what type of interrogation he meant.

They got out and walked along a little pathway to the front door. Ryan knocked a few times, and was about to reach for the handle when it swung open.

'Ryan, my boy. You're here.'

A woman in jeans and a patterned blouse stood before them with her arms open. Her blonde hair was soft around her shoulders and Jaz had a glimpse of how Steph would look in twenty-five years. Ryan's mother was beautiful, tall and thin. She latched onto Ryan and hugged him tightly. When she finally pulled away, Jaz could see her eyes shining from tears of joy.

'I'm so glad you could make it. And this is Jaz, your friend?' she asked as her gaze settled on Jaz. A smile radiated across her face. 'Come in. I'm Kathy. When Steph mentioned you, we all got excited. It's so wonderful of you to come.'

Kathy wrapped her arms around Jaz and hugged her tightly. Jaz instantly liked her.

'Thank you for having me,' said Jaz, as Kathy stepped back to let them in the house.

'Come, everyone's in the dining room.'

Jaz followed Ryan down the narrow corridor, but slowed upon seeing family photos along the wall. Kathy's home felt so warm and loving, not big and cold. It was a massive change from Marcus's house.

'Is this Ryan?' said Jaz stopping by a photo of a boy about six with a cowboy outfit on, two plastic guns in his hand.

'Oh yes. He loved those guns. Didn't you, sweetheart? And this one is Ryan at his graduation.'

Jaz followed Kathy's finger to the next photo on the wall. God, Ryan at seventeen was still a hunk. Jaz wished she could be back there at that time and be the girl hanging off his arm.

Jaz didn't get to study the picture further. Ryan had come back and was now pulling her arm. 'Enough of that or Mum will have you going through everything. Dinner's waiting.'

'Spoilsport,' said Jaz as she glanced back to Kathy, who gave her a secretive wink.

Ryan let go of her arm when they reached a doorway into a small dining room. There was an archway on one wall into the kitchen. Again, the rooms were small, covered with photos and things collected over the years. The wood-look flooring looked new though.

'Yay, you made it,' said Steph who was sitting at the small six-seater table. Beside her was a handsome guy with shaggy brown hair and dimples that made his smile even cuter. At the head of the table sat Ryan's dad. He had to be. Strong and solidly built, with a presence that commanded respect. Jaz felt drawn to him, whether it was because Ryan was so much like him or because he made her feel safe and protected. But the way he was looking at Steph was every part the doting loving father.

Ryan's dad turned to follow Steph's gaze and the grin that spread across his face upon seeing his son was momentous.

'This is my dad, Frank,' said Ryan, who was trying to introduce them, but his dad only had eyes for his son. He got up from his chair and hugged Ryan. It was like two bears colliding. When Frank pulled back he gently gripped Ryan's face in his hands. 'I can't believe you're here. It's a miracle,' he teased.

'Come on, Dad, it hasn't been that long,' said Ryan, shaking him off.

Frank scoffed in disbelief. 'Sure. You probably don't even remember Gazza,' he said waving towards Steph's boyfriend.

Ryan leaned over the table to shake Gazza's hand. 'Of course I do. How are ya, Gazza?'

'All right. And you?'

Gazza's eyes went to Jaz and Ryan turned, as if remembering she'd actually come with him. 'Oh, everyone this is Jaz. Jaz, my dad, Frank, and Steph's boyfriend, Gazza.'

'Hi, nice to meet you all.' Jaz felt like a fish in a tiny glass bowl as they all stared at her. Had she sprouted an extra arm overnight?

'Sorry, Ryan hasn't brought anyone home since he left school. Please, grab a seat and I'll bring dinner out,' said Kathy, indicating the closest two chairs.

'Yeah, Ryan,' said Steph. 'Mum wouldn't serve dinner until you arrived. I thought I'd be starving all night,' she teased.

Ryan pulled a face at Steph, and Jaz realised how much she was enjoying this night already.

'So, we hardly see you, son, and then here you are with a beautiful girlfriend as well. We are so happy to meet you, Jaz,' said Frank, as Ryan started waving his hands at his dad. 'We've been hoping Ryan would find himself a lady. He's never brought anyone home before. How long have you two been together?' he asked, looking directly at Jaz. Frank hadn't even seen Ryan's attempts to stop him.

But right now all eyes were on her and Jaz could feel a red hot flush working its way up to her face. It was going to contradict everything she was about to say.

CHAPTER 25

'Oh, um, we're not dating,' Jaz said, shaking her head. 'We're just friends. I actually have a boyfriend.'

'Yes, I remember. The guy you went to the ball with. Did you take photos?' asked Steph.

Jaz pulled out her phone and pulled up a photo. 'His name is Marcus,' Jaz said to the others as she handed her phone across the table to Steph.

'Wow, he's cute,' said Steph. 'Sexy with the long hair.'

Ryan fidgeted in the chair beside her.

Kathy put a great big lasagne on the table next to the large bowl of salad, before leaning over Steph's shoulder to see the photo. 'Oh Jaz, you look gorgeous. Did you see this, Ryan?' she asked.

Ryan cleared his throat and busied himself with the salad, his eyes down.

Steph showed Gazza and Frank instead.

'A long-haired lout?' said Frank teasingly.

'No, he's really sweet and caring. Always puts me first and always thoughtful. Steph, flick the photos forward a few,' said Jaz. 'There are some of the pictures he's drawn. A real talent.'

'Oh my God, that's amazing. He's captured you perfectly, Jaz. I can tell how much he cares just by this drawing,' said Steph, who then showed the picture around.

'So, Dad, how's Rusty going? Still getting around?' said Ryan.

Steph ignored Ryan's attempt at a new conversation and pushed Jaz's phone over the table to him. 'Check it out, Ry. Look at Jaz.'

Ryan took the phone with a sigh. Jaz thought he'd just pass it straight back to her, but instead, once he saw it, he paused. He sat staring at the drawing of her; Jaz was dying to know what he was thinking.

'See, he's read her well, right?' said Steph.

Ryan passed the phone back to Jaz while his eyes remained on his plate. 'Ah, yeah. It's good.' His voice was strained.

Steph watched her brother while Gazza loaded up his plate. Kathy returned from the kitchen with a bottle of wine and filled up Frank's glass.

'So, Dad, how's Rusty?' Ryan asked again.

'Oh, Rusty's fine. Still kicking on.' He turned to Jaz. 'He's fifteen now. Not bad considering he got hit by a car last year. He's a Labrador, tough as nails. He was Ryan's dog – got him for his ninth birthday?' He glanced to Kathy to confer and she nodded as though it was close enough. 'But then he became our dog after Ryan moved out.'

'I told you I couldn't look after him. My work is too hectic and Rusty wouldn't get the love and care I know he gets here,' said Ryan. 'I s'pose he's overfed and fat?'

'No, he's not,' said Kathy.

Steph snorted. 'Mum, he *is* fat. That is not muscle around his mid section,' she said with an eye roll.

Kathy shrugged and then turned her focus to Jaz. 'So, if you and Ryan aren't dating, how did you meet?'

Jaz assumed this was another one of those curly questions Ryan wanted avoided but she was sure she could explain it quite truthfully. 'Well, I work at my local gym and Ryan came in. We both love staying fit and working out, so we became friends from a mutual love, I guess you could say.' Jaz turned to smile at Ryan and found him watching her intently. 'Right?'

He smiled back. One of those smiles that took her breath away. One he usually kept for special occasions. It confused her that she was getting such an honest smile now, considering how unreadable he'd been lately.

'That's right,' he agreed.

A shiver spread throughout her body and Jaz hoped no one could notice just how one smile and the deep velvet of his voice could affect her.

Jaz needed a distraction, and quickly. 'So, Gazza, how did you and Steph meet?' she asked him.

He finished his mouthful and glanced at Steph. The adoration shone brightly from his vivid green eyes. 'We both love football and Steph was helping out at our local club. It was impossible not to notice her,' he said blushing a little. 'I knew I had to make my move quick before my teammates spotted her.'

Steph put her fork down and held Gazza's hand. 'I only ever had eyes for you,' she said. She mouthed the word 'Now' to him and he grinned. 'I guess now is as good a time as any.' Steph smiled at her mum and then turned back to Frank, who gave a nod. 'Mum, I know it's your special anniversary dinner. You two are an inspiration for us and I hope we can reach the same milestones that you guys have. And to make tonight even more special… Gazza asked me to marry him and I said yes,' she said with an excited rush.

'Oh my God!' screamed Kathy, jumping up from her chair.

Madness ensued. There were hugs and handshakes all around as food was left to cool on plates. As Jaz gave Steph a hug, she had a weird feeling of inclusion, as if she'd been accepted into their family without hesitation as she shared their special news. 'Congrats, Steph.'

'Thanks, Jaz.' Steph held her shoulders and smiled at her in a funny way. 'Now we just need to find Ryan a girl,' she said with a wink.

Jaz had a feeling of déjà vu. It was as if Steph could read her just like Anna. A nervous laugh erupted from Jaz. 'Good luck with that, I don't think he wants one,' she said.

'Maybe he's just waiting for the right one to come along,' Steph whispered to her before Ryan came to congratulate her.

Well, Ryan wasn't waiting for Jaz, that much was real. He'd once said that they could never be together because they worked for MTG and the Agency didn't allow relationships between their operatives. Jaz was sure it was just some nonsense he was making up to keep her at a safe distance. It sounded like old-age crap. If he really wanted to be with her, Ryan was the kind of bloke who wouldn't let anything stop him. Obviously, she wasn't worth it.

After dinner, they sat in the lounge room and talked. Jaz was amazed at the way Ryan spun out fake details of his life and what he'd been up too. She wondered if any ever came back to bite him. And the scary thing was, Jaz was really no different with her family. They weren't operatives for MTG, they were actually just paid liars. Well that's what it felt like sometimes.

Jaz sat beside Kathy and Steph on the cream leather three-seater and listened as they told stories about Ryan when he was younger. Ryan sat by his father and Gazza discussing sports. Every now and then she'd catch his gaze and he would hold it for a moment, but she couldn't read his thoughts. Did he find it strange having her in his parents' house? Was he uncomfortable watching her chat to his family? She dismissed that thought straightaway. No, Ryan didn't look annoyed. He seemed content and reflective. It was better than the anger she'd seen earlier that night.

'So, how long have you and Marcus been going out for? Is it serious?' asked Steph.

All of a sudden, Jaz felt the room go quiet, as if all ears were tuned in to her answer. 'Um, for a few weeks now I guess.' Blood was pounding in her ears as her heart raced from being centre of attention and put on the spot. How much did she divulge? Then a wicked thought came to her. Setting up Ryan seemed like fun. 'He's actually making me a romantic dinner tomorrow night. He has the house to himself, so he's going all out,' she said, trying to keep her voice full of excitement at the prospect. Especially considering the thought made her feel a little anxious.

Jaz really wanted to glance at Ryan and see what he thought of this news but she couldn't do it.

'Oh, look out. Looks like someone's about to get lucky,' teased Steph.

Kathy scoffed at Steph, and Jaz tried hard to stop the flush she felt building.

But she also hoped Ryan had heard every word.

Jaz had had enough of the limelight. 'So, have you set a date yet?' she asked Steph.

'Not yet. Next year sometime. I don't want to wait too long. Maybe you can be Ryan's plus-one.' She smiled, and Jaz got that familiar feeling Steph was hinting at something.

'If he hasn't got himself a girl by then I reckon I'd try,' said Jaz truthfully. 'I've never been to a wedding. You'll look stunning.'

'Thanks, Jaz. And don't worry. Somehow, I doubt my dear busy brother will have found himself a girl. He's too work-focused. We're all amazed he managed to find you as a friend.'

Jaz laughed. 'Only because I run the place he frequents.' She realised how glad she was that Ryan had come into The Ring. Her life would seem so empty without him.

'But you can see why we eagerly jumped to conclusions,' added Kathy. 'We just want him to be happy.'

'Oh yes, I can understand that. Just having Marcus makes me realise how wonderful it is to have someone to hold you and love you unconditionally,' said Jaz. She loved the way Marcus freely gave himself to her and wished Ryan could be more like him, instead of giving her bits but then snatching them away again, each time ripping out a chunk of her heart. Didn't he realise? Pakistan had left her wounded in so many ways.

'You okay, Jaz?' asked Kathy. 'You look a little pale.'

'No, I'm fine. Just tired. I've had a few late nights,' said Jaz. She glanced at Ryan without thinking and found him watching her again. Damn, she wished he wouldn't do that.

'We should probably head off, it is getting late,' said Ryan, with concern.

Jaz really didn't want to go, she loved his family but she found trying to stay on her feet with the lies quite tiring. And his parents were endless with their questions. They seemed to be making up for lost time.

Everyone followed them out as they headed for the door.

'Make sure you both come back for dinner again. Jaz, can you make sure to bring him back?' asked Kathy as she hugged her goodbye.

Steph swapped phone numbers with Jaz before saying goodbye. Ryan didn't look impressed.

'This way, when you won't come I can get Jaz to herd you here. Either that or she can just come on her own,' said Steph, giving Ryan an evil eye. Steph put her hand on Jaz. 'Or we could just do coffee and talk about him,' she teased.

'Sure, I'd like that,' said Jaz. 'See you, Frank.' She hugged Ryan's dad and felt a lump in her throat. Ryan was so much like him. 'Bye Gazza. I hope Steph doesn't go all bridezilla on you,' she teased.

'Oh, I'm counting on it,' he said, smiling back.

They all waved them from the front porch as they jumped in Ryan's car and left.

'You have an awesome family. They miss you. You should make the effort to see them more,' she said softly.

A few seconds later, she only just caught his words. 'I know.'

Ryan drove her straight back to her house but, as usual, parked a few houses down.

'Thanks, Ryan. I had a great night. You're very lucky,' she said.

She reached to open the door but as she went to move, Ryan's voice pulled her up.

'Jaz?'

He sounded desperate.

'What?'

Ryan sat holding the steering wheel, looking straight ahead. 'Tomorrow… don't do anything you'll regret.'

Her chest tightened and her breathing shallowed. Was he warning her? He'd really been listening at his parents' house. 'I'm sure I won't regret it,' she said with a smile. Jaz felt like she was poking a sleeping dragon. What would Ryan do?

She made to move again, but this time Ryan's hand stopped her. It was hot against her arm, spreading a sensation through her like a dizzying drug. He was her addiction. How did she quit? Did she want to quit? She wished he would hurry up and say what he wanted to say.

'Jaz, just don't do it. You don't have to. You have nothing to prove.'

'Why not? Anything to help the mission, right?' she said. When he didn't answer, Jaz wondered just how many times he'd done that for a mission and with whom. It made her green with envy. And a little sick to her stomach.

His continued silence began to make her angry. Who was he to tell her what she could and couldn't do?

'Promise me, Jaz,' he said softly.

'No,' she said shaking off his hand. 'Why should I. What's it to you what I do anyway. You don't care, and quite frankly it's none of your business.'

'I don't want to see you get hurt.' His voice was still gentle and it just pissed her off even more.

'Well, don't watch then,' she said. He was back gripping the wheel like it was a stress ball. His voice had seemed calm but his body said otherwise. 'I might get hurt but I'm prepared for that. I'm willing to take certain risks for reward, Ryan. Are you?' Jaz gave him a few seconds, and when he didn't reply she opened his door and got out. She stopped herself from slamming his door and walked to her house without a backwards glance. She would not give him the satisfaction.

CHAPTER 26

Jaz pulled up outside Marcus's house and sat in her Jeep for a long while. She still hadn't decided where tonight was going to go. She knew what she wanted. Ryan. But he didn't want her. And Marcus? He was perfect and sweet. There was nothing wrong with him. Well, besides his dad was dodgy. And he wasn't Ryan. But in any other life, one in which Ryan didn't exist, Jaz would jump at the chance to be with Marcus. Except, this was her life and these were the facts she had to deal with.

Finally, she decided to just wing it, and climbed out of her Jeep. *Live in the moment*, she told herself. *Just see where her mood takes us both.*

Her car wasn't the only one in the driveway. She ran a finger along Carl's sleek car, and just knowing he was inside scared her. Would there be any chance he'd noticed her at the fish-and-chip shop? She'd been sure she wasn't recognised, but still, her pulse raced on as she reached for the door buzzer.

It opened seconds later. Jaz hoped for Marcus, but it was Carl.

'Hey, Jaz. Good to see you again. You look nice,' he said, eyeing off her vintage blue dress. He was all smiles and the good vibes of a nice guy who cared for his family – and who thought nothing of dealing in drugs that killed people every day.

Jaz forced a smile as thoughts raced through her mind. *Does he keep a gun in his office? Should I look?*

'Thanks, Carl,' she managed to say. 'You heading back to work?'

'Sure am. No rest for the wicked,' he said, and let her in before heading to his car.

Jaz watched him go and wondered just how wicked he was.

'Hey gorgeous.' Marcus's arms wrapped around her waist. She leaned back against him as his lips pressed against her neck. 'I'm glad you're here. Come inside. Dad'll be gone for ages.'

Marcus had everything set up. Popcorn to go with a movie, then he'd pasta pre-made for dinner – and Jaz didn't want to think what came after that. She prayed for ice-cream or chocolate.

She tried to relax through the movie but she felt cold in their large house, especially after being at Kathy and Frank's warm and cosy place the night before. Even when she was snuggled into Marcus's arms.

Jaz tried hard to focus on the movie but she missed chunks of it, even though she was staring at the TV. How late would Carl be? What was he doing? Should she go through his office again? What should she do tonight with Marcus? Did he expect it? Should she heed Ryan's warning? Were Anna and Taylor okay?

It didn't help that Marcus was running his fingers over her arm in a rhythmic motion. It was making her sleepy, but she didn't want to think about bed right now.

Jaz pushed herself up in the couch so she was more alert, and tried to watch the movie. But it finished five minutes later and Jaz still missed the whole plot.

'You okay? You're very quiet,' he asked as they walked to the kitchen to start on dinner.

'Yeah I'm fine. Just a little tired. Anna kept me up most of the night. We'll blame her,' she said laughing. She watched as Marcus held up a bottle of wine.

'A glass with dinner?' he asked.

'Thanks, that would be nice. But only one, I have to drive home and mum will kill me if she knows I had a glass.' Maybe she needed something to take the edge off her nerves. One would be her limit; she needed her wits in case she went off snooping.

The wine did relax her and she enjoyed chatting with Marcus over the macaroni cheese he'd made. It wasn't quite the roast she'd smelt at Ryan's house a while back but he did have more years under his belt. It was about nine o'clock when they finished and Jaz took their dishes to the dishwasher. 'Will your dad be home for dinner?' she asked.

'Who knows? I'm sure when he's out late he eats at the office.' He must have seen Jaz's expression and taken it for something else. 'He's not always out late. Usually only a few nights a month when a big shipment comes in and needs cataloguing.'

'Don't worry, my dad practically lives at his office. Some people work because they have to, but I think Paul works because he just loves it. Simon takes after him. Me, I like to Mars Bar it: work, rest and play,' she said with a laugh.

Marcus pulled her to him and laughed. 'I like to play too.' Linking his fingers with hers, he led her back to the lounge. He changed the TV channel to a music one before sweeping her up in his arms to move to the beat. Lana Del Rey's voice was soothing and romantic. Jaz laid her head on his shoulder, closed her eyes and swayed with him.

His soft lips pressed against her shoulder, slowly working their way up to her neck and below her ear. His hands ran over her back, down to her bum and squeezed her closer. Jaz let herself go. She welcomed him when he finally found her lips. As she kissed him back her hands snaked up his shirt as if searching for something, maybe the ripple of a scar, but she didn't find anything but smooth skin. Marcus stepped back, pulled off his shirt and reached for her again, cupping her face in his hands. Jaz kept her eyes closed as her hands roamed over his chest and down to the top of his jeans. A fire was beginning to ignite inside of her, the pressure of a hand against her breast, another one under her dress squeezing her backside. Finally, she could feel herself trembling.

Marcus pulled back a fraction, his lips leaving hers moist. 'Was that your phone?'

Jaz pried her eyes open as his words registered. 'Oh, maybe.' She slipped her hand into the small pocket on her dress and pulled out her phone. 'Yep, it was.' Damn, it was on vibrate.

Jaz froze when she saw who the message was from. It was from 'Dark', her code name for Ryan and his dark, mysterious eyes. She swallowed as a sweat broke out. Was the heater on? Jaz tapped to open his message. Just three words.

I do care.

Her heart lurched and her legs lost all strength.

'Are you okay? Is it bad news?' asked Marcus.

Jaz brought her eyes up to his while her mind raced. Why had Ryan sent this now? To stop her? To tease her? What did this mean? Did he *care* care or just care enough not to want her to sleep with a target? Oh, what did all this mean! Either way it had probably done its job. Jaz had lost any interest in being here with Marcus.

'It is. I'm sorry, I have to go. Simon's had an asthma attack.' Yet another lie trickling from her lips. Jaz took small comfort in the fact that Simon did actually have asthma, but he hadn't had an attack since he was four.

But it still made her feel terrible when she saw the real concern on Marcus's face. He wasn't worried that their night was interrupted. 'Can I do anything? Drive you home?'

Jaz put her phone away and touched her hand to his cheek. His deep sea-green eyes were so alive and bright. 'Thanks, but I'll get home okay. Thank you for being so understanding.' She leaned forward and kissed him with everything she could give him. He deserved so much more.

'Wow,' he said as she stopped. 'Can we pick this up another time?'

Jaz didn't know what to say, so she just nodded and gave him a reassuring smile. Then he walked her to the door, not even bothering to put his shirt back on.

'Thanks for an amazing night. I'm sorry I have to rush off.'

'No, go to your brother. He's important. Text me, let me know how he's going?'

'I will.' Jaz squeezed his hand, and then ran to her Jeep while fishing for her keys in her other pocket.

It wasn't until she was back home, parked in the driveway, that she pulled out her phone and read Ryan's text again. How could three little words throw her so much? She was angry with him. So angry. Why did he do it? Did he enjoy toying with her emotions? Was he serious? Her heart refused to believe he was admitting he liked her. It hurt too much when he pushed her away last time. He was clever; he knew those words would upset her enough to leave Marcus.

Jaz got out of her Jeep before she screamed or hit the steering wheel. She stomped to the house. She told her parents she was just getting some stuff and staying the night with Taylor.

'Why? Did something happen?' Tasha asked, getting up and walking to her.

'No. Well, kind of. I just want to cool things with Marcus, and Anna is with Taylor, so I'm sure they can help me feel better,' she said.

Her mum seemed relieved the moment the words 'cool things with Marcus' were uttered. 'Okay. I'm here if you need me.'

'Thanks, Mum. I'll be okay.'

Jaz sprinted up the stairs to her room and changed out of her dress. She put on black leggings, black boots and her black skivvy. She chucked a jumper over the top just in case her mum saw her on her way back down. Then she packed her black beanie, gloves and a change of clothes into a bag, along with her Canon camera. She stopped in the kitchen, checked everyone was still busy doing their own thing before she raided the freezer for meat, and hid that in her bag too.

She needed enough to keep a snarling dog happy. She also took the Swiss Army knife from the top drawer, just in case.

CHAPTER 27

Jaz drove to Taylor's house and left her car nearby on the road. Taylor was home, along with his dad, which Jaz was happy to see his car at home for once. Without disturbing them, she called a taxi. She didn't want to risk her car being found near the warehouse in case they linked it back to her, so it was safer left near Taylor's house. When the taxi picked her up, she took only the things she'd need: her phone, beanie, the bag of meat camera and the switchblade.

'Just here, thanks,' she directed the driver when he was close to the warehouse. He dropped her in a residential area, but now she had to leave the safety of streetlights and homes to walk towards the darker industrial space. It was gloomy and getting late, probably around ten o'clock, she guessed. She was too scared to check her phone for the time incase the brightness of the screen gave her away. She stuck to the shadowed bush line so passing drivers – especially Carl – couldn't recognise her in their headlights.

When she reached the trees that edged his warehouse area Jaz pulled her skivvy up over her chin and then put on her beanie, pulling it low. It managed to cover most of her face. Her hair was piled up on her head so the beanie covered it all. She'd morphed into a black ninja, something Anna had always called her when she accidently dressed in black. Tonight she just hoped she could live up to the name if needed.

Jaz looked out over the yard. It was black but she could see the building and the outline of the sea containers. No outside lights were on, just the glow from the inside ones. From her last visit she knew there was a light sensor near the office, so she'd have to go the other side, near the toilets. She only wanted to look in a window and see if she could witness something naughty.

As she moved closer to the fence she saw that the main gate was ajar. On closer inspection, it had been loosely locked, leaving just enough space for her to squeeze through.

Her pulse was pounding in her wrists, and she seriously wondered if she should be doing this. Maybe they were complacent and maybe they wouldn't think to look outside and she could remain undetected. She knew that if they gave chase, she could at least get back through the gate, whereas they would have to unlock it first. Jaz squished her body through the small gap. Every movement was careful and when the chain rattled against the gate, she paused in fright, half-expecting Cujo to bark the alarm. When she was satisfied that all she could hear was her frantic breaths and the soft thrum of voices from the warehouse, she continued through the gate. Each step was carefully placed so the gravel wouldn't crunch loudly.

Jaz made her way to the left, trying not to trip over the pallets that were stacked by the warehouse wall. Her hand was holding the bag of defrosting meat, ready to throw at anything hairy and snarling. Cujo was tied up last time she visited, so she hoped he was only let off when no one was here. With a bit of luck, the dog was inside with Tommy.

The only window along this side of the warehouse was to the toilets. Damn, she wouldn't see much through that. Jaz didn't want to go to the other side of the warehouse near Cujo or the open shed door: that would be too risky, and she was nowhere near ready to be mauled by a dog or get caught. She glanced up at the toilet window; it was black so it must be empty. It had bar work over it but the slats of glass could be removed. Jaz felt a plan forming in her mind.

She felt to the side where the pallets were. Would she be able to stack them quietly? With as much stealth as possible, Jaz put her bag of meat down and picked up a crate. It wasn't light, but it wasn't heavy either. It was difficult to carry because of its shape. She moved one under the window and realised she'd need at least another six.

Another pallet down. Jaz stopped. Listened. When all she could hear was the adrenaline pumping through her body, she continued. Another pallet. When she had seven stacked, she lifted her leg and climbed on top of them. It gave her just enough height to reach the windows with her hands if she stood on tippy-toes to see in. No wonder they didn't worry about this window; anyone would need a ladder. Jaz got down and stacked two more. Her arms were feeling sore from trying to control each pallet quietly. When she got back up this time she had a much better view, but she couldn't see anything without a light on. The wooden architrave around the window was rotten and wobbly. Some of the screws holding the bars up over the window were loose, so Jaz took the switchblade from her pocket and used the Phillips head to unscrew the bar work. It wasn't easy with her gloves on, but there was no way she was taking them off and leaving evidence.

Jaz pulled the bars free and nearly fell back as the stack of pallets rocked. If she'd been game enough to speak she would have sworn. With the bars held up over her head, she regained her footing and then slowly pulled out each slat of glass from the window.

As she heaved herself up into the open window, she had a frantic thought: how would she get back out? She took out her phone out and checked it was on silent before switching on the torch to see into the bathroom.

There were two toilet cubicles, and right under the window was the hand basin. That was her exit. She could work with that. Sliding her phone back into her leggings she climbed through the window frame. It wasn't graceful and it took a while to manoeuvre herself around and ease herself down. *Please don't need to pee*, she chanted silently as she watched the door of the toilets. Unless she suddenly morphed into Spiderwoman, there was nowhere for her to hide in the window.

Once she was inside, she collected her breath before stepping to the door. The handle was cold as she gripped it and turned it as calmly as possible. She could hear metal being moved and tools dropped to the floor, along with voices, and hoped that these would cover any noise she made.

She pulled it slightly ajar, just enough so she could see through it. Inside, the warehouse was flooded with light. It looked much the same as it did when she had visisted with Marcus: bubble wrap, boxes and the sea container. Only, this container was a different colour. A new one?

A skinny man dressed in blue workman's clothes and a beanie came out of the container. Jaz looked for any features she could lock away for later. She couldn't see his eye colour but he was unshaven and he did have a funny walk, as if his back were sore. He carried something, and Jaz followed his path to where another, similarly dressed, man stood. His lips were moving but she couldn't hear what he was saying. Something about, 'This is it. Last one,' if her lip-reading was right. He passed the package over to the other guy, who turned. Jaz instantly recognised the bald head and face. Tommy.

'Let's go,' she heard him say. Lights were then turned off, and the screech of a metal door being slid closed pierced the night.

Jaz stayed frozen behind the door, listening as the truck drove off, then waited another five minutes before carefully opening the door.

Using her mobile as a torch, Jaz stepped towards the sea container. She didn't dare make a sound in case she stirred up Cujo, and she was a little worried they might have other sensors or alarms. Anything was possible with drug dealers. Taylor's dad had told them many stories of the booby traps set up around drug crops, but they were out in the middle of the bush. At least here it was all locked up. Well, except for the bathroom. Jaz didn't dare crack a smile, she was not out of this yet. And she didn't have anything to show for her break-and-enter either.

She shone the light into the sea container. It was empty. She moved the light around the warehouse. There were no masses of artwork or sculptures. Where did it all go so quickly?

She focused on the fact that the skinny guy had walked out with something in his hands. So, Jaz took a few steps inside the sea container. About three quarters of the way down she saw welding gear. Moving the light, she noticed some metal panels. Long and skinny, just like the size of one of the ripples in the sea container. Jaz got closer and trod on something squishy.

'Please don't let it be a body part,' she whispered as she took a look.

A black mouldy lump. It could be anything. Jaz squatted down for a better inspection and found a few more, and then a pile near the wall of the container. Where her foot had squished this one she could see a familiar pattern. Oranges? Really old and rank oranges.

Jaz moved up the ripple panel on the container. If that had been welded closed and filled up with drugs – well, that would be a lot of drugs.

Jaz wondered how it wasn't picked up. Maybe the oranges killed the scent of the drugs for the dogs? Didn't they X-ray these containers? Jaz would have to ask Ryan. She was sure he knew a lot more about the process than anyone else in her world.

And realistically, who would see anything wrong with some welded bits? This sea container was bashed and dented all over. Jaz took her phone and did a circle along the walls of the container and found a spot on the other side where another panel may have been. Whoever had cut the panel off hadn't bothered to make it neat. No doubt this sea container wouldn't be used again. Is that why the others were outside? They had done their job. Is this why Carl was interested in that sea container sale?

Jaz moved to the outside of the container and looked for its number. It wasn't the same as the one he'd written down in his office, so did that mean there was a container waiting at a yard for the sale with drugs in it?

Had she just figured out how Carl's operation worked? Could they catch them in the act with the next container? Jaz felt an excited buzz jump through her body. Two seconds later, she was telling herself to get the hell out of here after taking a few photos. But not many as the flash freaked her out and felt like a bloody beacon that any passing ships could see from far out at sea.

The only way back out was the toilet. She crept back in, shut the door and then scaled the wall.

Using the basin to heave herself up to the window didn't go according to plan, as it let off a crack, pulling away from the wall. 'Shit.' *Please don't notice that*, she thought.

Jaz didn't get far before she heard Cujo start barking. And what was worse was that she could follow the barks as he ran around the warehouse to her window.

She wasn't going to make it down in time to reach the meat and open the bag. Jaz decided to stay still and hope he left or found the meat himself. Cujo settled down and Jaz risked taking a look.

She couldn't see much in the darkness outside and had to wait for her eyes to adjust, but she could make out the outline of a dog by the pallets she'd stacked. It was hard to tell if he was eating the meat or not, but after a minute she heard the rustle of a bag. This might be her only chance.

Lifting herself up again she got halfway out of the window. Cujo began to snarl. Was he protecting his food now? This wasn't how it was supposed to go. In the movies you throw the dog some steak and it's happy. Cujo wasn't an easily pleased pooch. Jaz got a leg out and was going to try to get down anyway while Cujo was at least half-occupied. Turning herself in the window she began to lower herself slowly so not to spook Cujo. Somehow she didn't think talking to Cujo softly and calling his name would settle him or make them lifelong friends.

Jaz heard the movement just before she felt the tug on her foot. Cujo probably would have barked if her foot wasn't in his mouth. The bloody dog was jerking himself backwards, trying to pull Jaz from her hold. If she went down, there was no knowing what he would do. Using her strength, she tried to shake off Cujo and lift herself. The weight of the dog dangling from her foot didn't help. Luckily her commando boots were heavy duty; anything else and her foot would be shredded by now.

Jaz broke free and got herself back inside the toilet cubicle, where she sat on the floor to gather her breath. Her foot was fine, apart from feeling like it had been squished in a vice. So much for this night being a simple recon mission. Had she blown it? Should she suck up her pride and call Ryan? Right now Jaz couldn't see a way out of this that didn't involve taking on a dog. And she wasn't going to stay here all night just to get caught in the morning. She needed help. She needed Ryan.

Taking a deep breath, she tried to calm her nerves and ready herself for Ryan's angry onslaught. She pulled off a glove and rang his number, hoping to God he was at home and not out on a mission. Worse than Ryan answering his phone was hearing it ring out and go to his message bank. No, she didn't want to leave a message. What would she say anyway? *Come help me, I'm trapped in a loo by a vicious dog.* The only other person who knew what she was up to was Pax, and ringing him would only worry his heart, and she didn't think he'd be especially nimble on his feet if they had to run. Did Pax even have a gun? She'd never thought to ask him. But she knew someone who did. Someone she trusted and knew would help.

She pressed his number and waited for him to pick up. 'Hi Tay. Don't talk, just listen. Can you come and get me? I'm in trouble. Bring a gun, some bolt cutters and steak.'

Jaz knew she'd probably have to repeat her request to Taylor. It's not every day your friend rings up asking for those three things.

'What the hell have you got yourself into?' he asked.

'I've no time to explain. Just come to that address, make sure you park away in the dark so your car can't be seen. And bring a loaded gun. We may need it to shoot the dog if the steak doesn't work, or in case the bad guys come back.' The phone went quiet. Taylor probably thought she'd taken something hallucinogenic. 'Look, it's all got to do with Ryan and his work. I promise I'll fill you in later, but right now I need you. Can you do it?'

'Of course, Jaz,' he said without hesitation. 'I'll be there a quick as I can.'

'Thanks Tay. Oh, and wear black. And a beanie,' she said before they hung up.

Talking with Taylor had lifted her mood. She would be all right now. He would be sneaking around the house unlocking the gun cabinet and finding bullets. Jaz just hoped they didn't need them.

Five minutes later, she heard a vehicle approaching. Taylor was quick. Then Jaz realised it couldn't possibly be her friend because he wouldn't be able to drive straight up to the warehouse. *Oh shit.*

She could hear voices muffled next door in the office section. What the hell should she do? Taylor would be walking right into trouble. Did she text him? What if his phone wasn't on silent? Could she risk it? Jaz stayed hidden in the toilet cubicle while she tried to figure out what to do. How long until they left?

Maybe now was her chance to escape. Maybe they had retied Cujo?

There was only one way to find out. Jaz scrambled back up the wall, trying not to crack the sink any more than she already had. With half her body leaning outside the window she waited for her eyes to adjust and kept her ears strained for noise. She couldn't see Cujo or hear any movement from the other side of the warehouse.

Quickly she manoeuvred herself out and onto the pallets. They rattled slightly with her weight, the glass panes clinking against each other.

All of a sudden, her legs were being crushed together and dragged off the pallets. She fell to the ground with her attacker still clutching at her legs.

'What the hell are you doing here?' growled a man's voice as he held her tightly.

She could not be caught. Using her free arms she lashed out at him, trying to break his hold. He was thin and scrawny and she knew which bloke it was. They rolled around on the gravel, pushing and pulling, punching and dodging in the dark.

Jaz got an elbow to her cheek, but she managed to get a knee free and aimed for his groin.

He groaned, and Jaz worried that Cujo or Tommy might come looking. She had to move quickly. But just when she felt like she was winning the fight, landing all her blows, he pulled out a gun from the back of his pants. The moonlight glistened on its metallic form.

Instantly Jaz jumped onto his chest, both hands pushing the gun away. The man's breath was rank, like stale cigarettes and scotch. She arched back and then headbutted him, causing the gun to relax from his grip and go sprawling off into the dark. Jaz tried to crawl over him to reach for the gun but his fingers wrapped around her jumper. Her hands scratched at the ground, searching for the gun, a rock, anything she could use. Her wrist banged against something solid and hard. A brick. Grabbing for it she felt a nail rip off, but the pain wasn't there. Just this life and death adrenaline feeding her to fight. Jaz pulled back with all her might, lifting the brick in both hands. Closing her eyes, she brought it down hard on the man's head. The crunch sickened her, and for a moment she fought the bile rising in her throat. His hands went slack, dropping from her waist. Dragging herself off him, she crawled along the gravel, grabbed the gun and got her breath back. She didn't know if she'd just knocked him out or whether it was much worse. Could she have killed him? Was he bleeding out? She couldn't tell anything in this dark. Before she could stand, the sound of footsteps froze her. Was it Taylor?

A beam of light came around the edge of the warehouse. 'Digger, what the hell are you doing and why does Cujo have a steak? Bloody dog won't move from his kennel.'

His torchlight hit the body. Jaz tried to stand in the dark, hoping to move behind the pallets.

'Holy shit, Digger,' said Tommy, before she heard a gun cocked and the beam of light flicked around, searching.

Jaz turned to run as the bright light swept in her direction. A shot rang out and simultaneously she was thrown to the ground, a dull ache coming from her leg.

'Turn over slowly. Who are you and what are you doing here?' he demanded.

Jaz tried to sit up but moving her leg caused pain. She reached down and felt a gooey wetness. She'd been shot!

'Did you hear me? I said turn around.'

But she didn't want to turn around and let Tommy recognise her. Plus she was struggling with the relisation she'd been shot. Bloody hell.

'Put your gun down,' came a familiar voice. Jaz had never been so happy to hear Taylor.

Tommy swung around, dropping the torch. Its light sprayed against the warehouse wall. Tommy and Taylor were facing off, guns pointed.

'You're just a kid,' said Tommy. 'You wouldn't even know how to use that.' As Tommy's arm flexed to fire, two guns went off.

A body fell to the ground as Jaz looked at Taylor. Both of them still had their guns trained on Tommy. 'I don't think he's going to get up,' said Jaz eventually.

'Not with two bullets in him.' Taylor picked up the torch so he could see Tommy's wounds. Then he felt for a pulse. 'Shit. He's dead.' His face was pale, his eyes filled with confusion.

'Thanks for saving my life, Tay, but we need to get out of here now.'

'There's another guy. Did you...?' He stepped over to the skinny guy and she heard him dry-retch. 'Oh, he's not good either.' He staggered back to Jaz. The light from the torch picked up the slick shiny blood running down Jaz's leg. 'You're shot.'

'Ya think. Can you help me back to the car?'

Taylor tucked his gun into his pants and then got under Jaz's arm to help her.

'Is your car far?'

'Not far, can you make it?'

'I hope so. People will have heard those gunshots. We gotta move.'

'What about them?' he asked.

'Not much we can do. Maybe they'll think it was a break-in?'

Taylor shone the way while Jaz tried not to drag her leg. They'd probably follow her marks. The gates were open. They kept moving towards the tree line on the other side of the road where Taylor had hidden his car.

'Wait here,' said Taylor, as Jaz leaned against the Mustang.

'I'm not going anywhere,' she joked dryly.

Taylor had pulled a shirt off his back seat and tied it around her leg.

'Ouch, careful. It hurts.'

'I bet it does. Let's get you to a hospital before you bleed out,' he said, opening the door and helping her in.

Jaz still had the man's gun in her hand. The solid form of it between her fingers usually wasn't so scary. Not at the range it wasn't, but holding one that had just been fired and taken a life? That was a whole different ball game.

Taylor started driving and they didn't look back. 'Take back streets and take me to Ryan's house.'

'What? No. You need a hospital.'

'Taylor,' said Jaz, feeling rather woozy. 'We can't go to a hospital, they'll find us. Promise me you'll take me to Ryan's.'

He nodded. Relieved, she put her hand to her head. It was sore from the headbutt and the elbow she'd taken. Her face felt swollen. Life felt like it was leaking out of her as she drooped in the seat. She didn't know if she'd have enough energy to get out of the car. Then she thought of Tilly, who had driven them through Pakistan after being shot in the arm.

'I'm sorry if I get blood in your 'Stang,' she said.

'Oh Jaz, you worry about the weirdest things.' He glanced at the gun she was holding in her lap. 'What are you going to do with that?'

'See if Ryan wants it.' She shrugged. *Man, is Ryan going to be pissed.* 'I hope he's home, if not we'll just have to wait.'

Jaz instructed Taylor to park his car a block away and then walk to Ryan's house. She was sure that if anyone saw them, they'd think they were just a couple of drunk kids staggering home. Jaz had the staggering part sorted.

'You're heavy, Jaz,' teased Taylor. 'Too many muscles.'

She laughed. 'I wish.'

Jaz unlocked the gate and they slipped into Ryan's yard. She was struggling to stay lucid with the blood loss. Taylor knocked on the door while trying to hold Jaz upright. They both had guns hiden down the front of their pants and probably looked ridiculous. In the glow from Ryan's outside light Jaz could see Taylor's white shirt soaked with red blood. Would Ryan think they were off to a costume party? She almost giggled at the thought. Maybe the adrenaline overload was making her a little loopy.

'What if he's not here?' asked Taylor as he banged on the door louder. Then he checked his watch. 'It's late, maybe he's asleep.'

They heard the *thunk* of the door unlock, and moments later the door swung open.

Ryan stood there in just trackpants, which hung low from his waist. His hair was a little ruffled from sleep and his eyes still waking up. For Jaz, just seeing his naked chest was the right amount of morphine. She forgot all her aches and pains.

'Sorry to wake you, but we need your help,' said Jaz.

Ryan's eyes focused properly on her face wounds, the guns and then her bloodied leg. In that instant he was wide awake.

Without a word he stepped out and scooped Jaz up into his arms. 'Taylor, can you take the gun?'

Taylor did as he was told and yanked it from the band of her leggings.

But Jaz didn't care about anything. She was feeling woozier and she wasn't sure if it was from the blood loss or the way Ryan was carrying her into his house. His eyes never left her face as he navigated his way with his peripheral vision. Jaz had her arm around his neck, holding on to his straining muscles. He smelled so good. She didn't care if he yelled at her. Jaz pressed her face into his warm skin. Right now she felt like she was home and safe.

CHAPTER 29

RYAN TOOK HER straight into his bathroom and sat her on the bench by the sink. Jaz had a feeling of déjà vu. He'd stitched up her arm in here, and now he had to stitch her up again.

'You're such a good doctor,' she said dreamily. Everything was going to be fine now that she was with him.

Ryan was tugging at her laces, trying to take her boots off. He lifted one and pointed to a series of teeth marks.

'A friendly dog called Cujo did that.'

Ryan glanced at Taylor, who shrugged. He threw her boots to the floor then opened a cupboard and pulled out his first-aid kit. After taking off Taylor's makeshift bandage, he used scissors to cut her leggings around the gunshot wound. The lower half of the material was soaked with her blood, so Ryan pulled it off, exposing her leg stained red.

'I didn't like them anyway,' said Jaz as Ryan poked around in her wound, causing Jaz to grimace and grip her leg. She risked a glance at it and felt her stomach roll. Was that her flesh?

'I was going to ask if you know what you're doing, but it looks like you're familiar with this kind of stuff,' said Taylor, looking at the scars along Ryan's back.

Jaz pulled up her sleeve and stuck her arm out at Taylor. 'He stitched me up here, see,' she said proudly. Taylor's eyebrows shot up but he didn't say anything. Instead, he watched Ryan work.

'Have you got anything for the pain?' Taylor asked when Jaz sucked in a breath.

'No, but Jaz won't need it. She's tougher than she looks.' He looked her right in the eye as if challenging her. 'But I have some painkillers in the kitchen, last drawer. Not the aspirin.'

Taylor opened his mouth to protest, but Jaz waved him off. 'I'll be fine, Tay. A bullet wound, some gravel rash and a swollen face won't stop me. See, wasn't this more fun than sleeping?' she said with a forced chuckle.

'Yeah, totally.' Taylor pulled a face before retrieving the pills and a glass of water for her. Jaz swallowed them and grimaced as Ryan lifted her leg gently so he could see the back. 'Clean through and through, no major arteries, just a flesh wound. You'll live.'

Ryan began to clean the area on her leg. 'So, which one of you wants to tell me what happened tonight?' His voice remained calm but Jaz could see the fire in his eyes. He was boiling mad.

'We killed someone. Actually, quite possibly two people.' She hadn't meant for it to sound so blasé and cold. It didn't even sound like her. Feeling fatigued, she let her shoulders slump and felt her body tremble. Shock? Her vision became blurry with tears as she began to remember the night. Seeing Ryan had momentarily made her forget the dramas. But the gun going off in her hand was real. The recoil. The thud as the bullet hit Tommy's back. Poor Tommy. What would Marcus think? What would the police think when they found them? What would Carl think? Did Tommy have a family? Jaz felt a wave of sickness and began to lean to one side. Ryan caught her, holding her shoulders.

'Are you okay? Just a little bit longer,' he promised.

Jaz nodded as a tear fell down her cheek. She put her head down and clung to the benchtop.

Ryan squeezed her arm before he continued to fix her up. 'Is she right, Taylor?' he asked. 'Did she kill someone?'

Taylor sat on the closed toilet with his head in his hands. He was looking less than peachy.

'Are you all right?' asked Ryan.

Taylor ran his hands over his face, causing it to go whiter. 'Not really.' His Adam's apple bounced. 'I never thought I'd actually have to fire a gun to kill someone. But he was dead. We both shot him before he shot us.'

Jaz counted maybe three seconds before Ryan exploded. 'What the fuck kind of mess did you two get yourselves into!'

Jaz almost welcomed Ryan's anger. She needed to feel something, and his anger was better than the horror.

'What's the address?'

Jaz gave it to him before he stormed out. She could hear him on the phone to someone, giving a short sharp message.

'I've got someone to drive by and see if the cops have turned up. Should I be worried?' he asked

Reaching out, Jaz put her hand on his arm to calm him. 'No, it should look like a break-and-enter gone wrong. We left no prints, no one saw us except for the dead guy. And the other man, if he recovers, didn't see my face.'

Ryan's dark eyes were scary dark, like a dangerous hurricane. 'I really want to throttle you both, but I can't when you're bleeding in my bathroom. Again, I might add. You're making a habit of this,' he said through clenched teeth..

So many feelings surged through her, but they all disappeared when she realised how much she needed him and how close she came to dying tonight and never seeing him again. The anger she had for him earlier vanished. How could she stay angry with him? She loved him.

'Want me to start from the beginning?' she said softly. Ryan glanced back to Taylor, uncertain about letting him listen. 'He may as well hear it. He already knows about you, sort of.'

Ryan rolled his eyes. 'Any of your other friends you want to tell? You do realise that this is all meant to be secret?'

Taylor sat up. 'I would never tell anyone. Jaz, Anna and I would never do that. I've got shit happening to me too, with my dad, and Jaz said you would be able to help. I wanna know, and you have my word, it stays here.'

Jaz had never seen Taylor look more dead serious about anything before.

'Righto.' Ryan was pressing the sterile gauze to her wound and she felt herself fading. She had to stay strong, so she focused on the night's events.

'Not long after I got your text, I went to see what Carl does late at night in his warehouse. So, I got in through the toilet window and then his workers left. I had a look around and worked out they were bringing the drugs in by using the sea containers. In the walls with a fake lining.' He looked up, she could tell he was a little impressed with her news.

'Nice one, Jaz.' He lifted her leg so he could clean the exit wound and then pressed more gauze to that one.

She smiled but looked away quickly as he continued his work. 'Anyway, I went to leave, and they'd let Cujo, the dog, off his chain, so I couldn't get out the window without help. I rang you – no answer, so I called Taylor. I knew he could help and he had access to a gun, just in case. But the guys came back, probably forgot something, and I think they saw Cujo had been eating the steak I'd brought, because one guy came around the warehouse for a look and grabbed me as I was getting out. We fought, he pulled a gun, I hit him with a brick.' Jaz shivered as she heard the crunching sound replay in her mind. But she forced herself to continue. 'Then the next guy comes and shoots me, I go down and just as I think I'm a goner, Taylor turns up. Both of them faced off. He didn't think Tay would pull the trigger, but we both did.'

There were so many more details Ryan would want but they were the main bits.

'Why did you go there alone, Jaz? I thought we'd had this talk before? No risking your neck. Remember?'

Jaz yawned, and pretended not to hear him. 'How're you holding up, Taylor?' He was staring at the floor and Jaz almost thought he'd fallen asleep.

His voice was weary. 'All right. I s'pose I should go home in case Dad wakes up and notices I'm gone. I don't want him to panic. What're we going to do about this?'

'Tell no one. Get some sleep and come back here tomorrow and we'll talk. Jaz can stay here for the night. You can cover for her?' Ryan asked.

'Yep.'

Ryan finished wrapping the bandage around her leg to keep both wounds clean and then washed his hands. When Taylor got up, Ryan gripped his shoulder and shook his hand. 'Thanks for saving Jaz. And I'm glad you didn't get shot in the process. Will you be all right to get home?'

'Yeah. Thanks. Thanks for looking after her.' Taylor stepped around

Ryan and wrapped his arms around Jaz and they gripped each other like there was no tomorrow.

'I love you, Tay. Thanks for coming to my rescue.'

He kissed her head. 'What are friends for, hey? But tomorrow you owe me a massive explanation.' He looked as if he'd aged ten years in one night and Jaz felt horribly responsible for it.

She brushed the hair back off his face. 'Try to get some rest and I'll see you tomorrow. Text me if you need.'

He squeezed her hand and then left the bathroom. Seconds later, she heard the door shut. Now it was just her and a half-naked Ryan left in the tiny bathroom.

'You two care a lot for each other,' said Ryan.

'That we do. Been friends for a long time.' Jaz was staring at the bandage over her leg, only because she was avoiding the big elephant in the room – and that was Ryan.

'Let's get you cleaned up.' Ryan washed the blood off the rest of her leg and helped her to stand up.

Before she could take a step, he'd lifted her up and carried her to his bed. The doona was already thrown back from when he'd got out to answer the door. Jaz felt a tingle spread through her at the thought of being in his bed. He pulled the cover back over her and then sat down beside her on the floor, his dark eyes watching.

'What will I tell everyone about my leg?' she said, turning her face on his pillow so she could see him. Everything smelled like Ryan, it was better than any painkillers. Her eyes felt heavy as she strained to keep them open and focused on him.

'That you pulled a muscle at the gym during a fight with me? I don't know, I'm sure you'll come up with something convincing,' he said, brushing her swollen cheek. 'I should get you some ice for that.'

Jaz reached for his hand, hardly able to cope with him touching her. She still had things to say. 'I have the number of a sea container coming up in a sale. I think it has more drugs in it. Carl had it written down on his desk.'

'Jaz, Jaz. It's not important now. You need rest. We'll sort all that out later.' He went to move but then paused, his brow creasing. 'Jaz, you didn't answer my question before. Why did you go off without telling me?'

Oh that, thought Jaz, turning her head to the other side. But Ryan reached for her chin and guided her back.

He leaned against the edge of the bed, his bare chest taunting her with muscles. She wanted to reach out and touch him. Touch his scars. Feel his heartbeat. 'I was angry at you.' She may as well spit it out, it didn't look like he was going to move until he had an answer. 'I was with Marcus… we were having a great time and then you texted *that*.'

His face creased with tension at the mention of Marcus. 'You didn't…'

Jaz sighed as the truth fell from her lips. 'No. How could I. Even if what you said was a lie.' Her eyes closed tightly. She didn't want to read the truth on his face.

'Jaz.' His hand found hers, holding it tightly. 'I do care. Don't ever doubt that.' It was his deep voice, but the words surely didn't come from him.

'Yeah, right. You have a funny way of showing it,' she mumbled.

'I care for you more than I should.' Then he moved her hand, bringing it to his lips.

Jaz was floating, and any minute she would hit the ceiling, she was sure of it. His lips were better than any drug, and for the moment she forgot the horrors of the night and the painful throb in her leg. She opened her eyes and caressed his face with her other hand. Stubble was already shading his face. This time his eyes were closed as he pressed into her hand, as if her touch were magical. While his eyes were still closed, Jaz lifted her head and kissed his lips. He instantly let her in, deepening the kiss as if this were the last time they'd ever see each other. Moving her hand, she dropped it to his heart where it pounded beneath his warm skin. He covered her hand with his and she could sense his relief. But his release was only fleeting. He pulled back, but instead of walking away like he did in Pakistan, he brushed her lips with his thumb. 'You need rest. I'll get you some water.'

Getting up off his knees, he leaned over and kissed her temple and left.

Jaz fell back into his bed, into his warm sheets. Even after everything she'd been through tonight, she still lay there with a smile on her face. Tomorrow would be another day and another mission. But for now, as she tried to fight off sleep, her memories were firmly locked on Ryan's kiss.

The Recruit is the first in the MTG Agency series.

THE RECRUIT

From one of Australia's Queens of Romance comes the debut in a brand new YA series about secrets, strengths, and what lies beneath the surface.

Jasmine Thomas is your normal seventeen-year-old girl. She dislikes the rich, mean kids at her school but loves her two best friends, computer-savvy Anna and popular, gorgeous Taylor. Her spare time is spent at The Ring, a boxing gym where she practically grew up learning karate, boxing and street fighting. So, yeah, she can kick some major butt.

Life seems pretty normal until Ryan Fletcher enters her gym; mysterious, hot and oozing plenty of bad-boy charm. But she isn't prepared for what she finds out about him and before long she's drawn into his adult world of secrets and lies. Just how far is she willing to go? And could this be the life-fulfilling path she'd dreamed of?

Next in the MTG Agency series….

THE DECEPTION

Jaz is back in another explosive mission – but her hardest task is keeping her secret from her friends…

Jaz's last mission for the Agency had unforeseen consequences, and she is only now beginning to understand that the hardest part isn't the physical training. Her ongoing mission involves an undercover operation – pretending to be the girlfriend of the son of one of the Agency's most wanted.

What starts out as a chance to prove herself soon becomes a lesson in emotional detachment, as her pretend boyfriend starts to feel too real. Factor in Ryan, still sexy, still dangerous, and still irresistible, and Jaz is discovering that her love life is more treacherous than anything the Agency can throw at her.

9 780648 236818